W9-BXX-504

JUDITH STACY

has gotten many of the plot ideas for her nineteen romance novels while taking leisurely drives and long afternoon naps. When those methods fail, she is forced to turn to chocolate for inspiration. Judith is married to her high school sweetheart. They have two daughters and live in Southern California.

CHERYL REAVIS

is an award-winning short-story and romance author who also writes under the name of Cinda Richards. She describes herself as a late bloomer who played in her first piano recital at the tender age of thirty. "We had to line up by height—I was the third smallest kid," she says. "After that, there was no stopping me. I immediately gave myself permission to attempt my other heart's desire—to write." Her Silhouette Special Edition novel *A Crime of the Heart* reached millions of readers in *Good Housekeeping* magazine. Her books *The Prisoner* and *The Bride Fair,* both from Harlequin Historical, and *A Crime of the Heart* and *Patrick Gallagher's Widow,* both Silhouette Special Edition novels, are all Romance Writers of America's RITA® Award winners. A former public health nurse, Cheryl makes her home in North Carolina with her husband.

PAM CROOKS

While expecting her first child more years back than she cares to count, Pam read her very first romance novel. She has been in love with them ever since. Her childhood was spent in the ranch country of western Nebraska, where she became fascinated with the Old West and the cowboys who lived it. Pam still lives in Nebraska with her husband (who is not a cowboy), four daughters, one son-in-law and her very mellow golden Lab mix, Spencer. She loves to hear from her readers, and responds to each and every one. Contact Pam via e-mail from her Web site, www.pamcrooks.com, or snail mail at P.O. Box 540122, Omaha, NE 68154.

SPRING BRIDES

Judith STACY

Cheryl REAVIS

Pam CROOKS

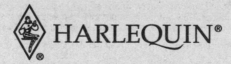 HARLEQUIN®

TORONTO • NEW YORK • LONDON
AMSTERDAM • PARIS • SYDNEY • HAMBURG
STOCKHOLM • ATHENS • TOKYO • MILAN • MADRID
PRAGUE • WARSAW • BUDAPEST • AUCKLAND

ISBN 0-373-29355-0

SPRING BRIDES
Copyright © 2005 by Harlequin Books S.A.

The publisher acknowledges the copyright holders
of the individual works as follows:

THREE BRIDES AND A WEDDING DRESS
Copyright © 2005 by Dorothy Howell

THE WINTER HEART
Copyright © 2005 by Cheryl Reavis

McCORD'S DESTINY
Copyright © 2005 by Pam Crooks

CONTENTS

THREE BRIDES
AND A WEDDING DRESS

Judith Stacy

To David for all our yesterdays and all our tomorrows.
To Judy and Stacy for all the joy you've given me.

Chapter One

California, 1887

Her husband. The man she would marry.

Anna Kingsley lurched upright on the train seat, her mind racing. Good gracious, what did the man *look* like?

His face. She couldn't picture his face.

Panic shortened Anna's breath as another thought surfaced. What sort of woman was she? What sort of wife would she be if she couldn't recall what her own husband-to-be looked like? Even if she hadn't seen him in months.

A wave of calm swept through her. Really, she already knew what sort of wife she would be. And the fact that she couldn't remember the man's face at the moment was the least of her problems—and his.

Anna leaned her head against the windowpane and gazed out at the awakening countryside. Spring had brought a faint blush of green to the landscape. She'd watched nearly two thousand miles of scenery pass by her window since leaving Virginia, and her journey wasn't over yet.

After so many days on the train, sleeping fitfully, washing from a bucket in the ladies' room, spending her money on the overpriced foods provided by vendors at the train stations along the way, Anna longed for the things she'd taken for granted, the things she'd left behind. A soak in a hot bath, a meal seated at a table and a feather mattress seemed like heaven right now.

Nothing about the trip was as she imagined it. Except her destination. That hadn't changed.

Henry Thornton. Anna mulled the name over in her mind, thankful that she had no trouble remembering at least that much about her intended.

Henry Thornton. Mrs. Henry Thornton. Anna Thornton. Little Thorntons to follow?

A chill passed through Anna and she forced away her uncomfortable thoughts about her journey to California. She consoled herself with the knowledge that whatever awaited her as the wife of Henry Thornton was far better than what she'd left behind in Virginia.

"Excuse me? Miss Kingsley?" a voice called.

Anna smiled as Mrs. Tomlin, another passenger on the train, sat down next to her. Throughout this westward trek, the one constant was the friendly passengers.

Mrs. Tomlin turned her cherubic face to Anna. "May I look over those catalogs of yours again, dear?"

"Certainly." Anna drew her satchel onto her lap and rifled through it. She'd packed her journal, writing supplies, a number of books and every catalog she could get her hands on to occupy herself on the long train trip. "Any one in particular?" she asked, holding up several.

"These will do fine," Mrs. Tomlin replied, taking them all. "Wish I had something more to trade with you."

Anna had already read Mrs. Tomlin's books, plus the newspaper her husband had bought at the last stop.

"I need to catch up on my journal," Anna said.

Mrs. Tomlin clutched the catalogs in both hands and sighed contentedly. "No wonder you brought so many of these with you. You'll be starting a brand-new life, just you and your new husband. You must be very excited."

During the long hours on the train the two of them had chatted and Anna had told her about her upcoming nuptials.

"Yes, I'm excited," she said, hoping she actually sounded that way.

Mrs. Tomlin sighed again. "And to think, all those women in California, and Mr. Thornton wanted *you*. You must have been very flattered when he proposed."

Stunned was what she'd been.

Anna had met Henry Thornton last year when he'd traveled to Virginia on business. After church one Sunday his host had invited Anna, her father and brother to supper. She'd found Henry pleasant and interesting as he'd shared stories of the highly successful lumber business he owned in California. The man had extolled the wonders of his adopted state, the freedom, the opportunities. He'd said it was a place where a person could find himself, and anyone could build something grand with his own wits.

Anna had found herself hanging on to his every word that evening at supper. Opportunities for *everyone?* Could such a place actually exist?

After Henry returned home, he surprised Anna by writing to her. They exchanged letters. Nothing personal, though. Nothing that prepared Anna for the day her father had appeared in the parlor and announced that Henry Thornton had written to him, asking for Anna's hand in marriage.

"Go ahead and marry him, if you want," Papa had said with the indifferent shrug she'd seen all her life.

Since Mama had died several years ago, Papa had struggled to keep the family business going. Her brother's help seemed no help at all. Neither of them allowed Anna to do more than fill in occasionally at the store. They didn't let her take over her mother's position there, even after Anna completed her courses at Miss Purtle's Academy for Young Ladies.

The two men had little time or use for her. Their family home was quiet and empty much of the time. She was almost twenty years old now, and her few brushes with romance had come to nothing. None of the eligible men in town had showed any interest in her at all lately; she wondered, at times, if her father's poor business reputation and her brother's rumored gambling contributed to her lack of suitors. Anna was left to watch her friends marry and move on to their exciting new lives, leaving her marooned in hers.

Yet accepting Henry Thornton's marriage proposal—and the accompanying move to California—had been the most difficult decision of her life. How did any woman make this tremendous, life-altering choice? How could she assure herself that she could be a good wife? She'd asked her friends, her aunts and cousins, but no one had given her any help. In the end, she'd decided to take a chance and marry Henry.

Anna hoped with all her heart neither she nor Henry would regret her decision.

Her friends had given her bridal gifts at a tea in her honor. Papa had commissioned the finest seamstress in Richmond to make the wedding dress of her dreams. Anna had turned her hope chest into a hope trunk, stuffed it until the hinges strained, and headed west.

Mrs. Tomlin patted Anna's hand now, jarring her from her thoughts. "You're nervous. I can tell. We all were. It's understandable. I'm sure you'll make a fine wife."

Anna managed a small smile but no reply. She had no idea whether she'd make a fine wife or not. How could she know? Even now, as the time drew near, she didn't know. She'd fretted about it endlessly.

Henry Thornton hadn't swept her off her feet with wild romantic notions, and she hadn't pined away for him after he left Virginia. But he was a good, decent man and Anna intended to be a good, decent wife to him.

Even if she didn't yet know how to do that.

Even if she couldn't remember what he looked like at the moment.

Cade Riker didn't bother to look up from the stack of papers on his desk when he heard his office door open, then slam shut. Another problem. He knew it. And he'd already had all the problems he could take for one day.

"Not now," Cade grumbled.

"There's a problem."

The familiar voice of his brother caused Cade to look up. Ben was only a year younger. Tall, dark-haired and blue-eyed, he looked like Cade. From a distance, most people couldn't tell them apart.

"Whatever it is," Cade told him, "it can wait."

"No, it can't," Ben said. "You've got to do something about this—now."

Cade's jaw tightened. "Like hell I do."

Ben glared right back at him, one of the few men at the company—or in the town of Branford, for that matter—who'd dare do so.

"You know I wouldn't be here if it weren't important," Ben said, in that reasonable way of his. He waved his hand, encompassing the office. "I know what's going on around here, same as you."

Cade couldn't argue the point, although Ben didn't know the huge problem Cade had stumbled onto only this morning. He and Ben had run the business together for two years. Neither kept secrets from the other. Until now. Cade didn't dare tell anyone what he'd discovered.

Ben dropped a telegram atop the papers piled on Cade's desk. "Henry's wife is coming."

"Christ…" Cade squeezed his eyes shut for a moment.

"Today."

Cade rocked back in his chair, his gut tightening as it did lately when Henry Thornton came to mind.

"Cousin Henry's wife is coming?"

Cade's gaze swung across the room as the voice of his youngest brother, Kyle, drew his attention.

"When did you get here? Aren't you supposed to be in school, boy?"

"His *wife?*" Kyle asked, walking over, the broom clutched in his hand.

Cade looked hard at Kyle. "I expect an answer when I ask you something."

"We've got a bigger problem to deal with." Ben tapped his finger against the telegram. "Ol' man Latimer at the express office just gave me this telegram addressed to Henry. It's from *her.* She's coming in on the afternoon train. And she's expecting to marry Henry when she gets here."

Cade shoved out of his chair. "What the hell do you expect *me* to do about it?"

"Somebody's got to tell her," Ben said.

"Can we keep her?" Kyle asked, his eyes wide.

"Get the preacher to do it," Cade said to Ben.

"Henry's our cousin," Ben said. "It's up to us to handle this."

"Then you go talk to her," Cade declared.

Ben drew back a little. "You know I'm courting Emma Stokes. I can't be seen in public with another woman."

"We're keeping her, aren't we?" Kyle asked again.

Cade turned away from his desk and paced across the room and back. He rubbed his forehead, then looked at Ben.

"You need to do this," Ben said softly.

Cade glared at his brother for a moment, then bit back another curse, grabbed his hat from the peg beside the door and headed outside.

Ben was most always right, and he sure as hell was right about this.

Chapter Two

Anna pressed her face against the window as the town of Branford came into view. The noise level rose as passengers prepared for their arrival at the station.

The farmland, the mountains, the deep river they'd crossed all gave way. Wooden houses on the edge of town passed, then finally Branford itself appeared.

Henry had assured her the town was very prosperous. How else could he have built his lumber business into the biggest in the state?

The locomotive's whistle pierced the air as the train rolled to a stop at the platform outside the depot. Steam hissed from the engine, sending up a cloud of mist.

She scanned the faces of the people waiting on the platform. Henry? Was that him? Yes—no, that wasn't him. Anna bit her bottom lip. She didn't see Henry. At least she didn't *think* she saw him. Surely she'd recognize her own husband-to-be when she actually saw him in person.

As the other passengers made their way to the doors at either end of the car, Anna moved into the aisle. When she passed the conductor, he spoke before she had the chance.

"It's fine. Perfectly fine. It will be unloaded with the other baggage," he told her, none too kindly, then pushed ahead of the other passengers and out the door.

Anna supposed she couldn't blame him. She'd made a bit of a nuisance of herself, worrying over her trunks back in the baggage car.

But why shouldn't she worry? Inside one of them lay her beloved wedding dress, which her father had purchased for her. Anna wasn't about to abandon her grand gown to the leaky, drafty baggage car and not check on it. Even if it annoyed the conductor, who had to escort her back and forth.

Stepping down from the passenger car, Anna planted her feet firmly on the platform. People rushed into the arms of loved ones, laughter rose. Folks pushed past, anxious to claim baggage and be gone.

Anna noticed a knot of young women about her own age giggling, obviously anticipating someone—or something— grand to emerge from the train. Would these women be her friends? Had Henry told them about his new wife?

Anna remained near the passenger car, holding her satchel, watching and waiting. The crowd thinned. Passengers continuing to the train's next stop disappeared, presumably searching the town for a decent meal. Baggage was carted away. Supply wagons pulled up to the boxcars as porters unloaded cargo.

A wail rose from the crowd of young women, followed by groans and rising chatter. The conductor waved his hands for silence, but to no avail. Still Anna waited.

A little knot of worry grew in her stomach. Had Henry not gotten her telegram? She'd sent it from the last stop; the train schedule was too undependable to send it any earlier. She'd thought that would give him plenty of time to get to the station and meet her train.

Or had Henry suspected her shortcomings?

Minutes dragged by. Anna's gaze swept the platform, the station. Her worry intensified.

Henry would be as anxious as she to start their new life together. The opportunities roamed through Anna's mind now as they had during the long train trip.

He'd probably stopped to pick flowers for her, she decided. He'd do that, wouldn't he?

She pushed the thought aside. In truth, she didn't know if he would or not.

Time slipped by. Should she go inside the station and speak to the stationmaster? Find the sheriff? Or maybe—

A man strode around the corner of the depot heading her way. Anna gasped.

This certainly wasn't Henry.

Tall, good gracious he was tall. With broad shoulders. A wide chest. Dark hair and piercing blue eyes. He was handsome in a rugged way, Anna decided. He wore dark trousers, a vest that fit snugly over a snowy white shirt and his black hat rode low on his forehead.

Their gazes locked and he stopped still in his tracks. He looked at her—hard.

Anna couldn't move. She couldn't even tear her gaze from his. Her mouth went dry and her heart pounded in her throat, and suddenly she became conscious of every wrinkle in her dress, every errant strand of hair, every flaw in her appearance from her long days on the train.

He hung back for another moment, then seemed to gather his strength. He walked over. Anna had to tilt her head back to see his face. Goodness, he was even more handsome up close.

Heat warmed her cheeks and she lowered her gaze, admonishing herself for having the thought. She had trouble remembering what Henry looked like at times, and here she was thinking another man attractive? What was wrong with her?

"Miss…Miss Kingsley?"

Anna dared raise her gaze once more. The man looked slightly dangerous, and none too happy about seeing her.

"Cade Riker," he said. "Henry's my cousin."

"Oh." A thread of relief wound through her. Yet her heart

hadn't slowed and she wasn't sure she could compose a co-herent sentence beneath the man's blistering gaze.

"I, ah, I—" Cade stopped, cleared his throat, then jerked his chin toward the depot. "You need to come inside."

Anna glanced around. The few people who remained on the platform took notice of Cade, then her, then every one of them ducked their heads and turned away.

"Is Henry—"

"Just come in here."

Cade strode to the station door and waited. When she walked toward him, he watched her every step, making her oddly nervous. Heat rolled off of him as she passed by. She felt his gaze on her back; it made her knees unsteady.

A few people milled around the waiting room, while others slouched on the wooden benches. They all glanced at Anna, then looked away. The ticket agent behind his barred window did the same. When Cade opened the door to the sta-tionmaster's office, the man inside cast her a quick look, mumbled something to Cade, then hurried away.

Anna hoped the other people in Branford would give her a warmer welcome.

She stepped inside the small office. A row of windows opened to the street. Pedestrians passed by, along with horses, wagons and carriages.

The door closed behind her. Anna turned to face Cade. They were alone in the room. He still didn't look happy.

"I'd like to see Henry now," she said, her sense of unease rising.

Cade planted himself in front of her. He took off his hat and pressed it to his chest, then drew in a deep breath.

Still, he didn't speak.

"Really, Mr. Riker," Anna began, a little annoyed now. "If you don't mind, I'd like to see Henry—"

"Henry's gone."

Anna blinked up at him. "He's—"

"Gone."

She glanced around the office, as if she might spot Henry lurking in a corner. "Gone where?"

"Just gone," Cade told her. "He's not coming back."

"Not—"

"Ever."

"But…."

Cade pulled a folded handkerchief from his shirt pocket and thrust it at her. "Three days ago. Left a note. Not coming back. Said to tell you he's sorry."

Anna just stared at the man frowning down at her, holding out a handkerchief. Henry had left three days ago?

Three days ago she'd been on the train, trying to remember what he looked like.

Three days ago she'd been fantasizing about walking down the aisle in her grand wedding gown.

Three days ago she'd been imagining how she would use all the lovely gifts her friends had given her.

Three days ago—and many before and after—she'd suffered fits of anxiety wondering how she'd ever discover the secret of being a good wife.

And all the while Henry had been gone?

A wave of dizziness came over Anna, but she refused to give in to it. She couldn't, however, fight off the awful feeling of shame.

Henry must have figured it out. He must have reread her letters and realized how unprepared she was to be a wife.

Humiliation washed over her. Somehow, Henry had *known*.

Cade stared down at his cousin's intended, more than a little put out with the woman. Here he'd gone and taken time out of his busy day to meet her at the station, to break the news about Henry, news that caused so much pain to himself. He'd gone home first, washed, put on a fresh shirt. He'd remembered to bring a clean handkerchief for her. He made arrangements with the stationmaster to let them use his private office.

He'd even thought up some consoling words, some nice things to say about Henry.

And the woman had yet to bat an eye or shed a tear. Here he stood with his hat in one hand and a clean handkerchief in the other, and she acted as if nothing were wrong.

"Try to calm down," he told her.

That got a reaction. Her head snapped up and anger flashed in her eyes. "What's that supposed to mean?"

"It means you don't seem very upset about the fact that your husband-to-be is gone," Cade told her. "I took the afternoon off and walked over here to break the news—"

"Oh, well excuse me for causing you so much inconvenience. I traveled two thousand miles, spent weeks on that wretched train, expecting to have a husband and a new life waiting for me. And all I find is *you.*"

"Henry's my cousin. That makes you my responsibility," Cade declared. "So I'm paying for your ticket back home out of my own pocket. I already checked the schedule and the next eastbound train will be through here in about an hour."

Everything in Anna revolted. How could she go back to Virginia and face her family and friends after *this?*

"Keep your money, Mr. Riker. I have no intentions of going anywhere."

"You're staying? What the hell for?"

Why on earth wouldn't this man leave her alone with her humiliation?

Anna dug deep, finding anger beneath her embarrassment.

"I'm staying because I *choose* to. Not that it's any of your business," she informed him.

Cade shook his head and mumbled a curse. "Fine, then. If you're hell-bent on staying, I'll find you a new husband."

Another husband? Anna's mind reeled at the thought. Henry hadn't wanted her—in fact, he'd walked out on her before she'd even arrived. Would any man in town—or anywhere—be interested in her?

"You've just told me Henry is *gone*. Do you think I could marry someone else tomorrow?" Anna demanded.

"Well, hell, I don't know." He sighed tiredly. "All right, I'll find you a job somewhere. Can you do anything?"

"I can do *this*." Anna spun around, marched out of the office and slammed the door.

Footsteps pounded the boards of the platform behind her as Anna left the station. She knew it was that awful Cade Riker. Honestly, the nerve of the man. Why didn't he just leave her alone?

She quickened her steps but he caught up easily and planted himself in front of her, stopping her in her tracks.

"Look, Miss Kingsley, I've got no time for this foolishness. You're my cousin's wife-to-be, so I'm willing to do the right thing. I'm taking responsibility for you."

"You are not responsible for me!" Anna blurted the words, surprised to hear them come from her own mouth. "I'm responsible for myself."

Cade looked at her as if he didn't really comprehend what she'd said.

"Good day, Mr. Riker." Anna stomped away, fuming.

She just wanted to get away. To have some privacy. To sort through what had happened.

"What are you doing?" Cade called.

From his tone, he was no happier with her than she was with him. Anna clomped down the steps into the alley that ran past the depot, and looked back, but refused to answer.

Cade stopped at the edge of the platform, the extra height making him tower over her. "You don't know where you're going. Hell, you don't even know where you *are*."

"I'll figure it out."

"I can't let you just roam around town by yourself," he said, coming down the steps, frowning.

Anna glared up at him. "Listen good, Mr. Riker, because I don't intend to tell you this again. I don't want your help.

Stay out of my way or I'll go to the sheriff. I'm sure he'll be glad to help me once he finds out who I am. Henry Thornton was an important man in this town, you know."

Cade paused. "He was?"

"Yes." She threw the words at him. "He owns—owned— the lumber company, the biggest in the state."

One of his eyebrows rose sharply. "Is that a fact?"

"It most certainly is. And not that it's any of your business, Mr. Riker, but if I need any help, I'll go to the lumberyard and speak with Henry's employees. I'm sure they'll be glad to assist me. Why, I'm sure they would even give me a job, if I ask."

Cade pressed his lips together. "You think so?"

"I'm sure of it."

"You've worked at a lumberyard before, have you?"

"Of course not. But I completed a full course of study at Miss Purtle's Academy for Young Ladies in Virginia."

"Miss Purtle's Academy for Young Ladies, huh?" Cade nodded slowly. "I guess you'll fit right in with the boys down at the lumberyard."

"I'm sure I will." Anna spun around and stomped away.

She walked two blocks, dodging men and women on the boardwalk, hardly seeing them, her mind in turmoil. She couldn't remember ever meeting a man who instantly made her as angry as that Cade Riker did.

When she reached the next corner, Anna stopped and her anger drained away. She looked around. Businesses, people, wagons and horses. Nothing familiar. Nothing.

A rush of emotions rose in Anna. She didn't know where she was. She didn't know where to go. She'd left her family and home behind and come here expecting a new life, a new opportunity. And now she had none of that.

She'd been abandoned at the altar—almost. Left to suffer searing humiliation heaped atop the abandonment she felt.

Anna gulped quickly, trying to force down her emotions.

A single tear escaped. Then another. She glanced around, spotted the entrance to another alley, then ducked inside.

The late afternoon sun cast long shadows across the dirt lane. She dropped her satchel and gulped again. She'd never been able to hold off her tears. Anna folded her arms against the wooden building, buried her face in them and cried.

She sobbed until her tears ran out, then lifted her head and gasped.

Cade Riker.

He stood at her side, legs braced wide apart, hat pulled down low. Looking solid. Sturdy.

Their gazes locked. Cade stepped forward. He didn't offer her a handkerchief this time. Instead he brushed away her tears with his big thumb. Anna let him.

He slid his arms around her. She let him do that, too.

The hard muscles of his chest and arms sapped her strength. Anna moved against him and turned her face up. She smelled his scent—soap and cotton. She saw the dark whiskers on his chin.

He leaned down. His mouth hovered above hers; his hot breath puffed against her lips. She didn't pull away.

Cade kissed her.

His mouth covered hers, hot and moist. He deepened the kiss and drew her closer, holding her against him, their bodies, their mouths melting together. Anna curled her fists into his vest and held on.

He pulled away, finally, and the cool air in the alley drifted between them. He held her gaze for another moment, then turned and walked away, leaving Anna alone once more.

Chapter Three

Cade stepped up on the covered porch of the building that housed his office, and went inside. Much of his time was spent here. But this morning something rebelled in him, urging him to go elsewhere. He didn't know where.

Or maybe he did.

Cade shook off the unwelcome thought and decided he was just tired. He hung his hat on the peg beside the door and crossed to the little stove in the corner. He hadn't slept much last night. Worries about the business had kept him tossing and turning, along with visions of Anna Kingsley.

He'd kissed her. Cade warmed at the memory. Yet what the hell had he been thinking?

He took a cup from the shelf and poured it full of thick coffee from the pot atop the stove. He'd kissed Anna Kingsley. On the mouth. Kissed her and held her, and felt her soft—

"Did you get Miss Kingsley taken care of?"

Cade whipped around at the sound of Ben's voice, sloshing coffee from his cup, and saw his brother sitting at his desk across the room. Cade hadn't realized he was there.

"What the hell is that supposed to mean?" Cade demanded.

Ben raised an eyebrow. "What's wrong with you?"

"Nothing," Cade barked.

Ben rose from his desk, grabbed a linen towel off the peg beside the stove and handed it to Cade. "You're a bear this morning—even worse than usual."

Cade took the towel, dried the lukewarm coffee from his hand and mopped up the spill from the floor.

"I've got a lot on my mind, that's all." He stewed for minute, then blurted, "I kissed her."

Ben frowned. "Kissed who?"

"Miss Kingsley."

"You *kissed* her? You were supposed to tell her about—"

"I know, I know." Cade winced. "I don't know what the hell happened. One minute she was yelling at me—"

"She yelled? At *you?*" A little grin pulled at Ben's lips. "Damn…"

"Then the next thing I know, I'm kissing her."

"Was it a peck on the cheek? A brotherly sort of kiss?"

"Not hardly," Cade grumbled.

"This just proves what I've been telling you," Ben said, shaking his head. "You're spending too much time worrying about the business."

Cade didn't answer, just moved to his desk and dropped into his chair. Courting a woman was the farthest thing from his mind. Even with Ben's help, he could barely handle the daily operation of the fast-growing company, the problems with customers and orders, the situations that constantly arose with employees. He had Kyle to look after, too.

And, of course, the latest problem, which he hadn't any idea how to handle.

"I thought that you telling her about Henry yourself would…" Ben stopped and shook his head. "I thought it would help you deal with…what happened. So did you finally get around to breaking the news to her about Henry?"

Cade nodded. "Yeah, I told her. She didn't even cry."

"Guess you got off lucky, not having to go through a crying jag with her," Ben mused. "Sounds like she's a strong woman. No wonder Henry wanted her for his wife."

Cade had thought it odd when Henry had announced that he'd found himself a wife in Virginia. He'd spoken of this Anna Kingsley after returning from his trip, but never indicated he and the woman had deep feelings for each other.

Cade had been surprised when Henry told everyone that the woman had agreed to marry him. Surprised and a little suspicious. The whole thing just didn't sit right with Cade.

But he went to the saloon that night along with the other men to toast the groom-to-be. Cade didn't drink, usually, but he made an exception on this occasion.

Now, after meeting Anna Kingsley, he wondered if his unease that night had been caused by something else entirely.

He shrugged. "I offered to help her, but she wouldn't hear of it. Claimed she could handle things herself."

"Somebody who didn't want something from you?" Ben uttered a short laugh. "That must have been a relief."

Actually, it annoyed him, Cade realized. The woman was out of her element here in the West. She knew no one, had no place to live. He doubted she'd learned anything useful in that academy for young ladies she claimed she'd attended.

But she'd insisted she could handle things herself. Shouted it at him, actually.

Suspicion once again crept into Cade's thoughts. Was there another reason Anna had refused to return to Virginia?

"So what are you going to do?" Ben asked.

Cade had already mulled it over and knew there was only one thing he could do. He owed her an apology.

Surely she'd been in shock when he'd delivered the news of Henry's abandonment, and that was the reason for her odd reaction. He'd judged her too harshly.

He wasn't very proud of himself for the way he'd handled everything. He'd lain awake last night thinking about what had happened at the train station and in the alley.

Mostly about what happened in the alley.

Cade shifted in the chair as the same stirring that had kept him awake made itself known. Strong, urgent desire.

"I'm going to find her. See how she's holding up. Make sure she's all right," Cade said, deciding to keep his planned apology to himself.

"Better make it quick. She'll head back East soon."

"Didn't sound like she wanted to," Cade said.

"She'll go," Ben said. "She's got no reason to stay here. I'd give it a week or two and she'll be gone."

A week or two? Gone, never to return?

Cade drummed his fingers against his cold coffee cup. Maybe Anna Kingsley could do him some good before she left.

Cade Riker.

Anna came awake, annoyed that after her first night in weeks snuggled in a real bed, Cade Riker would pop into her mind right away.

She rolled over, enjoying the feel of the soft feather mattress. When she'd stumbled out of the alley yesterday afternoon, Anna had spotted the Harrington Hotel. The woman at the registration desk, Mrs. Harrington, had gasped aloud when Anna explained why she was there. She'd come around the desk, hugged Anna and expressed her sympathy over Henry's desertion. Most everyone in town, according to Mrs. Harrington, knew Henry was expecting a bride from back East.

Which meant everyone in town knew Anna had been abandoned. She cringed inwardly. What must the town think of her? Or worse, what did the town *know* about her? What had Henry said to everyone before he left?

Mrs. Harrington's words had been kind. Anna had been grateful when she'd set to work making her comfortable. A hot bath, a tray in her room, then, thankfully, solitude. Anna had slept straight through the night.

Only to awaken to thoughts of Cade Riker.

She sat up and pushed her dark hair over her shoulder. After all she'd been through, why would she think of that man?

A tremor jolted her as she realized that she hadn't been very nice to Cade yesterday. He had, after all, come to meet her at the station. He'd offered to help, even if he'd acted as if she didn't have sense enough to take care of herself.

And then he'd kissed her.

Warmth grew inside Anna as she recalled lifting her head after her crying spell and seeing him standing in the alley. He'd followed her. Wiped away her tears.

She touched her finger to her cheek, remembering the feel of his thumb against her skin. And those strong arms of his wrapping around her, pulling her close. His hard chest. Everything about him was muscular.

Except his lips.

A little sigh escaped from Anna's mouth, jarring her from the recollection. She got to her feet, reaching deep for a different emotion. She settled on anger.

How dare Cade Riker kiss her like that? How dare he kiss her at all?

Of course, she'd let him.

A sharp hunger pain drove all other thoughts from Anna's mind. She went to the window and pulled back the eyelet-trimmed curtain. Outside, the street was crowded and the sun shone brightly. The day was already under way.

Anna braced her hands on the sill and leaned out the window. She spotted a bank, general store, bakery and restaurant. All looking neat, clean and well-kept.

She'd walk through the town today, she decided. Stroll the boardwalk, duck into a shop, sample a cookie from the bakery, eat at the restaurant. Her insides warmed at the thought. She could do anything she wanted.

Not like back home. Papa insisted on knowing everything she did, every person she spoke to. Her brother quizzed her on the details of her days. Not that either of them cared or were interested. They simply thought it their duty to keep track of her.

Would Henry, as her husband, have done the same? Anna wasn't sure.

No one had kept track of her on board the train. A smile came to Anna's lips as she recalled the freedom, the joy of making her own decisions and doing as she pleased.

She turned her head the other way, taking in the view to the east. A feed store, hardware store and the train station. And beside it was the alley where Cade had...

That kiss again. Anna pulled her head back inside and turned from the window, willing away a sudden rush of warmth.

She freshened up at the washstand, then opened one of her trunks to select a dress. Yards of white satin lay before her, causing a little ache to tighten around her heart.

Her wedding dress. Would she ever get to wear it?

Anna straightened away from the trunk. Yesterday she'd made a point of insisting to Cade Riker that she could take care of herself. Maybe she should get on with it.

Downstairs, Anna found Mrs. Harrington sweeping the lobby. The front door stood open, letting in the breeze.

"Good morning, Miss Kingsley. Sleep well, dear?"

"Yes, the room is wonderful. Especially after being on the train for so long."

"Oh, I know what you mean." Mrs. Harrington laughed gently, then her expression sobered. "It's a difficult thing you've been through, dear. Coming all this way only to hear the news about Henry. You must have been devastated."

Kissed. She'd been kissed upon hearing the news.

Good gracious, what was wrong with her? Anna fought off the recollection, hoping the kindly hotel keeper hadn't noticed the warmth she felt gathering on her cheeks.

"I suppose Henry had a reason for what he did," Anna

said, though deep in her heart she knew there was no *supposing* about it. He'd somehow realized she'd never make an acceptable wife, and had left. "But I really have no business being upset. Henry's family, his friends claim that right. Everyone here in Branford surely knew Henry better than I, and are truly upset by his leaving."

"You've a generous spirit." Mrs. Harrington took up her chore again. "You're not thinking of going home, are you?"

"I have a cousin near San Francisco. I might go there."

"I hope you'll give Branford a chance. We have—"

Mrs. Harrington stopped her sweeping and squinted out the front door. Then, with a look of smug satisfaction, she turned to Anna. "I knew Her Highness would be along. Vida Kendall, the mayor's wife. I knew she'd be over to see you right away." Mrs. Harrington leaned a little closer to Anna. "You were supposed to be the fourth, you know."

"The fourth what?"

"Bride," Mrs. Harrington explained. "It wasn't enough that Vida's own daughter was getting married. Oh, no. She decided to put on a wedding festival so that all the young ladies in town who'd planned to marry this spring could celebrate together. Four couples—three, now that Henry's gone—in one grand ceremony. A day-long festival so that the whole town would turn out. You ask me, Vida Kendall just wanted to stage the occasion so that her daughter would outshine the other brides."

"And they wanted me to be part of the ceremony?"

"Oh, yes. But your not being there won't deter Vida. Not one little bit. She's going to have her grand wedding, regardless." Mrs. Harrington lowered her voice. "Some of us are wondering if it's *her* wedding or her daughter's."

"Three weddings at once?" Anna shook her head. "That's quite an undertaking."

"The whole town is flush with wedding fever." Mrs. Harrington rolled her eyes. "Edgar Talbot might end up getting run out of town before it's all said and done. He owns Talbot's General Store, just down the street. Vida Kendall insisted the brides—meaning her own daughter, of course—have the finest fabric available for their dresses, so she had Mr. Talbot send all the way to England for it."

"England? Oh, my…"

"Yes. Can you imagine?"

"The fabric must be beautiful."

"We may never know," Mrs. Harrington predicted. "We've not seen the fabric. It should have arrived but hasn't."

Anna gasped, imagining how the brides must feel. The scene at the train depot yesterday flashed in her mind. Were the distraught young women gathered around the conductor the brides, disappointed that their fabric hadn't arrived?

"Time is getting short. If that fabric doesn't get here…" Mrs. Harrington's words trailed off, but Anna knew exactly what she meant.

"Why don't the brides order fabric from somewhere else?" Anna asked.

Mrs. Harrington's eyes grew round. "Do you think Vida Kendall would allow her daughter to marry in a dress made of just *any* fabric? Why, I can tell you right now that—"

Mrs. Harrington cut off her words abruptly as two women entered the hotel lobby. Anna knew, even without an introduction, that they were the mayor's wife and daughter.

The older woman wore a garnet-colored dress and a hat with a black feather sticking out the side, her dark hair graying slightly. The younger was a mere wisp of her mother, tall and slender, with golden hair gathered under a blue bonnet. Anna guessed the girl was no older than herself.

Mrs. Kendall introduced herself and her daughter, Rachel, then got down to business.

"Too bad about Henry Thornton." She said the words kindly enough, yet dismissively. "But don't think you've come all this way for nothing."

"You're from Virginia?" Rachel asked with a shy smile.

"And you made the trip by yourself? It must have been very exciting. I'd love to hear about it."

"No time for that now," Mrs. Kendall declared. "Just because Henry up and left is no reason for you not to participate in the wedding festival. Come by the house tomorrow morning. We're discussing preparations."

Anna didn't respond. She didn't think it necessary. The invitation sounded more like a command than a request.

Rachel cast an uncomfortable glance at her mother. "Mama, maybe Miss Kingsley doesn't want to be part of the festival."

"Nonsense. Of course she wants to," Mrs. Kendall declared, then turned to Anna. "You've just come from the East with firsthand information about the latest fashions. You must share it with us."

"I did bring quite a few catalogs with me," Anna said.

"Then you absolutely must be there."

Rachel gave Anna an apologetic smile. "It's a perfect chance for you to meet everyone."

Anna didn't know if she could face the women tomorrow. She had no idea what Henry had told the townsfolk about her. Had he given a reason for leaving? Had he told them something unflattering about her? She couldn't be sure, judging from Mrs. Kendall's invitation. The woman, it seemed, wanted her for her catalogs, regardless.

"Tomorrow morning," Mrs. Kendall declared. She headed for the door. "Come along, Rachel. I'm paying a visit to the mercantile to see what's going on with that fabric."

"But Mama, I'm sure Mr. Talbot is doing the best he can," Rachel said.

"We'll just see about that."

Rachel offered Anna a quick wave as she followed her mother out the door.

Mrs. Harrington gave Anna a telling look, then went back to sweeping. Anna stepped out onto the boardwalk.

Townsfolk passed, some of them nodding, some smiling faintly, others staring. What were they thinking? Anna wondered. What did they know?

If only she had some hint of what Henry had told folks before he left town. Had he ruined her reputation before she'd even arrived?

Something that awful Cade Riker had said to her yesterday drifted into her mind. A letter. Henry had left a letter. Anna had to learn what he'd written.

She sighed heavily. Much as she hated it, she'd have to find Cade Riker.

Chapter Four

Anna located the Branford Lumber Company on the west edge of town. Oxen dragged gigantic logs through the sprawling site, mule teams pulled wagons and men worked at a steady pace. There were barns and animal pens, storage buildings and sheds. A railroad spur from the main line snaked through the yard. Saws buzzed relentlessly.

Wood lay everywhere. Piles of logs. A maze of perfectly piled stacks of boards. Heaps of scraps. Sawdust mounds. The sweet smell of just-cut wood filled the air.

Henry had owned this business. The biggest in the state, he'd said. Surely the workers were concerned about their jobs, their futures.

Anna worried about her own. Though nearly everyone in Branford was a stranger and she could leave at any moment, she didn't want to be forced away. She wanted to take her time deciding what to do with her life. She needed to give it considerable thought. Her last decision hadn't been a good one, obviously.

Back home in Virginia, facing a marriage proposal, Anna had thought she and Henry shared a respect and fondness for each other. Even with her own feelings of inadequacy, she'd thought those qualities were enough to keep them together until she figured out how to make him happy.

They weren't. Henry had made that perfectly clear when he'd run out on her before she'd even arrived in Branford.

What did a man expect from his wife? She'd wrestled with the question. She'd observed other marriages but had gleaned nothing. None of those unions seemed to work well.

Her parents, for one. They had merely tolerated each other for several years before her mother died. Some of Anna's friends seemed to actually fear their husbands. Other husbands whom she had thought loved their wives were known to consort with all manner of women. Yet Anna had known men who doted on their wives. It made no sense.

She was left to wonder how a woman might discover these things in a prospective husband. Was there a way of finding out during the courting process?

To know the answer, a woman first had to understand what a man expected from a wife, what he thought, what he believed true and right in a marriage. Schools didn't teach it; Anna had found no books on the subject. Even the women she'd asked didn't seem to know the answer.

Gathering her skirts, Anna stepped up onto the long, narrow, covered porch of the lumber company's office. She'd come here to find Cade Riker. Someone at the lumberyard would know where she could find the man, since he was Henry's cousin. And, hopefully, Cade would let her see the letter Henry had left so that she might learn the answers she sought, as well as how much Henry had shared with the town.

Anna opened the door and stepped inside. Two desks sat at right angles in the center of the large room. Maps and charts hung on the walls. Windows on all sides let in sunlight and provided a sweeping view of the lumberyard.

Every flat surface in the office was piled high with crooked stacks of ledgers, and crumpled, dog-eared papers shoved haphazardly into them.

A door at the back of the office opened and a man walked

out of what appeared to be a storage room. Her heart rose in her throat.

Cade Riker. What was he doing here?

An easy smile spread across his face. "Afternoon, ma'am. Can I help you?"

Anna just stared. It wasn't Cade, after all.

"Ma'am?" he asked.

"Sorry," she said, giving herself a little shake. "I didn't mean to stare. But you look so much like—"

"Cade." He walked over. "I'm Ben Riker. Cade's brother. Most people get us mixed up."

"I can see why," Anna told him.

"You can tell us apart because I'm the good-looking one."

Ben's smile was wide and genuine. The resemblance between the brothers was uncanny. The difference lay in the soft, friendly lines of Ben's face.

"I'm Anna Kingsley," she said.

Ben's expression turned somber. "I can't tell you how sorry everyone is about Henry. I know this is a blow to you."

"I'm sure everyone here misses him," Anna said.

"Did you want to see Cade?" Ben asked.

"Why, yes," Anna said, wondering how he knew.

"I'll get him for you." Ben opened the back door, yelled Cade's name, then turned to Anna again. "He'll be right in."

She touched her fingers to her lips. "Mr. Riker—"

"Call me Ben. Keeps things simple that way."

"I didn't realize—"

Cade strode in the back door. He whipped off his hat and tossed it on the desk, then wiped his forehead with his shirt-sleeve. Anna's heart gave an annoying little lurch.

"You've got company," Ben said.

Cade turned, and just as he'd done at the train station yesterday, froze at the sight of her. Anna stilled, as well.

Some time dragged by while they both stared. Finally, Anna said, "I—I didn't know you worked here."

"Work here?" Ben chuckled. "Cade owns the place. Along with me, of course."

Heat swept up her throat and onto her cheeks. "I thought Henry…Henry told me he owned the company."

Ben shook his head. "Henry worked for us. He did the books, took care of the payroll, things like that."

Embarrassment burned her face. Yesterday, outside the train depot, she'd railed at Cade about how she could turn to Henry's employees in her time of need, since he'd been such an important man in town. And all along Cade knew the truth. He'd stood there and let her humiliate herself.

"You *own* the company?" she asked, stepping toward Cade.

"Well…yes," he admitted, and at least had the good grace to look uncomfortable.

She pushed her chin up. "You must have had quite a laugh yesterday at my expense."

"Uh, well, Miss Kingsley—"

Getting a look at Henry's letter didn't seem important at the moment. Anna drew herself up. "I came here, Mr. Riker, to thank you for your…assistance…yesterday when I arrived. So…thank you."

Anna yanked open the door and turned back. "For everything *except* the kiss." She stomped outside and slammed the door.

Anger and embarrassment rolled through Anna as she stopped at the edge of the porch, getting her bearings. She could burst into tears—if she wasn't so mad.

Behind her, the door opened. She glanced back to see Cade coming outside.

"Wait, Miss Kingsley," he called. "Don't go."

If he hadn't sounded a trifle contrite, she would have started walking. Instead, Anna waited. As Cade stepped in front of her, she wondered if she shouldn't have left.

Lord help her, he was handsome.

"Look, uh, I'm…" Cade pulled at the back of his neck. "I, uh, yesterday I should have, uh—"

"Is this some sort of attempt at an apology?"

He quit shuffling his feet and looked down at her. "I don't do it very often."

"Well, don't bother to do it now," Anna told him, her warring emotions draining away. "I probably deserved to be laughed at, after the way I carried on. I'm sorry."

"I'm sorry, too," Cade said, though the words didn't roll off his tongue very easily. "I'd just told you the man you'd come here to marry had up and left town. I couldn't see telling you he was a liar, too."

His reasoning made sense, though Anna didn't really want to agree with him.

Cade shifted again. "I want to apologize for the kiss, too."

"Well, you should. I can't get it out of my mind."

Cade raised an eyebrow. "You can't?"

Her cheeks flamed and she turned away, but he leaned down and caught her gaze. "Can't stop thinking about it, huh?"

Anna's eyes locked with his, and for a moment she thought he might kiss her again. Instead, he turned sharply and gazed toward the street. A frown settled over his face.

"What are you doing here, boy?" he asked.

A smaller version of Cade approached. Same dark hair, same blue eyes. His features were nearly identical, only softer. The boy stood almost as tall as Anna, long-limbed and skinny. She put his age at around thirteen.

She smiled. Surely this was exactly what Cade had looked like as a boy.

Instead of answering Cade's question, the boy stepped up onto the boardwalk. "Are you Miss Kingsley? I'm Kyle— Kyle Riker. Henry's cousin."

"It's a pleasure to meet you, Kyle," she replied, realizing this boy must also be Cade's brother.

"I'm sorry about Henry running off, and all," Kyle said.

"I'm sure you miss your cousin," Anna said.

"You're staying, aren't you?" Kyle asked. "Here, I mean. In Branford."

Anna couldn't resist giving Cade a defiant look. "I haven't decided what I'll do."

Kyle perked up a bit. "You've got a house here."

"I do?" she asked, completely taken aback.

Kyle threw Cade an accusing glare. "You didn't tell her about the house?"

"Look, Kyle—" Cade began.

"It's a nice house, ma'am," Kyle said. "You can live there and work for us. All you'd have to do is cook and clean a little. You can cook whatever you want. Cade and Ben will eat anything—and so will I. You can—"

"Whoa," Cade said. "Slow down, Kyle. We're not—"

"No." Kyle squared his shoulders and looked up at Cade. "She's supposed to be Henry's wife. Henry was our cousin. That mean she belongs to us. She's part of our family."

"She doesn't—"

"I'm the one doing all the cooking now," Kyle said, his voice rising. "And I'm tired of it. It's too much work. Nobody should have to do that much work. We need a woman!"

Cade looked at him for a long moment, then put his hand on Kyle's shoulder and urged him toward the opposite end of the porch. "Excuse me a minute?" Cade called to Anna.

Kyle remained on the porch; Cade moved to the ground so the two of them were closer to eye level.

Anna waited while their conference went on. Kyle did most of the talking. Cade nodded, said something that, from his expression, Anna suspected had to do with Kyle not being in school, then patted his back and sent him on his way.

He returned to where Anna waited. "Sorry about the boy."

"You were sweet with him," she said, genuinely surprised to see this side of Cade. "You let him speak his mind. You listened."

"Can't expect him to stand up and say his piece as a man if he doesn't learn as a boy."

"I take it you're raising him?"

Cade paused a moment, then glanced off down the street. "Our folks went down to Texas to visit our sisters a few years back. Train derailed. We lost them both."

The hard lines of his face softened, and Anna saw that the hurt lingered, even after so long.

"I'm sorry," she said. "So you took on the job of raising him?"

"A job that seems like it's never going to end," Cade said with a tired sigh.

The urge to touch his cheek, comfort him, nearly overcame Anna. It seemed the most natural thing to do.

She decided it was wiser to change the subject.

"I wondered about the letter Henry left," she said. "Could I see it?"

"Look, Miss Kingsley, there's no need in rehashing this thing. What's done is done."

"Yes, but I'd like to know the reason," Anna said, hoping she looked innocent. "You can understand, can't you?"

Cade gazed off toward town. Several moments passed, just long enough to bring a pang of guilt to Anna.

"I'm sorry," she said. "I shouldn't have asked. It's a painful memory for you, losing not only your cousin but a trusted employee. Forgive me for bringing it up."

"No, it's not that," Cade told her. He paused another moment, as if contemplating something, then said, "The letter didn't say much. Just that he was leaving for good."

"Nothing about…me?"

Cade turned his gaze on her. He looked angry, though Anna wasn't sure at what or at whom.

"He said to tell you he was sorry."

"Did he speak to anyone about his decision?" Anna asked. "To you? Or to someone—a friend, maybe—in town?"

Another tense minute crawled by with Cade's gaze turning even more harsh. "Look, Miss Kingsley, just let it go.

Henry made his decision. And he sure as hell didn't give any thought to you when he made it."

"But if it weren't for me, Henry would still be here." Anna waved her arm toward the office. "He'd be working. Instead, you've been left in the lurch."

"It's not your fault," Cade told her. He sounded a little angry, but Anna wasn't sure why.

"I want to get married…someday," Anna said softly. "I'd like to know why Henry didn't want me."

A flash of pain crossed Cade's face. Anna decided it best to leave the subject alone. She turned and walked away. After a moment, Cade fell into step beside her.

"You don't need to walk me back to town," Anna told him. "I can take care of myself."

"I seem to recall you shouting that at me yesterday." His voice hardened a little. "But just because you say it doesn't make it so."

Annoyed now, she picked up her pace a little, which did nothing to deter Cade. He walked alongside her until she stepped up onto the boardwalk at the edge of town.

Cade caught her arm. His long fingers curled around her gently and he leaned down a little.

"Another thing," he said. "Just because I apologized for kissing you doesn't mean I'm sorry I did it."

Anna gazed up into those blue eyes of his and, for an instant, lost herself in their intensity. And for that instant, lost *anywhere* with Cade Riker seemed like a wonderful place to be.

He backed off a little, releasing Anna from his hold. She huffed indignantly—simply because she thought she should—and walked away.

At the next block, she stopped and looked back.

Cade stood on the corner, still watching her.

Chapter Five

The Bank of Branford loomed ahead and, as always, its bold yellow-and-black sign caused Cade's steps to slow.

Paperwork. He hated it. Sorting through stacks of papers. Finding the right ledger, the correct column. Squeezing figures into tiny spaces. Making sure everything added up. He hated going to the bank, listening to that old windbag, Charles Proctor, while his tellers counted every cent—as if a nickel one way or the other made any difference.

Keeping the books, handling the money, paying the bills was the one thing—just about the only thing—Henry had been good at. And now Cade was stuck doing it.

Not that he hadn't tried to push the job off on Ben. But his brother had fought him on it. No one on the Riker side of the family had patience for bookkeeping. Cade had tried to think of someone he could pawn the task off on, but he didn't trust anyone outside the family.

He didn't dare let the problems at the lumberyard become public knowledge. A few months ago business had fallen off, surprising both Cade and Ben. The lumberyard had always been on sound financial footing. Neither had seen it coming.

Cade had secured new contracts and stepped up production, but it hadn't helped. Finances were stretched almost to the breaking point. If things didn't improve soon, he'd have to ask Charles Proctor for a bank loan.

Cade would rather take a beating than do that.

A flash of green caught his eye. Anna? She'd had on a green dress when she'd been at the lumberyard earlier. Was that her? And where was she going all by herself?

Cade headed down the boardwalk after her.

She'd made a point of telling him she didn't want his help, but Cade wasn't so sure she didn't need it. He had a responsibility to keep an eye on her, whether it suited her or not.

Cade wove through the crowd, watching Anna's backside just up ahead. She skirted around the folks on the boardwalk. People got out of Cade's way.

He wondered, not for the first time, why Anna had agreed to marry Henry. Why she'd come so far, left her family and friends.

At the train station yesterday, Cade had readily seen why Henry wanted to marry Anna. Aside from being pretty, fit and healthy looking, she was smart. She had spirit, too. The kind of vitality that would make for some long sultry nights in a marriage bed.

Cade grumbled under his breath as the mental image brought with it a swift and strong physical reaction.

His steps slowed when he saw Anna stop at the window of Talbot's General Store and look at the wedding display. Was she dreaming of the wedding that wouldn't take place?

Damn that Henry Thornton for running off, Cade thought. But he knew Henry wasn't solely responsible for shattering Anna's dream, and that knowledge hung like a weight around Cade's shoulders.

He held back, wrestling with his conscience—and his desire to see Anna again. He wasn't sure he ought to go to her, yet he couldn't seem to stop himself.

The light breeze blew at Anna's skirt as she stood gazing at the display window. Her head was tilted, giving her chin a jaunty angle in the late afternoon sunlight.

Cade stopped next to her and she turned, favoring him with a look from those big brown eyes. Something inside his chest grew warm, then dived low, predictably.

"Do you follow all the single women in town, Mr. Riker?" she asked, pushing her chin up a bit. "Or is it just me?"

"So far, it's just you."

Anna wasn't surprised by his honesty. Nor was she surprised to find him standing next to her. As in the alley yesterday, Cade suddenly appeared. A wall of strength.

"I wish you wouldn't feel bad about Henry leaving," Cade said. "It wasn't your fault."

He sounded so sincere, so concerned that Anna couldn't hold back her feelings. She'd walked the town for hours, thinking, trying to come to terms with what had happened. Something about Cade standing next to her made her want to confess everything.

"I didn't love him. I was fond of him, though," Anna said. "I suppose Henry figured that I wouldn't make a very good wife."

"The hell you wouldn't."

The depth of Cade's voice sent a little tremor through Anna. She fought to suppress the warmth flooding her cheeks—and elsewhere.

"I don't really know what it takes to be a good wife," Anna said. "Maybe I shouldn't have agreed to marry Henry."

"Then why did you?" His words weren't judgmental. Anna hadn't expected they would be. Her decision to marry Henry seemed to have happened years ago now, yet her reasoning was just as strong.

"I wasn't all that happy with my life," Anna told him. "So I decided to build a new one for myself, and make it the way I wanted."

Cade grinned. "I'll bet you could do just that."

Hearing those few words of praise touched Anna's heart. "Maybe I was wrong to come here to Branford." She shook her head. "I don't know."

Cade shrugged. "You did the wrong thing by agreeing to marry a man you didn't love. Seems to me it's okay to admit it to yourself, decide how to do better next time, then forgive yourself and go on."

Straightforward advice. It sounded too simple coming from Cade.

"I wish it were that easy."

"Seems to me it could be, in your case," Cade said. "Just don't agree to marry a man again unless you love him."

"I don't expect to receive any marriage proposals anytime soon," Anna said, smiling a little. She turned back to the window display once more. "Before I left Virginia, my father bought me the most exquisite wedding dress, the dress of my dreams. I'd like to wear it someday."

A moment passed and Anna turned away from the window. Cade fell in step beside her as they headed toward the hotel.

"Must be hard for you seeing all this wedding business going on," Cade said.

Nearly every store displayed something bridal. The general stores featured gift suggestions. The sign outside Birdie's Restaurant announced a wedding special. Wedding cookies were offered by the bakery. Even the barbershop heralded a groom's haircut and shave deal.

"Mrs. Kendall asked me to help with the wedding festival," Anna said.

"Figures…" Cade said. "That woman is bound and determined to drag the entire town into the weddings."

"I'd like to help," Anna said. "If there is a wedding festival, that is. I understand there's a problem with the fabric. What a disaster that will be if it doesn't arrive in time."

"Yeah, well, uh…" Cade glanced around. "I need to talk to you about something. Come over here."

Anna hesitated as he stepped off the boardwalk into the dusky alley beside the hotel. Her heart rate picked up a little, but it wasn't from fear. It was…

Nothing, Anna told herself. It was nothing. Where was her mind these days? She joined Cade in the alley.

"There's a job offer on the table," he said.

Earlier, Kyle had asked her to come work for the brothers, but Anna hadn't taken him seriously.

Cade seemed to read her thoughts. "It's a legitimate offer. Kyle doesn't want to do the cooking anymore, so I have to find someone else."

"Kyle cooks for the three of you?" Anna asked.

"Off and on, whenever we need him," Cade said. "After my youngest sister was born, Mama had three more babies. None of them lived. You can imagine her joy when Kyle came along healthy. She held on to him a little longer than she should. Made him a bit of a mama's boy. That's how he learned to cook."

"Why don't you just hire someone in town?" Anna asked.

"There's plenty of women who want the work," Cade said. "Problem is those women are either nosing around for some gossip, or are husband hunting."

"Well, I'm certainly not looking for a husband." Anna managed a small smile. "Unless I find one I'm in love with, of course."

Cade smiled back, sharing her confidence.

"All you'd have to do is make breakfast and supper, and clean up afterward," he explained. "And you'd have your own place to live."

"Henry built a house for me?"

Cade paused as if he wanted to say something, but didn't. "It's at the lumberyard, next to our house."

Anna considered it. The job sounded easy enough, and would keep her from spending the money she'd brought with her on hotels and restaurants. It would help fill her time, too, until she decided what to do with herself.

"There's something else," Cade said, his voice hardening a bit. "If you come to work for me, you have to know that anything you see or hear is confidential. You can't go carrying tales all over town."

Anna was slightly miffed by his words. Did he think she knew nothing about the business world? Her own mother had been a bookkeeper. Then Anna realized that the other women who'd worked for him in the past—the husband hunters and the gossips—had probably done just that.

"You needn't worry," Anna assured him.

He raised his brows, as if needing more of a promise.

"It's the first thing Miss Purtle taught at her academy," Anna told him. She cleared her voice and quoted, remembering the schoolmistress's words, "'When one finds oneself in the role of employee, confidentiality is of extreme importance.' I'll be trustworthy. I promise."

Cade nodded. "I guess that settles everything."

"Not exactly," Anna said. "Just because I work for you, don't start thinking you are responsible for me, or have a say in what I do. Don't go trying to boss me around."

"Even if I'm the boss?"

"You know what I mean. We're simply employer and employee. Nothing more."

Cade leaned a little closer. "You're thinking about our kiss again, aren't you?"

"No," she insisted, then flushed because that's exactly what she'd been thinking about. How could she not? Every time she was near this man that's what came to mind.

"You said yourself we should be employer and employee," Anna said. "So it stands to reason there should be nothing more between us. Don't you agree?"

"No."

She looked up at him, unsure of whether he was teasing or taking her seriously.

"Do we have a deal or not?" she asked.

Cade hesitated, then finally nodded. "We have a deal."

"Good." Anna offered to shake hands to seal the arrangement.

Cade's palm slid across hers and his big fingers enveloped her whole hand. Warmth raced up Anna's arm, stealing her breath away.

Even in the dark alley, Anna saw his expression change. His breathing deepened. He angled his body closer.

Anna's breath quickened, too. She felt his heat holding her in place.

Cade kissed her. He covered her lips with his and blended their mouths together with an exquisite slowness that caused Anna to lean her head back and rise on her toes. Cade moaned low in his throat and deepened their kiss, caressing her with his tongue.

He pulled away but his lips hovered close to hers.

"I—I thought we agreed…" Anna began.

"You're not my employee until tomorrow," he whispered. Then he pulled away, escorted her to the hotel entrance and left her standing in the doorway.

Chapter Six

The chill of dawn quickened Anna's steps as she left the Harrington Hotel and headed toward the west end of town, her satchel swaying in rhythm with her walk.

Her first day on a job. A real job. A place where she could make decisions and work as she chose.

Unlike those disappointing days back home. Even after she got her certificate from Miss Purtle's Academy, her father hadn't let her lend a hand even with the books, as her mother had done. And he'd absolutely refused to listen to a single one of her suggestions.

Anna never understood why her father displayed not an ounce of faith in her, or a smidgeon of confidence or trust. So many unanswered questions.

Such as what to do with her life now, Anna realized.

Yesterday she'd decided to stay in Branford for a while. No sense running off somewhere, such as her cousin's place in San Francisco, without a clear plan. The last thing Anna wanted to do was make another mistake.

She had to figure out a new life for herself. A life that, one day, would include a husband and children.

She knew about the most intimate aspects of marriage, of course. The girls at Miss Purtle's Academy had whispered about it, sometimes in great detail. It was the other aspects of marriage that troubled her.

What did men want from a wife? What did they expect? That's what Anna wanted to know.

Of course, her lack of wifely knowledge wouldn't have been her sole problem with Henry, if he'd stayed in town and married her. He'd lied to her. He'd looked her in the eye and lied about the lumber business.

An old, much-too-familiar knot drew Anna's stomach tight at the thought. She'd believed Henry. She'd trusted him. And he'd lied to her.

She knew in her heart that their marriage would never have worked. If two people had no trust between them, what sort of life could they have?

Apparently Cade Riker, of all people, had trust in her. He'd offered her a job. Not the sort of work she'd been trained for at Miss Purtle's Academy, but Anna knew she could perform it well. Yet how good a businesswoman was she? Anna wondered. She hadn't even asked how much the job paid.

That was because she'd been busy kissing her prospective boss.

A warmth that defied the coolness of the morning swept over Anna. She ignored it and kept walking.

Her footsteps slowed as she passed Talbot's General Store, and Mrs. Harrington's dire prediction came back to her. If the fabric for the wedding dresses didn't arrive soon, the man could well find himself kicked out of town.

At the edge of Branford, Anna spotted two houses situated not far from the lumberyard office. She hadn't noticed them yesterday, set back from the road as they were. Each house had two stories, a covered front porch and a white picket fence.

Anna knew instantly which home belonged to Cade's family. It showed a little more wear, of course, since it was older, but its color gave away the residents. The house had been painted pale yellow and trimmed in white. A woman—Cade's mother, surely—had selected the colors.

The house next door boasted a coat of sky-blue. A man had chosen that color.

Lamplight burned in the upstairs rooms of the yellow house, so Anna figured the Riker brothers were up. She circled the house, found the door unlocked and went inside.

"Hello? Good morning?" she called.

She walked into the kitchen, a large room with a cookstove, cupboards, a sideboard and a big table. There was a warmth, a friendliness about the kitchen. Anna imagined many a meal had been prepared here.

Including this morning's.

Dirty plates, coffee cups, pots and pans covered the table, the stove and the sideboard. She put her hat aside and pulled an apron from her satchel. Her first day on the job and she'd made an impression, all right. She'd completely missed breakfast.

Anna gathered the dishes from the table and stacked them on the cluttered sideboard. What could she do to make up for this morning's mistake but prepare a fine supper tonight?

"Something spectacular," she murmured.

Anna turned away from the sideboard just as a door on the other side of the room opened. Cade walked out, naked from the waist up.

"Spectacular, indeed..." She breathed the words, frozen in place, staring at him.

He wore dark trousers, the top button unfastened. A suspender hooked over one shoulder, a small towel draped the other. The sleeves of his long johns dangled.

His chest was bare. Coarse, dark hair covered it, swirled around his nipples and arrowed down his washboard belly, disappearing into his low-slung trousers.

Anna's breath caught as she dragged her gaze from that unfastened button upward over his chest, to pause at his wide, straight shoulders. Then his chin, wet and smooth, and his jaw white with shaving soap.

None of the girls at Miss Purtle's Academy had whispered about *this*.

Heat coiled deep in Anna, then surged through her, bringing her to her senses. Good gracious, what was she doing? Standing in a kitchen, staring at a half-naked man who'd just walked out of the family washroom?

Cade's gaze bored into her with an intensity that caused her cheeks to burn. Yet there was no anger behind that look. No outrage, no indignation at being ogled. Anna didn't know what it meant, only that it called to her.

She might have answered, too, if Kyle hadn't clomped into the kitchen, hopping into his boots. Cade ducked back into the washroom and closed the door. Anna grabbed more plates from the table.

"Morning, Miss Anna. I sure am glad to see you here."

She nodded toward the cookstove. "I see I'm late."

"Cade and Ben are worse than animals," Kyle grumbled. "If you don't feed them early, they're grumpy all morning."

Anna laughed gently. "Are you ready for school?"

"Almost," he said, then shouted at the closed door. "If Cade will ever get out of the washroom, that is."

The kitchen erupted in chaos with Kyle explaining where everything was in the cupboards while yelling at Cade in the washroom. Ben appeared and helped himself to another cup of coffee as he talked to her and roughhoused with Kyle. Anna sought refuge in the corner and thought herself safe there until she looked up to find Cade standing across the room.

With his shirt on.

"It's about time," Kyle complained, then ducked into the washroom.

Ben snapped Cade's attention with conversation about

something at the lumberyard, then grabbed a biscuit from the basket and headed out the back door.

Kyle came out of the washroom, slicking down his hair with his hand. Cade caught his arm, stopping him at the door.

"I expect you to stay in school all day," he told him.

Kyle didn't say anything, just gave him a quick nod and hurried out the door. Cade watched him for a minute, then turned to Anna.

"I'll send a wagon to the hotel to pick up your things so you can get settled next door. There's not much furniture, but the place is livable," he said. "If you need anything, come to the office. Don't go wandering around the lumberyard. It's dangerous."

"I'll be careful," Anna assured him.

"Dangerous for my men," Cade said. His gaze heated a little and swept her from head to toe. "If they get a look at you, they sure won't have their minds on their work."

He took his hat and a set of keys from the peg on the wall and left.

Anna went to the door and watched Cade head toward the lumberyard office. He moved with confidence, almost arrogance. A man used to being in charge. Wide shoulders, long back, narrow waist, tight—

She closed the door and dashed to the table, admonishing herself for her blatant stares.

Anna made quick work of cleaning the kitchen, then sorted through recipes she'd brought with her, and planned supper. She pinned her hat on again, got her satchel and went back to the hotel.

"Glad you're staying in town," Mrs. Harrington said, as Anna stood at the registration desk settling her bill. "And working for the Riker boys? Good for you."

"I'm also helping with the weddings," Anna said.

"They'll need all the help they can get." Mrs. Harrington shook her head. "Vida Kendall and poor old Mr. Talbot got into a shouting match first thing this morning. There were some mighty ugly words exchanged."

Anna cringed. "Let's hope that fabric gets here soon."

She went up to her room and put all her catalogs into her satchel to take to Mrs. Kendall's house for the planning meeting, then repacked her trunks. Anna took a minute to push aside the tissue paper that covered her wedding dress.

Such a beautiful gown. A treasure.

A pang of longing rose in Anna. Her father had seen to it she had the wedding dress of her dreams. How thankful she was that the biggest day of her life wasn't hanging on the whim of a textile mill and the railroad delivery schedule.

"Come in, come in," Mrs. Kendall insisted, stepping back from her front door and waving Anna inside.

"Thank you for inviting—"

"Did you bring the catalogs?" Mrs. Kendall asked.

Anna lifted her satchel. "Yes, I—"

"Come inside, then."

Anna followed the woman down a short hallway. The Kendall home sat near the edge of town, a fine two-story house painted green, and Anna could see that Mrs. Kendall took pride in furnishing it.

The din of voices stopped as Anna stepped into the parlor. Nearly a dozen women turned to her. Mrs. Kendall made rapid-fire introductions of the brides-to-be, their mothers and the other women helping with the weddings. Then she relieved Anna of her catalogs and passed them out.

"I'm so glad you're here," Rachel Kendall said, coming to Anna's side.

The other two brides-to-be joined them—Mary Sumner, daughter of a local businessman, and Sarah Proctor, daughter of Branford's banker, if Anna remembered the introduction correctly.

Sarah's mother called to her from across the room as she

fanned through a catalog, leaving Anna to take a seat on the settee between Rachel and Mary. Anna talked with them until Mrs. Kendall rose to her feet.

"Ladies?" The woman raised her hand for silence. "I want to give you the latest on the fabric situation."

A rumble of interest went through the gathering. Anna thought she heard Rachel groan softly.

"This morning I spoke with Mr. Talbot *again*," Mrs. Kendall said. "He claims to have received confirmation that the fabric was shipped from England and arrived in New York."

"New York?" Mrs. Proctor's eyes widened in horror. "It's only now gotten as far as New York? But—"

Mrs. Kendall held up her hand for silence once more. "Mr. Talbot also claims that he has received notice from the railroad that the fabric was shipped here to Branford."

An expectant silence hung in the room. All the women leaned forward slightly.

Mrs. Kendall drew herself up slightly. "The fabric was shipped to Branford *weeks* ago."

The room erupted.

"Weeks ago?" someone called.

"It should have gotten here already," someone else declared.

The noise grew. Several women rose to their feet.

"I know what's going on!" Mrs. Sumner cried, bringing the room to silence. "I'll bet that Edgar Talbot never ordered the fabric in the first place! He was only boasting about his contacts in England! And now he's giving us this so-called confirmation story to appease us!"

Shrieks of horror arose, then Mrs. Proctor shouted, "I'll bet Talbot is deliberately holding the fabric! He's waiting until we become desperate so he can charge more!"

"How dare he!" another women called.

"It would be just like him!" someone else agreed.

"Oh, goodness…" Rachel groaned.

Anna turned to her. Color drained from the girl's face and she seemed to shrink more at each outburst.

"Would you like to get some air?" Anna asked.

"I'd like that, but…" Rachel glanced at her mother. "I don't dare leave."

Anna nodded in understanding. Seemed they were all trapped. She remembered her friends' weddings back home that she'd been a part of. Weddings seemed to bring out the worst in people, during the planning stage, anyway. These weddings, apparently, would be no different.

Heated accusations flew until the meeting broke up, with Mrs. Kendall and the other two mothers vowing to get to the bottom of the fabric scandal *no matter what*. As the women moved toward the door, Rachel touched Anna's arm.

"I really would love to hear about your train journey," she said. "Could we get together and chat?"

An escape—even a vicarious one—must seem appealing to Rachel. Anna understood her interest.

"Rachel!" her mother called.

The girl cringed slightly and hurried away.

Anna arrived at the Riker home before anyone else. She got supper started, then set the table with china she found in the cupboard that must have belonged to Cade's mother.

After the chaos of the Kendall home, Anna was more than ready for a quiet meal. She was anxious, too, to show off her menu planning and cooking, and demonstrate to the Riker brothers how capable she was.

Just as she placed a vase of fresh flowers on the table, Cade and Ben burst through the back door, looking tired and arguing over something. Neither acknowledged her as she placed the serving dishes on the table. Kyle showed up a few minutes later, shouting to be heard over their argument.

The three of them circled the table. Ben grabbed a chicken leg from the platter, took a bite, then pointed it at Cade, making some sort of point. Kyle broke off a hunk of corn bread and shoved it in his mouth, dropping crumbs on the floor. Cade picked up the vase of flowers from the table to set aside.

Anna watched in horror. She wanted—needed—a quiet evening. And she certainly didn't intend to let this sort of behavior set a precedence.

She picked up two pot lids and slammed them together. The men froze.

"If I intended to feed animals, I'd serve at a trough!" she declared.

All three of them shared a guilty glance.

She pointed at them. "Put that vase back on the table. And put that food on your plates. Go wash, all of you."

Ben and Cade hung their hats and a set of keys, which Anna figured belonged to the lumberyard office, beside the back door, then all three trooped into the washroom.

"Aren't you going to eat with us, Miss Anna?" Kyle asked when they came out again

She hadn't set a place for herself, thinking that she'd eat later. She was, after all, an employee.

"Yeah, come on and eat with us," Ben agreed.

They all looked at Cade, awaiting his approval.

"Sure," he said, and nodded toward the seat across the table from him.

Anna fetched a place setting for herself, then Cade and Ben bumped into each other as they both tried to hold the chair for her. Cade glared Ben into submission and they finally all settled down and started eating.

Anna decided her cooking met with their approval, since none of them spoke. Toward the end of the meal, they managed to make conversation. Anna told them about the meeting at the Kendall home and the accusations made against Mr. Talbot.

Afterward, Ben left to pay a call on the woman he was courting, while Anna cleared the table. Kyle helped her.

"Did you get settled next door?" Cade asked as, standing by the sideboard, he sipped a final cup of coffee.

The men from the lumberyard that Cade had sent had picked up her trunks and delivered them to the house. Anna had stopped by earlier and looked at the place.

"I have to unpack," she said. "It's a lovely house. I didn't realize Henry was such a good carpenter."

"Henry didn't build it," Kyle said, gathering a stack of plates from the table. "Cade did."

Anna's gaze swung to him. "You built it? I thought—"

"Your house would never have gotten built if it hadn't been for Cade. It was his idea. He did most of the work himself," Kyle said. "The Thornton side of the family is the laziest bunch of people the good Lord ever put the breath of life into. That's what Mama used to say. But they're family, so what can we do?"

Anna stared expectantly at Cade, waiting for further explanation, but all he did was set his coffee cup aside and head out the back door.

Outside, Cade walked a bit, then gazed toward the lumberyard. All was quiet at this time of night. He enjoyed the silence, the solitude.

After a while he heard the back door close, and turned to see Anna, lantern in hand, walk next door to her new house. His heart warmed at the sight of her—and so did the rest of him. It took everything Cade had not to follow her.

What a pretty thing she was, moving through the shadows with the lamplight dancing around her. Smart and caring, too. The supper she'd fixed seemed like the closest thing to a family meal he'd had in a long time. And she'd held true to her declaration of self-reliance. Not once had she asked for anything. Not yet, anyway.

Something about Anna still nagged at Cade's conscience. Touched something old, something ugly. Something he hadn't gotten over even after all these years.

Maybe it was better that way, he decided.

Light flickered through the windows of the house as Anna

made her way to the bedroom downstairs. Soon she'd undress, peel away skirt, petticoats and all the other trappings women wore. What sort of nightgown would she wear? Would she leave her hair down when she slid beneath the coverlet?

Cade let the images play through his mind. He thought again about going to her house, knocking on her back door, just to make sure she was all right. It seemed like a good idea.

Because after tomorrow, Anna might never speak to him again.

Chapter Seven

Had she done something wrong?

The notion came to Anna yet again as she left town, headed for the lumberyard office. This morning she'd gotten to the Riker house in plenty of time to prepare breakfast. Biscuits and gravy, potatoes, eggs, bacon, fried apples, steaming coffee. A meal hearty enough to please two grown men and one growing boy.

Or so she'd thought.

Just before he'd left the house, Cade asked her to come to the office this morning.

Was he unhappy with her cooking? Did it displease him that she'd used his mother's china?

An old, familiar mantle of worry swept over her. If she didn't figure out how to make a man happy pretty soon, how would she ever have a successful marriage? How would she ever be good enough?

Perhaps Cade would tell her. Anna's spirits lifted a little. If he was unhappy with something she'd done, she'd insist that he tell her how to improve.

Anna wished now she'd gone directly to the lumberyard office after cleaning the breakfast dishes. Instead she'd gone to town to pick up a few things she needed for her new house.

What she'd gotten was an earful when she'd walked past Talbot's General Store.

The din of men, animals and saws greeted her now as she drew near the lumberyard office. Even after so short a time, she'd gotten used to the noise. Anna caught her reflection in the window glass, straightened her hat and went inside.

The sounds faded—or maybe she didn't notice them anymore—thanks to the sight of Cade sitting at his desk. Ledgers were stacked up around him. One lay in front of him, unopened. He stared at the cover as if lost in thought.

An unfamiliar hunger claimed Anna. Now, and every time she'd looked at Cade since that first day on the railroad platform. She never felt it when she looked at any other man. Just Cade.

He glanced up at her and came to his feet.

"You're here." Cade fidgeted a bit, then waved her over. "Sit down."

"You look troubled," Anna said, and suddenly nothing seemed more important than learning what it was and finding a way to help him. She walked to his desk. "What's wrong?"

He stewed for a moment. "I stopped by the schoolhouse this morning. Kyle wasn't there."

"Why won't he stay in school?"

"I wish I knew. I've talked to him but he never gives me a straight answer."

"Are the lessons too hard?"

Cade shook his head. "Mama taught him to read before he ever set foot in a schoolhouse. The teacher has to give him special work to keep him occupied. I even told him not long ago that I'd send him to a college back East."

"Maybe there's a problem with one of the other students," Anna suggested. "A bully?"

Cade's expression hardened but not out of anger. More a protectiveness for his little brother.

"I'll see about that," he said, then seemed to dismiss the

subject by shoving aside the stacks of ledgers on his desk and clearing his throat. "So, ah, thanks for coming by this morning. There's something I need to…tell you."

A sense of unease crept over Anna. "What is it?"

"I, uh—just a minute."

Cade walked to the front door, checked outside, then slid the dead bolt lock in place. He did the same at the back door, then stationed himself at the entrance to the storage room.

"Come in here," he told her, then stepped inside.

Anna hesitated. How odd. What on earth was he doing?

"Anna?" He stuck his head out the door. "In here."

She ventured close to the storage room and peeked inside. A small, shaded window illuminated cluttered shelves and dozens of boxes and crates strewn haphazardly about. The tiny room didn't appear to have been cleaned in years.

"We don't have much time," Cade insisted. "Somebody might come to the door.

"But—"

Cade caught her wrist, pulled her inside and closed the door. He took up nearly all of the available space. Tall, big, strong. Warm, too.

Or was that *her?*

Anna backed up until she bumped the door. "What's this all about?"

"I want you to do something for me." Cade leaned across a stack of wooden boxes and pulled down the window shade, leaving the room in near darkness.

Anna's heart rate picked up a bit. But she wasn't sure if it was fear—or something different entirely.

Cade leaned close to her, towering over her. Heat wafted from him, cloaking her.

"You're working for me now, you know," he said.

Anna leaned her head back to see his face. She couldn't read his expression in the dim light. "Yes, I know that."

"And you remembered what we talked about when I offered you the job?" Cade asked. "Anything you see or hear has to be kept confidential. You gave me your word on that. Remember?"

How could she forget? He'd kissed her right afterward.

"Yes, yes I remember," Anna said, growing impatient and a little annoyed with herself that the memory of his kisses never left her. "Would you please just get on with whatever reason you have me in here?"

He looked at her for another moment, as if judging something in her, or making a determination, then turned and began sorting through the wooden crates. When he'd dug down to the largest one at the bottom, he straightened, gave Anna another look, then pulled off the lid and set it aside.

"There." He pointed.

She glanced inside the crate, saw nothing but packing paper. "Oh, honestly, Cade. You asked me to come over here, scared me to death thinking you were unhappy with my cooking, and all because of a crate of something? Why on earth—"

"It's the fabric."

Anna froze. She looked at the crate, then at Cade, then at the crate once more. "It's the—"

"Fabric. For the wedding dresses. It's—"

"*Here?*" Anna's eyes widened and her mouth fell open. "What is it doing *here?*"

"It must have gotten sent over from the train station by mistake, along with some other supplies. Henry took care of things like this, and with him gone, nobody realized it."

"How long has it been here?"

"I don't know. I just found it a few days ago."

"A few days ago?" Anna demanded. "And you didn't tell anybody?"

Cade winced. "I couldn't."

Anna flung both hands out. "The whole town is up in arms over this fabric. Accusations are flying. Just this morning I saw Mrs. Kendall, Mrs. Sumner and Mrs. Proctor in Talbot's

General Store. The sheriff was there. The women wanted the store searched and Mr. Talbot carted off to jail."

"I know things are getting out of hand." Cade pointed at the box. "But this isn't going to make things better."

Anna thought he'd taken leave of his senses. "Of course it will. I'm going to Talbot's right now and tell them the fabric is here."

She yanked open the door but Cade reached over her head and slammed it shut again. She spun around. "What is wrong with you? Why don't—"

"There's not enough."

Anna clamped her mouth shut, her gaze darting once more to the crate.

"The mill made a mistake filling the order. There's not enough fabric. See?" Cade picked up the bill of lading from atop the packing paper.

Anna angled it toward the feeble light creeping in around the window shade. Her blood ran cold.

"There's not enough fabric," she said, looking up at Cade. "The mill made a mistake. They didn't ship everything that was ordered. Only a portion."

"A *small* portion."

"Not nearly enough for three wedding dresses. Barely enough for two." Anna touched her fingers to her forehead. "Oh, dear. This is awful. Three brides and two wedding dresses. How will the fabric be divided up? Which of the brides will get it? And which one will get none?"

Cade shook his head. "Damned if I know."

"What are you doing to do?" Anna asked.

"Me? I'm not going to do anything." Cade reached around her, opened the door and strode into the office.

"Of course you're going to do something," Anna insisted, following him.

"No, I'm not." Cade swung around to face her. "You are."

"Me?" Anna stopped in her tracks.

"This is your problem now," Cade told her. "You figure it out."

She gasped in outrage. "You can't dump this in my lap."

"Yes, I can. You work for me, remember? It's your responsibility now."

"Not so fast." Anna advanced on him.

Cade backed up. "It's a woman's problem. A woman should handle it."

"This could get me run out of town!"

"Better you than me. God knows what those women might do if they find out the fabric was here all along. My business could be ruined. And I've got enough problems here already," Cade told her. He strode to the rear of the office, unbolted the back door and yanked it open. "I haven't got time to be fooling around with fabric and squabbling women. You handle it."

Anna's spine stiffened. "And if I refuse?"

"Suit yourself. But just remember your promise. You can't tell anybody the fabric is here." Cade plopped his hat on his head and went outside, slamming the door behind him.

Cade followed Ben into the kitchen, glad this long day was behind him. More than the usual number of problems had plagued him at the lumberyard—or maybe they just seemed worse after his confrontation with Anna this morning over the fabric. He'd gotten rid of the situation by dumping it on her, but that didn't make him feel as good as he'd hoped.

At least he'd get a good supper. Anna's cooking was the best. And he liked seeing her move around the kitchen, bending over to use the oven, reaching up to the cupboards. He'd caught her singing to herself when he'd come down for breakfast this morning. Such a sweet sound. Knowing she waited inside the kitchen right now made the day's problems seem a little less important.

Stepping into the room, Cade hung his hat and the office keys on the peg, then turned and saw his two brothers staring down at the supper table. Anna brushed past him.

"Leave the dishes. I'll clean them later," she barked, and disappeared out the door.

"What the…?" Cade turned to Ben and Kyle.

"What did you do?" Ben snarled.

"Yeah," Kyle snapped.

Cade had no idea what he was being accused of until he looked down at the supper table. It held a bowl of carrots, three slices of cold ham and the last of this morning's biscuits.

"What did you do to her?" Ben demanded.

"What makes you think that I—"

"Look at this meal," Ben declared.

"Yeah," Kyle said again, his anger rising. "Yesterday we got a great supper. She even made dessert. I like her. I don't want her to leave. And I don't want to go back to doing the cooking!"

"And I don't want to eat his cooking anymore." Ben pointed his finger at Cade. "Whatever you did, she's taking it out on all of us. You'd better fix this."

Cade grumbled under his breath, then slammed out the back door.

Fine thing. Couldn't even come to his own home and have a quiet supper. And then to have his own brothers turn on him. Well, that topped his day off just dandy.

Cade strode across the yard to Anna's house. He almost pushed the back door open and went inside, but caught himself and pounded his fist against the wooden planks.

"Anna!"

He raised his hand again but the door jerked open. Anna glared up at him, her cheeks flushed, her breathing heavy and her nose flared a little.

Lord, he wanted her.

Cade just stared at her, his anger gone, replaced by urgent and all-consuming desire.

She crossed her arms in front of her, pushing her breasts up a little. "What do you want?" she demanded.

What he wanted flashed through his mind in a heartbeat. Pull her against him. Kiss her senseless. Carry her to bed, make love until they were both exhausted. Then keep her beside him…forever.

Forever?

Cade backed up a step, stunned by his own runaway thoughts. He realized then that she was still staring at him, puffed up with anger and indignation, waiting for him to say something.

He gestured toward the house next door. "Does this mean we're not getting dessert tonight?"

"Oh!"

Anna slammed the door, but Cade was quicker. He caught it with his arm and stepped inside. This house was a twin of the one next door. Yet seeing Anna standing in the middle of the kitchen where she'd already added her own special touches made him feel entirely different about the place.

"What are you so mad about?" Cade asked.

Her eyes widened. "You don't *know?*"

"I've got a pretty good idea, but I don't want to admit to anything you might not know about yet."

"Oh, honestly…"

"Is it the fabric?"

"Yes. And I'm not really mad. I'm hurt."

Cade thought for a moment, trying to follow her reasoning. He failed.

"If you were just mad I could say I'm sorry and that would be the end of it," Cade said. "But this 'hurt' business is going to take a little longer, I just know it. Want to go outside?"

She hesitated a few seconds, then nodded and glided out the back door ahead of him.

The last of the sun's rays had already slipped below the horizon, leaving the sky with a few streaks of purple and the land banded with shadows. Anna lowered herself onto the top step of the porch. Cade sat down beside her.

The evening breeze was cool, and it carried the night song of a bird perched high in a nearby treetop. Cade let the quiet surround them; apparently, Anna was content to do the same.

He looked at her, though, studied her profile as she gazed toward the lumberyard. A loose strand of her hair lay against her neck. Cade wanted to curl it around his finger. He wanted to lean forward and bury his nose behind her ear, a sweet spot he'd discovered when he'd kissed her. He wanted to uncover other spots that he knew would be even sweeter.

"So, what's the problem at the lumberyard?" Anna asked without turning to him. "This morning in the office, you said you had your hands full with problems there."

Cade shifted, a little surprised that she remembered what he'd said.

"Business dropped off unexpectedly. But it will come back around," Cade said. "Nothing I can't handle."

"I'm sure that's true." Anna turned to him and the look of confidence in her eyes pleased him. Her expression hardened a little. "I'm hurt because you didn't trust me."

"I trusted you to come into my house, have free rein of the place with nobody around," he pointed out.

"But you didn't trust my judgment," Anna told him. "You dumped the fabric situation on me not because you knew I could handle it well, but because you didn't want to fool with it. And you did it under the guise of me being your employee, someone obligated to do as you said."

Cade thought about it for a minute, trying to come up with a way to refute her claim, but couldn't. "Yeah. I guess you're right about that. Trusting people outside the family isn't easy for me."

"No one in my family had any faith or confidence in me to help with the business, even after I graduated from Miss Purtle's Academy," Anna said.

Cade couldn't imagine how lessons on etiquette and table manners would help out in her father's business, but he didn't say anything.

"I tried so hard to figure out how to get my father and brother to accept me, but I never did." Anna gazed across the yard again. "I thought it would be different out here."

"It takes time to build up trust," Cade pointed out.

"And only a second to destroy it." She turned to him once again. "Who shattered your trust?"

He drew back a little, surprised by her insight. He wasn't sure anyone knew how much of that incident in Texas he still carried around with him after all these years. It showed in most everything he did. Ben understood. That's why the two of them made good business partners.

Sitting next to Anna, Cade experienced a comfort he'd never found with a woman before. Telling her what had happened didn't seem too difficult.

"We used to live in Texas. My pa ran a couple of businesses there. I wasn't much more than a kid when this girl came to town, visiting her aunt. Prettiest girl I'd ever seen. She took a shine to me right away. I fell head over heels for her, asked her to marry me. She said yes."

"You've been married?" Anna asked, surprised.

"No." Cade shook his head. "Her papa showed up in town, explained that she was already engaged to a business associate of his."

Anna seemed to consider what he'd told her. "So she was just looking for a way to get out of the marriage her father had planned for her."

"And I was her escape plan," Cade said. "She never loved me in the first place."

"Oh, Cade, that's awful."

Anna touched his hand, sending a wave of warmth up his arm. It was a comforting feeling. More than worth the lingering anguish of telling the hurtful story.

"I understand why you have trouble trusting people," she stated.

"Does that mean you'll take care of the fabric?"

"Maybe," she said. "I want something from you."

Cade's interest piqued as all sorts of thoughts skittered through his mind, but none, he was sure, that had anything to do with what Anna was likely to ask for.

"I want you to explain *men*," she told him.

His brows drew together. "You want me to do—what?"

"I want you to—"

"Miss Anna?" Kyle called.

Cade looked up to see his two brothers approaching. They stopped at the bottom step.

"Whatever stupid thing he did—" Ben said, jerking his thumb at Cade "—we're here to apologize for it."

"Yeah. We're sorry for whatever it was," Kyle said. "So will you still cook for us?"

"How about if I make you some hotcakes right now?" Anna got to her feet, then glanced back at Cade. She gave him a half smile. "I'll expect answers to my questions, starting tomorrow."

Chapter Eight

Time was of the essence.

Anna hurried out the back door of her house, anxious to find the prospective brides and their mothers, and get this unhappy chore over with. She'd thought about and could come up with no other way to handle it except to be honest. She'd announce the "good news," then let them figure out what to do with the fabric—or lack of it.

Noise from the lumberyard caught her attention as she crossed the yard. Work had been under way for nearly two hours now. She scanned the men moving about, then realized she hoped to spot Cade. An odd wave of disappointment washed through her when she didn't.

Had he come back home?

The back door at the Riker house stood open. Had Cade returned for some reason? And why did she keep thinking of him?

Anna stepped up onto the porch and glanced inside. Kyle sat at the kitchen table, reading.

He looked up as she walked in. "Hi, Miss Anna."

"Didn't I sent you off to school a few hours ago?" she asked, keeping her voice light.

Kyle shrugged. "I was there...for a while."

"Aren't you afraid of getting into trouble with your

teacher?" Anna asked. "Back when I was in school, a good swat with a hickory stick wasn't unheard of."

"Teacher's not allowed to hit me," Kyle said. "Cade told her not to. She's supposed to tell Cade if I cause trouble. He takes care of it."

Kyle seemed content with the arrangement, and not in the least fearful of his brother. It didn't surprise Anna.

For a moment she wondered what she should do with the boy, finding him here when he should be in school. Send him back to his teacher? Send him to Cade?

Really, she had no authority over him, just concern for his education and well-being. He wasn't causing harm to anyone, except himself, and he'd come home, of all places, to his own kitchen to read.

This was the oddest truancy Anna could imagine. She didn't envy Cade trying to figure it out.

"I'm going into town. Come with me?" Anna asked, thinking it better to keep him in sight.

"Sure." Kyle closed his book and followed her outside.

"Cade mentioned he wanted to send you to college back East," Anna said, as they walked. "That sounds exciting."

"Yeah, I guess…" Kyle murmured. "What are you going to town for?"

After much thought, Anna had decided the best way to break the news about the fabric was to invite everyone to the house. Surely the ladies would be on good behavior in someone else's home.

"I'm inviting a few ladies for refreshments this afternoon," Anna said.

"Mama used to do that," Kyle said.

Anna glanced down at him and saw the same hint of sorrow she'd seen in Cade's face when he'd told her about the death of their parents.

"My mother died a few years ago," Anna said softly. "I still miss her."

"Then how come you came here?" Kyle stopped abruptly, freezing Anna in place. His gaze came up sharply, the blue of his eyes showing bewilderment. "If you'd stayed at home, you could see the chair where she used to sit and the basket where she kept her knitting, things like that. It would be like she was still close by."

"I do miss those things," Anna admitted. "But I didn't get along so well with the rest of my family."

Kyle didn't seem to understand. "How could you not want to be around your family? Family is…well, family."

Anna smiled. "If I had a family like yours, Kyle, I'm sure I would never have left home."

He nodded thoughtfully as they continued on. When they reached town, Anna spotted Rachel right away. Rachel saw her at the same instant and walked over. A young girl, around Kyle's age, was with her.

"This is my cousin Ariel," Rachel said. "She arrived from Kansas last night with my aunt. They're here for the wedding."

Ariel could have been a porcelain doll standing on a store shelf, with golden hair and a magnolia-blossom complexion, dressed in a soft blue dress that matched her eyes. When Rachel made introductions, she dipped her lashes demurely.

"Pleased to meet you," Ariel said, her cheeks blushing.

"I'm so glad you're visiting," Anna said to her.

Kyle, however, couldn't seem to utter a single word. He stared, his mouth open slightly.

"Where's your mother?" Anna asked Rachel, expecting to see them together, as usual.

"She's gone with the preacher and his wife to visit the sick and shut-ins outside of town." Rachel nodded across the street and lowered her voice. "You might notice Talbot's is closed today. He's gone fishing. The sheriff's suggestion."

Anna nodded in understanding. She was disappointed, though, that she couldn't get everyone together right away and be done with the fabric problem. She didn't dare make the situation known without Vida Kendall present.

But at least the sheriff had stepped in and relieved the tension, for a day, anyway. And a delay that brief wouldn't adversely affect the brides who still needed to sew their wedding dresses. With every woman in town standing at the ready, the gowns could be completed in no time.

"Can you and your mother come by the house tomorrow afternoon?" Anna asked. "I'm inviting the other brides and their mothers, too."

"Certainly. Ariel and I were heading to the bakery. Would you two like to come along?" Rachel smiled dreamily. "I want to hear about your trip from Virginia. How wonderful it must have been for you to get on a train and just *go*."

Anna followed the two of them down the boardwalk but got no more than three steps before realizing Kyle hadn't moved.

"Come with us," Anna said. "I'll buy us cookies."

Kyle shook his head frantically. "I—I can't go. She's too… pretty."

A flash of memory took Anna back to her own youthful days of trembling knees and sweaty palms, of being too tongue-tied to speak.

Cade popped into her head. Maybe those days weren't so far in the past, after all.

She touched Kyle's shoulder. "Ariel is new in town. I'm sure she'd enjoy talking with someone her own age."

His eyes grew big as saucers. "You want me to *talk?* I can barely *breathe*."

Anna pressed her lips together to keep from smiling. "Just come with us. You don't have to talk if you don't want to. But you should keep breathing."

"Breathing." Kyle nodded. "Yeah, okay, I can do that."

Anna gave him a gentle push and they headed off down the boardwalk together.

* * *

When the knock sounded at her back door, Anna didn't need to answer it to know it was Cade. She'd heard the thud of his boots on the steps and porch, and knew it was him.

She opened the door, and though she'd just seen him a short while ago during supper at his house, her stomach warmed at the sight of him.

"Come in." She stepped out of his way, and closed the door behind him. "Coffee?"

"Yeah, sure."

He stood near the door, looking a little uncomfortable. Or perhaps he was tired. His days were long and he had more than his share of problems.

"You've got the place looking nice," Cade said, jerking his chin to encompass the kitchen.

Anna smiled as she poured coffee she'd just made, pleased that he'd noticed the work she'd done. Curtains, table linens and other items she'd brought with her from Virginia complemented things she'd gotten here in town.

"I'm working on the downstairs," Anna said, handing him a cup of coffee. "In fact, I've only been upstairs once."

On the day she'd arrived at the house, she'd gone to the second floor and found it empty, except for a few boxes of items that belonged to Henry. She'd had no reason to go upstairs since. The downstairs rooms were all she needed.

"Maybe you should sit down," Anna said, gesturing toward the table in the corner.

Cade froze, his cup halfway to his mouth. "Something tells me I'm not going to like the reason you asked me to come over here."

"Probably not," she admitted.

He heaved a tired sigh and set his cup aside. "Just tell me what's going on."

"Kyle wasn't in school today."

"Damn…" Cade dropped into a chair. "Why won't that boy

stay in school? I've talked to him over and over, and I can't get him to tell me what's wrong."

"There's another…situation." Anna placed his coffee cup on the table and sat down across from him. "I took him into town with me. We met Rachel's cousin, Ariel. She's a lovely young girl. Kyle seemed quite taken with her."

Cade frowned. "You mean…?"

Anna nodded quickly. "Yes."

"Great…" Cade blew out a heavy breath. "You got any more good news for me?"

"Actually, yes. Only this good news is actually good," She said with a quick smile. "I've invited the brides and their mothers over tomorrow. I'm going to explain what happened with the fabric."

He perked up, as if this news was actually something he wanted to hear.

"I'd like to receive them at your house rather than here, if you don't mind," Anna said. "Your mother's parlor has more breakables. It might keep a fight from erupting."

"What are you going to do about the fabric?" he asked.

"I'm simply going to hand it over," she said. "I don't know how else to handle it."

Cade just looked at her. Anna waited for him to say something; men always did. She'd yet to meet a man who kept his mouth closed long enough to hear a problem in its entirety before blurting out his solution.

But Cade said nothing. Somehow, the silence between them was comfortable. Just as his unexpected presence was. When she'd ducked into the alley to cry that first day she'd looked up and seen him there. As if he knew, somehow, that she needed him.

Anna supposed Cade was used to being needed. The demanding business he ran, his many employees, his brothers. He carried a lot of responsibility on his shoulders.

Wide, strong shoulders…

Anna gave herself a mental shake, anxious now to end the silence between them.

"Do you have a better idea?" she asked.

"I think you ought to have a plan in mind to divide up the fabric. Otherwise, things could get real ugly, real fast."

Anna thought about it for a moment. "That's a possibility. But if the fabric is divided among the three brides, there won't be enough to make a complete dress. If they use what's available for trim along with another type of cloth, for example, it won't do the fabric justice. Besides, I can't imagine any of the brides being willing to do that."

"Especially Mrs. Kendall."

Anna cringed. "Especially Mrs. Kendall."

"Then you'll have to find some impartial way to decide who gets it," Cade said. "Like playing a hand of poker, or cutting for high card."

"You expect brides to *gamble* for a wedding dress?" Anna shook her head. "That sounds like something men would do."

"Men would have a drinking contest or a wrestling match."

Anna rolled her eyes. "Women certainly aren't going to wrestle for fabric."

Cade grinned. "Might be kind of interesting."

"Oh, honestly…" Anna got up from her chair and walked to the sideboard. "This is what I get for asking a man what he thinks."

"I seem to recall you wanting to know about that sort of thing." Cade rose and followed her.

"So you're ready to answer my questions now?" Anna turned and found him standing so close they nearly touched. Yet she didn't shrink from his greater size. If anything, it drew her nearer, somehow.

"I'll tell you anything you want to know," Cade said, his voice soft and mellow. "But I can save you some time by saying that we only think about three things."

"That's all?"

Cade angled his body closer and glanced down. Anna shivered as his gaze flicked across her breasts.

"Okay. Four things."

Heat surged through Anna. She struggled against the desire to lean a little closer, to press her body to his. She realized those "three things" weren't proper conversation for an unmarried couple.

"It's more complicated than that. It has to be," Anna insisted.

Cade eased back, just a little. Anna fought the urge to follow.

"What are you trying to figure out?" he asked.

"Men. How do they think? What makes them happy?" Anna shook her head. "I tried so hard to please my father, to understand what he wanted so he'd let me help with the family business. I never did. I read books and magazines, talked with my married friends, trying to learn how I could please Henry, make him a good wife. But somehow, through reading my letters, he knew I didn't measure up."

"Your pa had his reasons for doing what he did and, I imagine, they had nothing to do with what you were capable of." Cade's expression hardened. "And Henry was a fool."

Anna turned away. "Maybe I should forget about ever getting married."

Cade touched her chin and brought her face around. "That would be a waste."

Anna saw warmth and hunger in his expression. The same grew inside her, threatened to overtake her. How easy, how delightful that would be. She'd experienced his hard body against hers, tasted his kisses. Dare she give in to desire?

"You're not really helping," Anna declared, moving out of his reach.

He didn't pursue her, yet somehow held her captive, leaving her unable to stray too far.

"Then how about this for some advice?" Cade asked. "Make yourself happy first."

Anna studied the open honesty of his face, the aura of trust and fairness that surrounded him. Though Cade himself was reluctant to trust anyone outside his family, it was easy to see why friends, employees and businessmen put their faith and confidence in him.

"When Henry was in Virginia and he talked about all the opportunities here in Branford, I thought maybe, just maybe, he would allow me to open my own business here," Anna said. To her own ears, the words came out quietly. Her own secret dream, greeting the light of day. And Cade.

He nodded. "You'd do a hell of a job."

"Do you think so?" Anna asked, her heart beating a little faster. She was thrilled in a way she'd never experienced.

"I sure do."

"Even after this fabric situation? If I don't handle it right, I could get run out of town by nightfall tomorrow."

A little grin pulled at Cade's lips. "I still think my wrestling idea is a good one."

Anna giggled. "It is not."

"Sure it is. Look here. Let me show you a few moves."

Cade looped his arm around her waist and pulled her against him. He caught her wrist with his other hand and held it out.

"Want to know what I'm thinking now?" he asked, his voice low and husky.

Probably the same thing she was thinking.

Cade leaned down and kissed her. His lips covered hers, then slid lower to taste her jaw, her throat, then to nuzzle the skin near her ear. Anna tipped her head to the side, reveling in the warmth of his mouth against her flesh.

She draped her arm around his neck and held on tight, certain her trembling knees wouldn't hold her up. He took her lips again. She kissed him back. Cade groaned as his hand went to her waist. His fingertips burned through her dress, scorching a trail upward until his palm captured her breast.

Anna gasped but didn't pull away. She leaned closer. Cade deepened their kiss.

When he finally eased back, he kept her locked in his embrace and rested his forehead against hers. His breath was warm. Everything was warm.

"I'd...I'd better go," he whispered.

Her first instinct was to tell him no, but Anna stepped away and followed him to the door. Cade hesitated, as if he wanted to say something—or wanted to stay?—then left, closing the door behind him.

Anna watched from the window as he walked past his house and continued on toward the lumberyard, disappearing into the shadows. A little piece of her heart went with him.

How she wished he'd given her that secret bit of advice she needed so she'd know the way to please him, to make him happy. Would her ignorance drive him away, as it had done with Henry, as it had distanced her from her father?

Suddenly, facing the brides and their mothers tomorrow, explaining about the fabric and figuring out what to do with it, seemed like a very small problem.

Chapter Nine

The parlor in the Riker home proved perfect for company, though Anna doubted it had seen a guest in years. Not one item in the room, she suspected, had been changed since the day the elder Rikers boarded their train for Texas.

Conversation buzzed among the brides-to-be and their mothers. Wedding talk, of course. Anna poured coffee and served the pastries she'd made, grateful that no one had yet noticed the large wooden crate sitting across the room.

Mrs. Kendall seemed more calm than Anna had seen her before. Apparently the cooling off period the sheriff had insisted upon yesterday had served its purpose.

"I'll get more cookies," Anna said, taking the tray into the kitchen. As she arranged them on the platter, the back door opened. Cade walked in.

"I didn't miss the fight, did I?" he asked, grinning.

"What are you doing here?" she asked. "Believe me, if *I* could hide out in the lumberyard that's what I'd be doing."

"I had an attack of conscience," Cade admitted, hanging his hat on the peg beside the back door.

"I haven't announced the *good news* yet," Anna said, heading toward the parlor with the platter of cookies.

Cade stepped in front of her, his gaze warm. "Maybe I

should demonstrate that wrestling hold again, in case a fight breaks out. You know, like last night?"

"You might need that for Mrs. Kendall," Anna told him.

"That old heifer? Damn, Anna…"

She grinned and scooted around him.

The ladies in the parlor greeted Cade as they helped themselves to the cookies. Anna perched on the edge of the settee and Cade positioned himself near the crate of fabric. The wedding talk continued while Anna gathered her courage. She glanced back at Cade. He gave her a little wink that made her smile. Finally, she got to her feet.

"Ladies, I have some wonderful news," she said, putting on a bright smile. "The wedding fabric has been located."

A stunned second passed before Mrs. Kendall demanded, "Where is it?"

"It's right here, actually. In that crate." Anna pointed. "It seems—oh!"

Mrs. Kendall lurched from the settee, the two other mothers hot on her heels. The brides squealed.

"Hold up a minute." Cade planted himself in front of the crate. "Miss Kingsley's got something to say."

The women turned to Anna, their gazes boring into her.

"Well, what is it?" Mrs. Kendall demanded.

Anna drew in a breath. "The mill shorted the order. There's not enough fabric for three dresses. Only two."

Wails and shrieks rose from the women as they went for the crate once more. Cade jumped aside.

"There's not enough fabric," Mrs. Kendall declared, waving the bill of lading in the air, as the other five women dug through the crate. More groans arose.

Anna exchanged a troubled look with Cade. He leaned down and whispered, "We'd better get these women to draw straws right away, before they have time to think about it."

"Good idea," Anna agreed.

Cade disappeared into the kitchen as the women turned to Anna once more. Mary Sumner had started to cry, while Sarah Proctor's face had gone white.

"How could this have *happened?*" Mrs. Sumner demanded of no one in particular.

"When did this fabric arrive?" Mrs. Kendall demanded. "Where has it been?"

Anna braced herself. "We're so fortunate that the crate was finally located, safe and sound. It had been put in the storage room at the lumberyard by mistake."

"The lumberyard?" Mrs. Proctor exclaimed.

Cade walked back into the room and all the women turned to him, riveting him with their gazes.

"When?" Mrs. Sumner asked. "When did you find it?"

"A couple of days ago," he said.

"Days?"

The women erupted in angry chatter until Mrs. Proctor's voice rang out above the rest.

"You intended to keep our fabric, didn't you," she shouted. "For when your brother marries Emma Stokes."

A chorus of accusations rose from the women.

"That's not true," Anna told them, raising her voice to be heard. "Cade discovered it and immediately brought it to my attention so I could—"

"So *you're* the one who wanted to keep it," Mrs. Proctor declared. "Keep it for your own wedding dress."

"No, of course not. I already have a—"

Shouts from the women drowned out her voice until Cade forced a piercing whistle through his teeth and the room went silent.

"Listen here. The fabric got sent to my supply room by mistake. Nobody tried to keep it from you, certainly not Miss Kingsley," Cade told them.

A little murmur went through the group. Anna thought the women had settled down until Rachel spoke.

"If there's not enough fabric for everyone," she said, "why don't we put off the weddings until we can order more?"

"No!" Mrs. Kendall screeched.

"We've got kinfolk coming from all over for the weddings," Mrs. Sumner said. "Some have already arrived."

"Oh, Mama, I can't wait to marry Jimmy," Mary Sumner said, crying harder now. "I can't wait."

"And I don't want to wait to get married, either," Sarah Proctor declared.

"We can't possibly postpone," her mother said.

Two of the brides nodded in agreement. Rachel said nothing.

"Fine, then." Cade held out his hand. In his grip were three broom straws. "Short straw loses."

All the women leaned closer, eyeing his hand.

"We should establish a criteria for who draws first," Mrs. Kendall insisted.

"Everybody together," Cade said. "It's the only fair way."

Mrs. Kendall looked as if fairness was the last thing that interested her, but she said nothing more. In quick succession, each of the brides drew a straw.

Rachel Kendall got the short one.

Her mother's face went white, then flamed to red. With a scathing look at Cade and Anna, she stormed out of the house. The other women lifted the crate and followed, leaving silence in their wake.

Anna shut the door and fell back against it. "I'd better start packing."

"You and me both." Cade pulled back the window curtain and gazed out. "Maybe I'd better stand watch tonight in case Mrs. Kendall comes back."

"Oh, Cade. This is just terrible."

"They could have postponed the weddings until more fabric was ordered, but they didn't want to," he said. "We did the only thing we could."

Problems always sounded less complicated and solutions so much simpler when Cade spoke.

He walked over to her. "Are you going to be all right?"

She forced a smile. "I'll be fine. Thanks for coming, for standing up for me."

She expected him to leave, but he didn't. For a long moment he just stood there looking down at her. Anna's heart warmed and she found herself wishing he would stay. Forever.

Anna got supper on the table just as Ben and Cade came through the back door. They both looked tired, oddly subdued, neither saying much as they washed up and came back into the kitchen.

"Rough day?" she asked them.

Ben glanced at Cade, then said, "The saw broke today. The big one, the one we need to get this order out for the railroad. We can't repair it. We're going to have to buy another one."

Anna didn't know anything about saws, but from the look on both their faces she figured it had to be expensive. Very expensive. Maybe more expensive than they could afford with the financial problems Cade had told her about.

"Then a hot meal just might make you both feel better," she said, thinking it wise not to dwell on their problem. Surely the two of them had wrestled with it most of the day.

Cade held a chair for her and they all settled around the table.

"Where's Kyle?" Cade asked, eyeing the empty chair to his left.

"I haven't seen him since this morning," Anna stated, hoping that meant he'd stayed in school all day.

"Talk of that wedding nonsense is all over town," Ben said, as they all filled their plates. "I went over to see Harlan at the blacksmith shop to ask what he thought about fixing the saw, and everybody is just tickled pink about the fabric being found."

"Everyone but Mrs. Kendall, I imagine," Anna said.

Ben chuckled. "When Mr. Talbot heard the news, he went

over to her house just to gloat. He offered to sell her some fabric from his store—at triple the price."

"Did anyone mention how Rachel is doing?" Anna asked.

The back door opened and Kyle came inside. He stopped short at the look Cade gave him.

"You're supposed to be home before supper," Cade said, his voice firm but even. "Where've you been?"

"Nowhere."

"What have you been doing?"

"Nothing."

"Did you stay in school all day?"

"No, sir."

"How am I going to send you to college back East if you don't stay in school and do your lessons?"

Kyle didn't answer, just drew up his shoulders and let them fall again.

"I told you what would happen if you left school again," Cade said. "So I'm walking you to school in the morning and I'll be there when school's out."

"Yes, sir. I remember."

"And then you can spend the rest of the day cleaning out the barn stalls and the animal pens."

"What?" Kyle's expression turned from passive acceptance to revulsion. "I *hate* doing that. It stinks—"

"Go wash up and have your supper," Cade told him.

Kyle fumed for another few seconds, then stomped into the washroom.

Once more, Anna marveled at the patience Cade displayed with his little brother. No shouting, no threats, no intimidation. Just steady listening and discipline. Especially commendable at the end of what had certainly been a long, difficult day for Cade.

When they finished supper Ben headed off to call on Emma, and Cade went outside with a cup of coffee. Kyle sat on the stool beside the stove and talked to Anna while she washed the dishes, then he got a dishcloth and helped with the drying.

"Mama and I used to do dishes together sometimes," Kyle said, picking up another plate to dry. "Being in the kitchen makes me think of her."

Anna's memories of her own mother came back to her. Pleasant recollections, just as Kyle's were.

"Have you seen Ariel in town?" Anna asked.

The plate slipped from Kyle's grasp, but he caught it before it hit the floor. "Yeah. Sort of."

"How's she doing?"

"Pretty." Kyle looked up at her, and his cheeks turned pink. "I mean, she's doing all right, I guess."

"Not talking to her yet?"

"I'm working up to it," he said, sounding more like a grown man suddenly, rather than a young boy.

They finished the dishes and Kyle went upstairs. Anna headed home.

On the back porch she paused, wondering if she'd see Cade. He liked coming outside in the evenings. It seemed to relax him and, after what he'd been through today, she thought sure she'd see him here.

But she didn't. Nor did she see lights burning in the lumberyard office. She didn't know where he was. A little disappointed, she went home.

If Cade hadn't been standing outside his own home, he might feel like a low-down varmint for lurking in the shadows, watching Anna walk home. He wanted to be close to her, be with her, craved the comfort her presence brought. He needed comfort tonight. Hell, he needed a lot of things tonight. All of which Anna could provide.

And that's why he held back in the shadows instead of going to her house. Something about that woman drew him in. He didn't know what it was or why he felt it. He hadn't known her long enough to figure it all out. But it was there and he didn't want it to be. Not now. Not yet. Not until he knew her better.

Lantern light glowed yellow in the kitchen window of Anna's house, then another lantern came to life in her bedroom.

Desire hummed in him, then grew stronger as another window glowed with lantern light. The washroom.

Images of Anna undressing, preparing for a bath, bloomed in Cade's head. The golden light against her dewy skin. Her silky hair loose, cascading down her back.

Cade gritted his teeth and struggled to remain where he was. Minutes dragged by, his imagination and his body urging him to go to her.

Finally, he gave in.

Chapter Ten

Cade climbed the steps to Anna's back porch, then turned, his gaze searching the outbuildings, the house next door, the lumberyard. He saw no one. He knocked on the door.

A few minutes passed and he wondered if he should leave. Want and need hummed through his veins. He couldn't go.

The door opened and Anna peeked out at him, half-hidden by the door. Cade's heart thundered in his chest. Her hair was gathered in a loose knot atop her head, tendrils curling around her neck. Her face was pink and moist from her bath.

"Is something wrong?" she asked.

Hell, yes. Everything was wrong. He wanted and needed her, yet something in him rebelled against that very desire. His head told him to turn and leave, but the rest of him...

"I—I don't know why I'm here, except..."

"How do you always know?" Anna asked, tears welling in her eyes. "When I'm upset, you appear. How do you do that?"

He'd come here for selfish reasons, but seeing Anna with tears swimming in her eyes made him want to break down the door, hold her, find out what was wrong and fix it.

Anna opened the door and he stepped into the kitchen. Lantern light cast her in shadows, revealing the curve of her hips through the nightgown and wrapper she wore. Her feet were bare against the wooden floor.

Cade's mouth went dry. Want and need surged through him. He ought to get the hell out of her house, away from her, but he couldn't bring himself to leave. Not with her upset, on the verge of crying.

"What's wrong?" he asked. It took some effort to keep his voice even, to let her explain things in her own way. He'd learned that with his little brother.

"Nothing serious, really." She whisked away her tears with the back of her hand. "I shouldn't have said anything."

He walked closer. "Tell me what's wrong."

She gazed up at him and sniffed. "I was feeling sorry for Rachel. And, I guess, for myself, too."

"Rachel, because she won't have the wedding dress she wants?" Cade asked. "And you?"

She gulped, trying to hold back more tears. "Because I have a beautiful wedding dress and—and no wedding. And it seems I never will. I still don't have the slightest idea what it takes to be a good wife, how to make a man happy. I've tried to figure it out, but I just don't understand."

"Any man would be proud to have you as his wife."

She drew in a ragged breath, still fighting back tears. "I'd hoped I'd have a daughter one day who would wear my wedding dress. But at this rate, I don't see how I'll ever get married. And the gown is so beautiful…."

"Can I see it?" Cade asked.

"Would you like to?" she asked, and seemed to perk up a bit. She headed down the hall toward the bedroom.

Cade followed her.

He stood in the doorway as she fussed with the wedding gown hanging from a peg across the room. He'd not been in here since construction had been completed on the house, when it was just walls and the essential pieces of furniture.

It looked nothing like he remembered. Anna had put a

rose-colored quilt on the bed, hung curtains and scattered rugs on the floor. Pictures adorned the walls. Vases of fresh flowers sat around the room, along with books and her writing supplies. Her hairbrush, mirror and all sorts of jars and small pots were on the bureau.

The room glowed with warmth and the attention she'd put into its furnishings. Cade liked it. A man could build a house, but it took a woman to turn it into a home.

He didn't know much about wedding dresses, but this one seemed special. White material, lace. Surely none of the brides here in Branford could make a gown as grand as this one, even with the English fabric they'd waited so long for. He couldn't imagine a prettier bride than Anna.

She touched the sleeve of her wedding gown. This afternoon when she'd hung it here her thoughts had been consumed with Rachel Kendall. What heartbreak she must feel since losing all chance at the wedding dress she wanted. Then, in an unexpected attack of self-pity, Anna had realized she might never get to wear her own gown.

"Beautiful," Cade said.

Anna turned, surprised to find him standing in the doorway. She'd intended to take the gown to him in the kitchen. That in itself was highly inappropriate, given her state of dress. Yet the need to be proper around Cade didn't seem so intense at the moment.

She ran her hand down the satin fabric. "Yes, it is beautiful, isn't it?"

"I meant you."

Her heart beat a little faster. A rush of warmth went though her. She'd felt it before when she was around Cade, or sometimes when she saw him from a distance, or simply thought about him. She'd first experienced it that day at the train station when she'd arrived in Branford. Since then it had only grown stronger.

She'd fallen in love with him.

She knew that now, looking at him across the room. Her heart thumped harder and her spirit soared at the realization.

She realized, too, why he'd come to her room.

Cade slipped his arms around her waist and eased her against him. For a long moment he gazed into her eyes. Then he searched for the pins in her hair and pulled them out.

"You are so beautiful," he murmured, threading her long hair through his fingers.

Anna's heart fluttered as she heard him say those words. No one had ever spoken them to her before.

He leaned down and brushed his lips against her temple, breathing in her sweet scent. One hand traveled up her back and burrowed into the hair at her nape. Anna's knees weakened. She looped her arms around his neck and swayed against him.

His chest was hard, strong, as were his arms wrapping her in a powerful grip. A deep masculinity flowed from him, seeping inside her.

Cade lowered his head and kissed her. She parted her lips. He groaned and pulled her tighter against him. Anna rose on tiptoes and pressed herself closer, soaking up the taste, the feel of him.

He broke their kiss. "I'd better go," he whispered. "If I stay…do you understand what that would mean?"

"Yes." She looked away, feeling the hot flush on her cheeks. "I know what it means. Well, that is, I don't know from personal experience, but…well, at school we talked about…it."

He touched her chin and turned her to face him. His brows drew together. "What sort of things was Miss Purtle teaching at that academy of hers?"

Anna smiled at his gentle teasing. "Maybe I'll tell you…someday."

"Or maybe I'll find out on my own," Cade said in a low, husky voice. He kissed her again. She tasted sweet, pure. He wanted more. He wanted all of her.

He deepened their kiss, then pulled loose the sash of her wrapper and slid his hand inside. His palm burned as it settled on the curve of her hip. He moved his hand upward, cupping her breast.

Anna gasped and clenched his hair in her fist. Her heart raced as this newly discovered heat consumed her. A heat that, with Cade, felt right.

He fumbled with the buttons of her nightgown. Her flesh was hot, welcoming. He touched her bare breast and she arched forward. His knees nearly gave out.

"Anna…"

She tightened her arms around his neck and locked her lips on his. Cade scooped her up and laid her on the bed she'd already turned down for the night. Looking at her in the lantern light, he wanted to bury himself in her body, in her soul, in her life.

Cade pulled off his boots, then stripped off his clothes and stretched out beside her. She snuggled against him and he saw the passion burning in her eyes.

He kissed her and pulled her nightgown off. His hands sought her shapely curves. She moaned against his chest and pressed her palms against the hard muscles. Her fingertips roamed him, shyly. Their bodies matched perfectly, her curves molding against his taut, straight lines.

Cade rose above her and eased himself between her thighs and into her body. Anna grasped his powerful shoulders, holding him with all her strength as he moved within her. She couldn't think, only feel.

Faster he moved, pushing her higher, driving her upward until the aching throb within her broke in great pulsing waves, consuming her.

Cade held back until his whole body screamed for release, for the exquisite relief only Anna could provide. Then he lost himself in the depth of her, over and over.

* * *

"I have to go."

Cade muttered the words against her ear as she lay curled in his arms. She'd fallen into a light sleep after they'd made love.

"I can't stay here," he said, easing away from her and sitting up on the bed.

Without him at her side, the night air chilled her. Anna drew the quilt over her.

"I know," she said, stroking his bare arm.

He rose and searched through the room, finding the clothing he'd thrown off only a short time ago.

"Don't worry about coming over to make breakfast in the morning," he said, pulling on his clothes. "We'll manage."

"Don't be silly," she said, pushing herself up on her elbow. "Of course I'll—"

"No. I don't want Kyle to see us together so soon…after, and get any ideas."

"Oh," she said, a little embarrassed, but not surprised that Cade's concern would be for his brother—and her, too, really. "I hadn't thought of that. I'll make supper."

Cade looked around the room, making sure he'd gathered everything that belonged to him, then blew out the lantern.

"Good night," he said, and left.

When he reached the back porch he closed the door solidly behind him and faced the darkness.

Cade pulled in deep breaths of fresh air. Good God, what had he just done?

Chapter Eleven

As Anna got supper on the table she glanced out the kitchen window, watching for Cade. She'd spent most of the day doing just that. She hadn't seen him since he'd left her bedroom last night, but he hadn't been out of her thoughts. All day she'd stolen glances out the window, hoping to catch a glimpse of him at the lumberyard. She hadn't.

Turning back to the stove, Anna pulled the roast from the oven. She'd taken extra care with tonight's supper, wanting to prepare something special for Cade. Her mother's recipe for roast with potatoes, carrots and onions was always delicious. She knew he'd love it.

Footsteps sounded on the back porch. Anna's heart thudded as she watched the door. She tried to steel herself, fearful she'd blush at the sight of him, but failed. After what they'd shared last night, Anna knew she could never keep her feelings in check around him again.

Disappointment swamped her as Ben and Kyle walked into the kitchen.

"Get washed up," Ben said to his brother, hanging his hat and the keys in their spot near the door. "And throw those clothes out the window. They'll stink up the whole place."

Dirty and sweaty, his shoulders slumped, Kyle stumbled

into the washroom and closed the door. It seemed the punishment Cade had given him for missing school had worn him out.

"Where's Cade?" Anna asked, trying not to sound anxious.

"I don't know. He's been yelling and grousing all day. He hasn't been in a mood this foul in a long time," Ben said, as he washed his hands at the kitchen pump.

"Is it because of the broken saw?" Anna asked.

"Maybe. He was going to see Charles Proctor at the bank about a loan. That's enough to put anybody in a bad mood." He dried his face and laid the towel aside.

They sat at the table together. A few minutes later Kyle staggered out of the washroom wrapped in a towel, and headed upstairs. Anna doubted they'd see him again tonight.

If Ben knew, or suspected, what had gone on between her and Cade last night, he gave no indication of it. He talked about the lumberyard, then stayed to help her with the dishes. After that, he changed clothes and left.

Anna lingered, anxious to see Cade, sure he'd be home any minute. She'd never known him to miss supper, or stay out late. But after an hour passed with no sign of him, Anna went home. He would come to her with he finished with his business, she knew.

She made a fresh pot of coffee for him, then busied herself rearranging the flowers in the kitchen window.

How she loved this house. Anna smiled as she recalled the wonderful moments she'd experienced, though she'd lived here only a short while. Times with Cade. Talking, laughing, having coffee.

And last night, of course.

Anna felt her cheeks heat at the memory. Yet she felt no shame, no remorse for what she'd done. Why should she? She loved Cade.

How could she ever leave him, or this place? She'd left her

own home in Virginia so easily. Anna couldn't imagine not living here forever.

Kyle flashed into Anna's mind as she got two coffee cups from the cupboard and placed them beside the stove. A smile grew on her lips, sure she knew the reason now that he wouldn't stay in school.

Suddenly, she couldn't wait to tell Cade. She wished he'd hurry over. She wanted nothing more than to tell him she'd solved this problem, to relieve his worry, make things better for him.

In that instant, she wished, too, that she could buy him the new saw he needed for the lumberyard, solve all the matters that troubled him.

Of course, she could be facing matters of her own that needed attention, Anna realized. She touched her palm to her belly and smiled. Was she carrying his child?

She couldn't think of a better place to bring a baby into the world. Here, in this house. With Cade, who'd shown, through his care and patience with Kyle, that he would make a wonderful papa.

Anna went up the staircase to the second floor. She lit the lantern on the wall and stood in the doorway, images of a child's bedroom filling her mind.

The stacks of boxes in the corner caught her eye. On the day she'd moved in she'd realized these were Henry's belongings. She wanted to return them to Cade.

Carrying the lantern, she knelt and dug through the boxes. Books, a couple of shirts, a pair of boots that had seen better days, and several thick stacks of papers.

Thinking them family correspondence, Anna pulled the papers from the box, intending to tie them with ribbons. Her hands stilled when she read the top sheet.

Receipts. Dozens of them for supplies ordered by the Branford Lumber Company. Why weren't these at the office?

Anna's mother had kept the books for her father's business

and Anna had been so intrigued she'd learned the trade herself at Miss Purtle's Academy. She could think of no reason why this record of company expenses would be here.

Unless…

A chill swept up Anna's spine. Henry had lied to her about owning the business. Cade had said the financial problems at the lumberyard started a few months ago.

Would a liar limit himself to one single lie? One deception? She thought not.

Anna flipped through the receipts, debating on what action to take. If she suspected Henry had been skimming money from the company, she needed to find out for sure. Her heart soared at the possibility of solving Cade's problem, being the one to help him, end his worry.

Yet she couldn't take unfounded suspicions to him. Henry was, after all, family. Cade valued family above all else. She wouldn't accuse his cousin without proof.

And, too, she needed to keep this possibility quiet in case she proved it correct. What would happen if word got out that he couldn't handle his employees, his money, his finances? A lack of confidence from prospective customers might ruin his business.

Anna gathered the receipts, took the lantern and left the room. She'd find out for herself. And once she knew the truth, she could present her findings to Cade.

He would be so happy with her.

"Oh, Henry…" Anna whispered in despair as she sat behind Cade's desk at the lumberyard office. She'd used the key that always hung by the back door at the Riker house, and let herself in. The lantern beside her cast a flickering pool of light as she went over the company books.

Just finding the ledgers had been a difficult task. Neither Cade nor Ben, it seemed, put much stock in organizing such things. And they hadn't kept up on the entries, either, she noticed after she finally found the ledgers and went through them. No entries had been recorded since Henry left.

But his presence was felt now, long after his abrupt departure. As she'd suspected, Henry had stolen money from the company. A great deal of money.

Using the receipts she'd found in her upstairs bedroom—which, surely, Henry had forgotten all about when he'd left town in such a hurry—she compared the amounts due each supplier to the figure Henry had entered in the ledger. They weren't the same. Henry had consistently written a higher figure in the ledger and, apparently, pocketed the difference.

Anna's heart ached at the discovery. Cade had trusted Henry because he was family. And Henry had taken advantage of that trust to the point where it now jeopardized the very existence of the company.

Why would Henry do such a thing? Anna's stomach knotted as she realized the worst. Had she played a part in this deception? With her on the way to California to marry Henry, had he needed more money?

She looked back through the entries once more, this time paying closer attention to the dates. A chill ran up her spine. The thefts had started not long after she'd written to Henry, accepting his marriage proposal.

What sort of man would steal from his cousins in order to provide for a new wife?

And what sort of person was she to have been so completely taken in by Henry?

Anna sat back, drawing in a heavy breath. She'd wanted proof of her suspicions and she had it. Now, at least, Cade could see the cause of his financial troubles. With this money drain ended, the company would pull itself out of the hole in short order. She'd solved the problem, yet the thought of breaking the news to Cade brought her no pleasure.

Maybe she should tell Ben first? Maybe he would rather handle the situation himself, tell Cade in his own way—

The back door burst open with such force that Anna jumped and spun around in her chair. Cade stood in the doorway.

"Oh, it's you. Thanks goodness…" She pressed her hand to her chest as if that might still her runaway heart.

"What are you doing in here?" he demanded.

A sharp edge hardened his voice, one Anna had never heard before. It alarmed her.

"I'm…I'm checking on something," she said, not wanting to blurt out the truth.

Cade circled the desk, glaring down at her. His gaze bounced over ledgers, the receipts, the pencil in her hand.

"What the hell are you up to?"

The venom in his tone and the glare in his eyes took Anna aback. What was he thinking?

"I'm going over the company books," she explained. "I—"

"You're *what?* Who said you could come in here? Who told you to look at the books?" he demanded. "How did you get in here?"

"I took the key from the house," she said. "Look, Cade, look at what I've—"

"I knew you were up to something." Cade drew away, looking at her in a whole different way now.

Anna's blood ran cold. "You think I'm sneaking around here, looking at your books so I can do what—steal from you? Is that the kind of person you think I am?"

"I wondered why you agreed to marry Henry," Cade told her. "You thought he owned the company, that he had money. Is that what you're in here checking on? Trying to find out if I was telling you the truth about our financial problems?"

Anna sprang from her chair and opened her mouth to speak. But no words came out. Raw emotion filled her—hurt, anguish, disappointment, outrage. Plus the very old feeling ingrained in her since she was a child—that she was unworthy to be trusted, relied upon or counted on for help. Useless.

Anna left the office without a word.

* * *

"Where's Miss Anna?"

Cade glanced up from the pan of eggs he was scrambling as Kyle came into the kitchen. "She's not here."

"She wasn't here yesterday morning, either," Kyle said, concern in his voice. "Why not?"

Cade held on to his patience as he lifted the eggs onto the plates alongside a slice of ham. The last thing he wanted was to explain anything to Kyle.

"She's just not coming over this morning," Cade said.

Ben strolled into the kitchen, then stopped when he saw Cade at the stove. "Where's Anna?"

"She's not coming," Kyle said, none too happily.

"Why not?" Ben asked.

"Because she's not." Cade slammed the pan down on the stove and stormed out the back door.

He felt like hell. He hadn't slept last night. Everything hurt—his stomach, his head…his heart.

How could he have been such a fool—again? Fallen in love with a woman he barely knew, let his heart overrule his head? Just like before. He'd let his guard down, let Anna into his life. And she'd betrayed him. Just like in Texas.

"Cade!"

Ben approached, causing Cade to wince. He didn't intend to tell anyone about this, not even his brother.

"What's going on?" Ben asked.

"Nothing."

Ben didn't say anything more, just looked at him. Patience and family ties ran deep and strong among the Rikers, and Cade was too weary to fight it.

"I was such a damn fool …." He looked away, shaking his head. "I caught Anna in the office last night, going over our books."

"What was she doing that for?" Ben asked, genuinely puzzled.

"I had a bad feeling about her right from the start," Cade said. "I shouldn't have trusted her."

"What reason did she give for going through the books?"

Cade shrugged. "None."

"Did you ask her?"

"I didn't have to. It was obvious to me that she came here in the first place because she thought Henry owned the business and had money. She was checking up on it."

"Oh, that's nice, Cade. Smart, too." Ben shook his head in disgust, then headed toward the lumberyard office.

Cade walked the other way.

He spent most of the morning yelling at people who didn't deserve it, throwing things and taking his foul mood out on anybody unfortunate enough to cross his path. He told himself over and over that he'd done the right thing. Even if it hurt like hell. Even if he loved her.

Cade finally ended up at the lumberyard office. He found Ben at his desk, ledgers and papers spread out around him.

"You are an idiot," Ben declared with a woeful shake of his head. "I can't believe I'm related to you."

Cade wasn't in the mood. "Shut the hell up."

"You're going to listen to what I have to say."

Cade just glared at him, then headed to the stove in the corner and picked up the coffeepot.

"Henry was robbing us blind," Ben said.

Cade put down the pot and swung around. "No, he wasn't. Henry wouldn't do that."

"It's all right here." Ben gestured to the ledgers and papers. "He took the bills for company expenses, inflated them, entered the higher amount in the books as if the company had paid that amount, then pocketed the difference."

Stunned, Cade approached the desk. "That's why we've been having financial problems?"

"Anna figured it out," Ben said. "She must have."

"But how…how would she know what to look for?" Cade asked, shaking his head.

"Maybe she learned something useful in that academy she attended." Ben rose from the chair. "But that's not the real problem here. The real problem is what's going on with you and Anna."

"There's nothing going—"

"I saw you go to her place the other night. I can guess what went on," Ben said. "So what happened afterward? You got scared and ran?"

"I didn't get scared," he insisted.

"Trusting someone—especially a great woman like Anna—isn't a bad thing."

Cade turned away. "I shouldn't have gotten involved with her the way I did. It was a mistake."

"No, it wasn't and you know it," Ben said.

"Don't tell me what I know," Cade declared.

"Okay, then, let me tell you what *I* know," Ben replied. "I saw the way you looked at Henry when he talked about his new wife coming out here. I know you were envious—hell, I was, too. I know that's why you pushed Henry so hard."

Cade just looked at him, unable to say anything.

"Then when you met Anna, it was plain as day that you'd fallen in love with her." Ben shook his head. "But you're so damn stubborn that you can't get over the past. You can't keep measuring every woman you meet by that one in Texas. You're getting ready to lose the best thing that ever happened to you."

"It's not that easy," Cade said.

"Who ever said being in love would be easy?" Ben asked. "You love her, don't you?"

"Yeah, but…"

Ben shook his head. "Damn, Cade, I can't believe I'm related to you. Sometimes you can be so—"

The front door burst open and Kyle strode inside, jaw set, shoulders squared.

He glared up at Cade. "What did you do?"

Cade's temper flared. He couldn't take any more today. "Why aren't you in school? I swear, Kyle, if you don't stay in school I'm going to—"

"She's crying." Kyle threw the words at him. "Miss Anna. She's crying and—"

Cade's anger vanished, replaced by a aching stab in his heart. "She's crying? When did you see her?"

"I don't want her to go," Kyle told him. "She's nice and she cooks good, just like Mama used to do."

"Who said she was going anywhere?" Cade asked, a little alarmed.

"I just saw her!" Kyle pointed toward town. "She took her wedding dress and gave it to Miss Rachel, and she was crying the whole time."

"That doesn't mean she's going anywhere," Cade told him.

"Then she got Harlan at the blacksmith shop to bring a wagon and load up her trunks, and she was still crying," Kyle said. "She cried all the way to the train station."

Chapter Twelve

"Thank…you …."

Anna squeezed the words out between sobs as she stood in the railroad depot clutching a damp handkerchief in her fist.

"Yes, ma'am," Harlan said, as he backed away.

Anna knew he was glad to go, to be rid of her, and she couldn't blame him. She'd done nothing but cry.

She collapsed onto a wooden bench in the waiting room, too distraught to stand. Tears poured down her cheeks. She'd cried all night and all morning. She couldn't stop.

She didn't care, though. She deserved to cry. She'd never been so hurt in her life. Nothing—absolutely nothing—had crushed her the way Cade had.

So she was leaving. She'd decided this morning that she couldn't bear to stay in Branford another day. She'd given Rachel Kendall her treasured wedding gown, cornered poor Harlan at the blacksmith shop, packed her things and come to the depot. She'd leave on the next train.

As soon as she could gather the strength to walk to the ticket window.

Sobbing into her handkerchief, Anna looked around the room. The half-dozen people waiting there stole occasional glances, thinking she'd taken leave of her senses, no doubt.

But Anna didn't care what they thought. She didn't care what anyone thought anymore.

The depot door opened and Cade walked in, sending Anna's emotions skyrocketing. How did he always know when she was upset? And why did he still have to look so handsome? She sobbed harder.

Tucked beneath his arm was a large box. He set it aside and approached her.

"Anna?" he said quietly. "Anna, are you all right?"

"No! I'm not all right! Of course I'm not all right!" she screamed, rising to her feet. "Why would you think I'd be all right?"

He drew back a little. "Maybe you should try to stop crying."

"I don't want to stop!"

"Okay, then, that's fine. Just keep on crying." Cade shifted uncomfortably. "Uh, well, Ben took a look at those ledgers and receipts you had in the office last night. He told me that Henry had been stealing from the company. But I guess you figured that out already."

"Yes, I did!" Another torrent of tears claimed her. "I'm an excellent bookkeeper! And an excellent cook! And a first-rate housekeeper! And I even figured out why Kyle keeps leaving school!"

"You did?"

"Yes!" Anna wailed anew, then drew in a long ragged breath. "I was so anxious to tell you about Kyle, and about what Henry had done so I could make things better for you, so I could relieve you of some of your problems, so I could help you and be important to you. But you wouldn't let me!"

Cade pulled at the tight muscles in his neck. "I know I jumped the gun last night. I shouldn't have said what I said. I shouldn't have assumed the worst in you."

"But of course you should have! It was foolish of me to expect anything more of you!" Anna flung out both hands. "I tried with all my heart to make my father happy, but I couldn't. I worried endlessly about how I'd make Henry happy, but he wouldn't even stay in town long enough to let me try. I gave everything I had to make you happy—and you know I mean *everything*."

Cade glanced at the people in the depot, who'd all turned to stare. "Yes, I know what you mean."

"And where did any of my efforts get me? Nowhere!" Another racking sob shook her. Then she pulled herself up straighter. "So I decided…to hell with all of you!"

Cade's chest expanded and his nose flared. "Oh God, Anna, I want you so bad right now."

"Oh! I'm leaving!" Anna stomped to the ticket window. "Give me a ticket."

The agent behind the bars eased back a little. "Where to, ma'am?"

"I don't care. Anywhere." Anna fumbled with her drawstring handbag, tears blurring her vision.

Cade appeared beside her. "You're not leaving."

"Yes, I am." She turned to the ticket agent. "How much?"

"Don't sell her a ticket," Cade told him.

"How much?" Anna insisted.

The agent's gaze darted back and forth between the two of them. "Well, ma'am, that—"

Anna turned to Cade. "I'm through trying to make a man happy. Through! From now on I'm going to figure out what makes *me* happy, and that's what I'm going to do."

"I'm the one who told you that," Cade said, "if you'll recall."

"Of course I recall." She sniffed into her handkerchief. "I remember everything you said because you're a kind, caring, smart, handsome man. The man of my dreams."

"I'm the man of your dreams?"

"Yes! And look what happened! You turned out to be a—a typical man!" Anna turned back to the ticket agent. "How much?"

"Ma'am, I can't tell you the fare until you tell me where you want to go."

"She's not going anywhere. Not yet, anyway." Cade laid his hand on Anna's arm. "At least hear me out, will you?"

More tears seeped from her eyes as a new wave of emotion overtook her. She couldn't tell him no. She just couldn't.

She walked with Cade to the other end of the room and sat down on the bench beside him, wiping her nose.

"First off, I want to tell you Henry's decision to leave had nothing to do with you," Cade said. "It was my fault."

"Your fault?"

He nodded. "Henry is a Thornton, and that branch of the family was never hell-bent on accomplishing much. When I found out he had a wife on the way, I pushed him. I made him build the house. I told him he'd have to learn the lumber business, not just bookkeeping, so I could make him a partner. He needed more money to take care of a wife."

"And he thanked you by stealing from you?"

"I guess my help wasn't any help at all. Henry wasn't up to learning the business or being a good husband. So he left." Cade leaned a little closer. "I was envious of Henry when he told me he had a wife coming. I fell in love with you a little bit at a time, whenever Henry talked about you. And then you arrived and I got a look at you…. Anyway, my life had been empty for a long time, but I couldn't—"

"Trust anyone? Because of what happened with that woman back in Texas?"

"It made me do a stupid thing, Anna. It made me suspicious of you, made me mistrust you, and you'd given me no call to do that." Cade took her hand in his and squeezed. "I'm sorry."

Anna soaked up the pleasure of having his hand around hers, the warmth, the strength. How good it felt.

"I brought you something," Cade said.

She sniffed again. "You did?"

He fetched the large box he'd carried into the station with

him. She'd forgotten all about it. Cade knelt in front of her, holding it between them.

"It's a dress," Cade said.

"You got me a dress?" Anna asked, pulling loose the ribbon from around the box.

"And I know that every woman likes to wear a new dress to someplace special," Cade said. "So I was hoping you'd wear this one down the aisle and become my wife."

Anna pulled off the lid. Inside lay her wedding dress. She burst out crying again.

Cade put the box aside and took her into his arms. She sobbed against his shoulder, then leaned back.

"Do you actually think I'd marry you?" she asked. "After what you did? The way you treated me?"

"Well, sure."

"You're impossible...."

"Okay, well, maybe not right away. But soon? Anna, I love you so much."

"Well, you should."

"And I do," Cade said.

"You'll have to learn to trust me," Anna told him.

"I can do that," he assured her.

Anna glanced at her wedding gown. "How did you get my dress back from Rachel?"

"Turns out she didn't really want to get married, anyway. She called it off. She gave the dress back to me right away, after I explained things. All I had to do was break the news to her mother."

Anna's eyes widened. "And you did that?"

"Yep," Cade said. "So you'll marry me?"

"I guess I have to marry you," Anna said, "since I finally found a man I love."

"After all, I am the man of your dreams," he said with a grin.

Anna smiled. "Yes, you are. But I just told you I'm through with trying to make a man happy."

"That suits me fine," Cade told her. "Because as long as you're happy, I'll be happy."

Laughter and music rose from the church fellowship hall as the wedding guests danced, ate, joined in the celebration.

Cade caught Anna's elbow and leaned down. "Let's go over here for a while."

The satin, lace and silk of her wedding dress rustled with each step. In the most quiet corner still appropriate for newlyweds to occupy, they stopped.

Cade slid his arm around her waist. "You're beautiful."

"And you're quite handsome yourself," she said, thinking he did look wonderful in his dark suit and snowy-white shirt. Anna gestured to the hall decorated with flowers and white bunting. "Was it worth the wait?"

"No," he grumbled.

They'd decided to give themselves six months to get to know each other better. They lasted three. In that time the financial problems at the lumberyard had ended and Anna had started keeping the books. Neither Cade nor Ben harbored any ill feelings toward Henry. He was, after all, family.

Anna nodded across the room to Kyle and Ariel. With the wedding festival over and Rachel departed for Kansas, Ariel and her mother had decided to stay in Branford to console Mrs. Kendall. It was proving a long task, which seemed to suit Kyle fine. He'd overcome his shyness around her, presenting Cade and Anna with another situation to handle.

"Can't say I blame the boy. She's a pretty little thing. But…" Cade called to his brother. Kyle didn't look pleased about being interrupted, but walked over. "I've got my eye on you and Ariel, along with nearly everybody else in the room. You remember what we talked about?"

Kyle looked back at Ariel with deep longing. "I remember."

"Be sure you do," Cade said, and sent Kyle on his way.

Anna eased closer. "What did you talk to him about?"

A little grin on his lips, Cade planted his hands on her waist and urged her against the wall.

"I told him how to find a dark corner, how to smooch her on the neck." He leaned down and nibbled Anna's ear.

She giggled. "Oh, Cade, you did not."

He smiled down at her. "And I told him that when you find the woman you love, marry her quick. Before she comes to her senses."

"Sounds as if you've got everything figured out."

"Not quite," he admitted. "You're the one who realized why Kyle wouldn't stay in school."

"It made sense to me that he wouldn't want to leave home and go the college you wanted to send him to. Home and family are too important to him. He figured that if you saw he wouldn't stay in school here, you wouldn't send him to college." Anna gave him a saucy grin. "Any other problems I can solve for you?"

"Yep." He wiggled his eyebrows at her. "Later on tonight when we get to San Francisco."

"I'm sure I can make you happy."

Cade took both her hands in his and held them against his chest. "I'm sure you'll always make me happy."

* * * * *

THE WINTER HEART

Cheryl Reavis

For Denyce and Terrie
Thank you for your excellent help
with all my "schoolmarm" questions.

Chapter One

⁓⁓⁓⁓⁓⁓

Wyoming Territory
June 1869

He thinks I'm a lady.

Or so Eleanor Hansen hoped. The man carried himself with a certain wariness as he walked in her direction, like someone concerned about losing his advantage—or losing face. Several other men stood on a section of wooden sidewalk nearby, looking on with more interest than the situation could possibly warrant.

The sun was going down, and she pulled her heavy wool shawl tighter against the wind and against the men who would be overly interested in the dimensions of her bodice, given the opportunity. It was cold here for June, something for which she was prepared, at least intellectually, because of her correspondence with an anonymous man who had signed himself only as the secretary for the Selby Cattle Company. It was the Englishman, Colonel Vandereau Selby himself, who had hired her—or, more accurately, his brother's widow, Lavinia.

Eleanor had been standing by the wayside waiting for someone to claim her for what seemed a long time, and she had hopes that this man would at least have some information as to what she should do. She glanced down the empty railroad track that disappeared into the horizon, wondering if whatever had felled the great Union Pacific locomotive that was supposed to get her this far had been discovered and remedied. The Platte Valley Route had just opened, and the men who ran the train had clearly been alarmed by the sudden breakdown of the new rail service—enough to send someone up a telegraph pole to relay a message to alert the army of the problem and to request that a wagon come fetch the passengers. The latter had arrived before the former, but only she and a drummer from Cincinnati had wanted to leave the train and take the wagon on ahead. And it was a *wagon*—a standard farm variety with a makeshift wooden roof added and open sides that made her long for the rough stagecoaches she'd traveled in days earlier, just to be out of the wind, if nothing else.

She looked back at the man who was still making his way down the hill in her direction. She was more than a little aware that she was the only woman in sight. There must be others somewhere, she thought, of some kind. Too many men milled around for there not to be, but clearly, there were not enough to make her arrival ordinary.

She didn't know quite what she'd expected to find here— not these few random wooden buildings clinging to the side of a low hill in the middle of nothing and nowhere. She wondered both at the reason for building them halfway up the rise and at their being scattered so far apart—the wind and the possibility of fires, perhaps? There was nothing of the connected row of structures she'd always thought of as a town.

Soul Harbor.

A strange name for a place surrounded for miles and miles by nothing but a great expanse of grayish-brown…nothing. She had been assured by her fellow travelers on the train that there would be more grass later. Some of it would be tall, and would wave and undulate in the ever-present wind like the sea.

Some would be as short as a front lawn dying in the heat of August back home.

Except for the dunelike hills where she stood at the moment, the land was as flat as a table—several tables, of various heights. In the distance and to her left she could see a completely separate one, rising sharply upward and just as flat, but very far away.

Such a lonely, treeless place.

The man finally reached her.

"Ma'am?" he said as he took off his hat. He glanced at the men who were close enough to hear with that same...wariness, she decided again, but she couldn't tell if it had to do with her or them.

"They said you were looking for someone from Selby's."

One of the men behind her snickered.

"I'm looking for Colonel Selby's representative," she said, careful of her demeanor. If he thought she was a lady, as awkward as it might feel, she was determined to remember how to be one.

Even so, she allowed herself the liberty of looking directly at him. He had blue-gray eyes and jagged fair hair his hat had caused to stick to his forehead. He was perhaps younger than she had first thought, and he stared back at her gravely, with a bleakness in his eyes that was all too familiar and suggested to her that he had seen too many things he'd rather forget. Four years after the Civil War the world was still full of men with eyes like his.

If she were her old, previous self, if she were still "Nell," she would have smiled at him boldly, flattered and teased and charmed him until he found the smiles he had apparently misplaced. But she was "Miss Eleanor Hansen" now, the newly hired schoolteacher, who had come a very long way to impart some semblance of an education to the children who lived on or near the great Selby cattle ranch. She had spent some thirty hours on stagecoaches, a harrowing two hours on a river raft, followed by five days on a train and another three hours bouncing in a farm wagon. Her body ached all over and her eyes burned with the need for sleep. She was rapidly discovering that she had little stamina left for either of her incarnations.

She noted—in spite of her weariness—that this man had the look of someone who worked out-of-doors, the scratched, rough hands, the tanned skin, both of which clashed strongly with the fact that he was wearing a wrinkled, but very clean, white shirt. She wondered idly if she was the reason for it, if someone at the cattle company had thought it would reassure the new teacher if she were met by someone who had dressed up a bit.

"The name's Ingram, ma'am," he said, almost offering his hand until the roughness of it, and perhaps their audience, apparently made him change his mind. "The colonel knows you're supposed to get here today?"

"I sent him a telegram with the best estimation of when I'd arrive, yes. I have a letter telling me to come, if you don't believe me," she said, because she suddenly felt that he didn't.

"The letter was from the colonel?"

"From his sister-in-law, Mrs. Lavinia Selby. I also have two subsequent letters from the secretary of the Selby Cattle Company."

"The secretary," he repeated.

"Yes," she said pointedly.

He drew a breath and gazed somewhere over her left shoulder.

"I work for Colonel Selby. I can take you the rest of the way," he said, looking at her again. "Can you ride, ma'am?"

"I cannot, Mr. Ingram." Her only experience on horseback had been when she was a child—on a gentle mare that had been more a pet than a mode of transportation.

He looked away, and if he wasn't wondering what he'd gotten himself into, he gave a good imitation of it.

"I'm *supposed* to be here," she said. "I don't understand why there is a problem."

"Not for me to say, ma'am. I…don't suppose you could drive a wagon. I would drive it myself, but I need to be on horseback in case—" He abruptly broke off and frowned.

"I'm aware of the troubles out here with the tribes," she said. She was aware—and she had come anyway.

"Colonel Selby has his own treaty with the Indians—Mrs. Selby saw to that. So far they're trusting her more than him or the United States government."

"Then what are you worried about?"

"Well, you never know, ma'am. There's not much law out here. Stealing cattle and horses is pretty common, for one thing," he said, as if he wanted to see her reaction to such a revelation.

"Treaties get broken," she said, because she was more concerned about that than about common thievery. There had been times in her life when she would have stolen a cow or a horse gladly, given the opportunity.

"Not by Colonel Selby's people. Not yet, anyway. Have you got a trunk, ma'am?"

"I had it taken to that building up there," she said, pointing to a two-story structure halfway up the hillside. "I was afraid it might rain."

"It doesn't rain that much here," he said, in spite of the muddy ground around them.

She could sense a certain element of reproach in his tone of voice, but for what she had no idea. For sending her trunk to an inconvenient place? For arriving at all? She just knew she didn't like it.

"Then where did the mud come from?"

"Late snow."

"It snows in June here?"

"Sometimes. And the late snows are pretty wet. The winter snows aren't."

"Are we leaving now?" she asked.

"No, ma'am. It's nearly a full day's ride to the colonel's ranch. I reckon we'll be staying the night here."

Someone in the nearby group of men guffawed at the remark, but Ingram paid no attention to him, in spite of the sudden redness of his ears.

"Don't worry, ma'am," he said again. "I reckon one of the railroad surveyors will give up his bed for you—one way or the other. We'll leave in the morning after the funeral."

"Whose funeral?"

He walked on without answering, and she followed, understanding now what the white shirt was likely for. Someone he knew had died here.

She tried to worry about his plan for finding a bed for her, and couldn't, in spite of the fact that nothing she'd experienced thus far left room for any expectation whatsoever that there would be decent accommodations for the female traveling public. All she wanted was a place to lie down, and she didn't much care where.

"Are you hungry, ma'am?" he asked over his shoulder.

"No," she said, because of her fatigue. "Yes," she immediately amended, because she suddenly remembered where she was, and that, out here, one did not forgo a meal of any kind and expect to soon find another.

She looked around at the sound of horses. A detachment of the U.S. Army—coming in from their ride to the stalled train, she decided. There was supposed to be a garrison in the vicinity, but she couldn't imagine where. She watched them pass, averting her eyes at the last moment and ignoring their rapt attention as decorum demanded. She realized after a moment that Ingram, too, was staring at her.

"You needn't concern yourself about them, ma'am. The captain has his wife and child with him. He keeps a firm hand on his men out of respect for them."

"I'm not concerned. I've lived in an occupied town as one of the conquered enemy for the last four years. I'm quite accustomed to what soldiers are like."

"That explains it then."

"I beg your pardon?"

"You've got a soft way of speaking. I reckon it's because of where you come from."

If there was a question in there somewhere, she made no attempt to find it. He looked as if he were trying to make up his mind about something.

"I don't want to stand here any longer, sir," she said. "And I'm not concerned that there's a saloon in the building where my trunk was taken." She started walking in that direction, leaving him to follow or not.

The truth of the matter was that there were all kinds of things in the building where her trunk had been taken. The drummer from Cincinnati had called it the "exchange"—which meant, as far as she could tell, a saloon, a general store, a telegraph office of sorts and a very limited, one dish restaurant—and probably a house of ill repute somewhere upstairs or in the back.

She walked along the muddy street, all too aware of the fact that the ground smelled more of manure than of wet dirt. But traveling cross-country had taught her to take pleasure in the small things—like stepping up out of the mud and onto an actual wooden sidewalk, even briefly.

A man lay on the rough planks next to the nearest building, his body curled as tightly into a ball as he could make it. She thought at first that he was humming, but then she realized that he was crying.

"Is he drunk?" she asked Ingram, who had caught up with her.

"More sorrowful than drunk, ma'am," he said.

"And lying on the sidewalk is his remedy for it?"

"I reckon so, ma'am. Now and again."

She didn't say anything more. Sorrow she understood—and the kind of despair that made a person want to lie down and weep.

"Most of the time he's all right," Ingram said. "He works

hard. He's a good hand—a good man to ride with when you're out looking for strays. He'd not leave you behind if things went bad."

The sidewalk abruptly ended, and she stepped bravely into the muddy street again. The next building was some distance away, and she noted with interest that the lawyer who occupied it, a man named Hapwell, seemed to be the local undertaker, as well.

But she made no comment. She begrudged no man his method of making his living, short of murder or taking advantage of women.

"Will you wait here, ma'am?" Ingram said. "I need to go inside a minute."

He didn't give her a chance to say whether she would or not, and after a moment she followed behind him, stepping up on the crude lean-to porch to wait out of the wind.

"Is she ready?" she heard him ask someone she couldn't see through the windows.

"She's ready. The baby, too. The reverend says he's not going to say anything over her. The girls want to know if you'll do it."

"Me?"

"That's what they said—ask Dan if he'll do it."

"I'm a long way from a preacher, Hap."

"Well, it's not like you haven't done it before. That's good enough for the girls. I don't think Lillyann and her baby would be offended by it."

No one said anything for a moment.

"You'll get your money. It might take me awhile—"

"I'm not worried about the money, Dan. I know you're good for it. What do you want me to tell them?" the man she couldn't see asked.

"Tell them what I said. I'm not a preacher."

She stepped back as the door opened. He looked startled to see her there, but he didn't say anything.

"Who has died?" she asked. He kept walking and didn't answer her. She had to hurry along to keep up. She kept glancing at him, but she didn't ask any more questions.

"I'd be pleased to know your name, ma'am," he said when she'd given up on any further conversation.

"Miss Eleanor Hansen."

"There are some crude men here, Miss Hansen," he said when they'd gone a bit farther.

"Are you one of them?"

"I've…been known to be," he said.

"Then I'd appreciate it if you didn't backslide until I'm safely delivered to Colonel Selby's place."

"I'll try not to, miss. The trouble with the straight and narrow, though, is you can't always tell where that is."

They walked in silence the rest of the way to the exchange—which was a good thing, because she was growing more and more out of breath. Finally, she had to stop altogether.

"You'll get used to the thin air," he said. "If you stay."

"Why—wouldn't I—stay?"

"Most people don't."

"You did—apparently."

"I like it. It suits me."

She glanced around her, still trying to get enough air, wondering what about this place could possibly suit him. She stood for a moment longer, then began walking again, and she still had the sense that he was being wary and watchful.

Given her breathless state, it would have been appropriate for him to offer her his arm the rest of the way up the steep slope, but he didn't. Once they reached the building, he did hold the door open for her to go inside.

She could see the telegraph office straight in front of her, the counters for the general store to her right, a potbellied stove, a few tables where one could eat. And, on her left, the swinging doors to the saloon. Someone in the saloon was playing the concertina, or trying to. She could see the stairs that led to the second floor, and two women—girls—standing on them, watching her with interest. She could hear the slap of cards just inside the doors and an occasional oath. The entire place was smoky because of the windy back draft from the stove.

It pleased Eleanor to know that she could send a telegram regarding her safe arrival—if she'd had anyone to send it to. Her mother had long since given up on her, and there was no one who would care but Maria Markham Woodard, her only friend left in this world and the one who had told her about Lavinia Selby's quest for a teacher brave enough to come to Wyoming Territory. It was Maria who had pointed out that, fallen woman or not, "Nell" had quite enough education to undertake the job of teaching children if she felt like it. And it was Maria who *didn't* throw it into her face that she was desperately in need of a new place and a new beginning as "Eleanor."

So here she was. Two thousand miles from home. Alone and, thus far, in spite of the mud and the thin air and the failed transportation, without regret.

Ingram was talking to the man behind the general store counter—who kept shaking his head. She spied her trunk sitting on the floor nearby. Her valise had been tossed on top of it. She had mistakenly assumed that both would be locked up someplace, and she went to get the valise, amazed that no one had walked off with it. She opened it, expecting to find half if not all the contents missing, but everything seemed to be just as she had packed it. Apparently, the thievery Ingram had mentioned was limited to livestock.

She opened the small velvet case lying nestled on the top, the daguerreotype of Rob Markham taken just before he went blithely off to war. Maria had given it to her the day she left to come to Wyoming Territory. Eleanor had destroyed her own copy, in a fit of grief and anger when word reached her that Rob had been killed at Gettysburg. She had hated Rob Markham then, in the same passionate way she'd always loved him. It was demented to hate a man for dying, but she had done so, and for a long time. How could she not? He wasn't a soldier. He was a man of books and learning, and their kind of love happened but once in a lifetime. They would have opened a school together, had children and grown old together—and he had thrown it away on a cause that had destroyed more lives than could ever be counted. She still couldn't bear to think of the terrible waste of it all, of him and of her. The pain had been unbearable. Seemingly without warning or conscious choice, she had become the flirtatious and irrepressible "Nell," a favorite of the Yankee officers. She had taken the enemy to her bed, taken their money and their favors—and sometimes their abject admiration. And she had felt nothing. No shame. No regret. It seemed to her, when she dared to examine her behavior, that she had wanted to punish Rob as much as she'd wanted to punish the men who had killed him. But the reasons no longer mattered. She had a choice to start over. Now, she hoped and prayed that she was "Eleanor" again—or what was left of her.

She snapped the case closed and looked up to find Ingram standing nearby.

"No bed," he said. He nodded toward where the man he'd been talking to was loudly hammering a nail into the wall. "He's going to string up a couple of blankets so you'll have some privacy. I'm not sure what you'll be sleeping on, but you'll be all right in here. The privy is out back. I wouldn't go wandering around in the dark, though. I told him to get you something to eat. He set it over there."

She looked at the small table he indicated near the stove, and nodded. Ingram walked with her and pulled out the chair.

"What happened to him?" he asked as she sat down.

"Who?"

"The man in the tintype."

"What makes you think something happened to him?" she

said, avoiding looking at him. The question unsettled her more than she wanted to admit. No one asked her about Rob Markham.

No one.

"You wouldn't be here if it hadn't." He didn't wait for a reply or for a criticism of his impertinent behavior. He left her sitting alone with her tin plate of beans and corn bread, and walked away, ultimately pushing through the swinging doors into the saloon.

The conversation inside and the concertina suddenly stopped. And all she could hear was the wind.

Chapter Two

The daguerreotype wasn't the only memento Eleanor carried in her valise. She had Rob's revolver, as well, a fancy pearl-handled model Mr. Markham had presented to both of his sons the day they marched away for glory. Rob had said the thing made him feel like a riverboat gambler, and some kind soul had sent it home with his personal effects months after the battle that had killed him. Maria had given it to her wrapped in a piece of linen the day Eleanor left Salisbury, just as the train pulled into the station. She hadn't wanted to take it; it was an even sharper reminder of Rob and his dying than the daguerreotype. But she understood the way of the world, too much had happened in her life for her not to.

She had placed the revolver in her valise, and she had been surprised by the degree of comfort she received knowing it was there. She removed her hat, then took the revolver out and stretched out on the sacks of flour that had been draped with a rough wool blanket for her to sleep on. The blanket was thick enough to keep her from breathing in flour dust and wide enough for her to cover herself. Even with a gun in hand, it was better than sitting upright on a stagecoach or a train.

She lay in the semidarkness, listening to the ever-present wind whistling through the cracks in the building and to the muttering of voices in the saloon and the occasional burst of forced, female laughter, the kind designed to flatter some man into thinking his feeble attempt at wit and charm had met with favor. Eleanor wondered idly if the giddy laugh came in response to something the terse Ingram had said.

She closed her eyes and drew a wavering breath, aware suddenly of the monumental step she had taken in coming to this place. It was likely that she would never see home again, and it surprised her that, expatriate by choice or not, it mattered.

For all her weariness, it took her a long while to finally fall asleep and what seemed like no time at all for someone to awaken her—a young girl with her blond hair in a long pigtail, holding a can of hot water and a piece of flannel.

Eleanor struggled to sit up, surprised that beams of daylight were coming in through the chinks in the walls.

"Danny said I was to bring this to you," the girl said, setting the can on the floor and handing Eleanor the flannel. If it bothered her that Eleanor slept with a gun in her hand, it didn't show.

"Who?" Eleanor said, trying to force herself awake.

"Dan Ingram. You know."

Ingram. Clearly he was more accommodating than she had first thought.

"I don't reckon you needed that gun," the girl said, after a moment spent staring at the rumpled dress Eleanor had slept in, and at her open valise. "Dan wouldn't let nobody bother you."

"I expect you trust in Mr. Ingram more than I do," Eleanor said, laying the revolver down beside her on the flour sacks.

"You don't look like a schoolteacher," the girl said. "Not any I ever seen, anyways. Can you sing?"

"Sing?" Eleanor said, thinking she'd misunderstood.

"Can you sing 'Farewell My Friends'? It was Lillyann's favorite song, only none of us knows the words to it. *She* used to sing it a lot, but I reckon none of us never paid that much attention. Just weren't thinking she'd die like she did and we'd be wanting it. That old preacher and his sister—I bet they know it, but he won't even come and say any words for her. Won't even come and stand there while she's put away." She gave a heavy sigh and made no attempt to leave. "I figure we can do without him, though. Would you come? To Lillyann's funeral?"

"I don't know the song."

"Well, that's all right. You don't have to sing or nothing. Just come and stand for a minute. Lillyann, she'd like that—a real schoolteacher paying her respects. She'd like that a lot. She was always wishing she could read and write. She said her baby wasn't going to be ignorant like she was—especially if it was a girl. Girls need all the learning they can get, she said. You can't go out to Selby's till Dan goes, and he'll be at the funeral."

"He was a...friend of Lillyann's?" Eleanor already suspected the nature of Lillyann's vocation. The question was inappropriate at best—and none of her business.

"Friend? No, not so much. But I reckon he'll be there so's he can kill Karl Dorsey if he shows up."

"Why would he want to do that?"

"It's Karl Dorsey's fault Lillyann and the baby died. Dan's said in front of everybody Karl's going to have to pay for it. Karl never could leave the bottle alone and him and Dan didn't ever get along much," she added.

"So Lillyann is a good excuse."

"Excuse? No, she ain't no excuse, miss. She's...just Lillyann. She was a good girl—you didn't never have to worry about her stealing things off you. Not like some around here. She was trying real hard to get Karl to the altar and working for Selby's—Mrs. Selby, she likes for the hands to be married men. It civilizes them, she says, and the sooner this country is civilized, the better. She even gets the married ones a little house to themselves—if they show they're willing to stay on and work hard. I reckon Karl won't be going over to Selby's after all this."

Eleanor listened with interest, in spite of her incomplete sleep. Her own presence here had to have something to do with Mrs. Selby's plan for civilization.

"Colonel Selby, he ain't much for Mrs. Selby's way of doing things, though. Mrs. Selby told him he weren't in India anymore—he couldn't lord it over people here in Wyoming Territory. He didn't much like that, but she don't care what he likes. She's a strange kind of a woman—but she's right a lot of times. I like a woman that's right about things, even if it does make the men all mad. She said women out here is going to get to vote. You reckon she's right about that—?"

"Hester!" a man's voice bellowed from the other side of the hung blankets, and the girl jumped violently, knocking the can of hot water over on both of their shoes.

"Oh, lordy, oh, lordy," she whispered as the blanket wall was suddenly jerked back.

A man reached in and grabbed her by the hair, and she began to shriek loudly. He let go, but only so he could slap her hard. She fell facedown on the floor at Eleanor's feet. When he would have kicked the girl where she lay, Eleanor fired the revolver into the floor an inch from the toe of his boot.

"What the—!"

"My goodness," she said sweetly. "You must excuse me, sir. I'm afraid I'm not all that used to firearms. These things *will* go off when you don't expect it, won't they? And I do find this one very heavy for a woman's hand. I can't raise it as high as I would like and hold it steady, so I'm afraid the next one might strike you sooner than I intend it."

The man had stopped in his tracks, not knowing if she was serious or not. Eleanor smiled.

"This ain't none of your damned—"

"The gentleman who taught me to fire a revolver was very adamant about one thing," she interrupted. "'Eleanor,' he said. 'A firearm is a great equalizer—especially for a woman. But you women have such tender hearts. You must forget your forgiving nature, Eleanor, and don't you ever, *ever* aim a gun at a man unless you mean to kill him.' I wonder if I can do that—forget my forgiving nature?"

She stared into the man's eyes, waiting. The girl sobbed loudly on the floor, then scrambled to her knees and crawled to hide against Eleanor's skirts. The man licked his lips and tried to decide if he could overpower her. Several men had come out of the saloon to watch. Eleanor ignored them.

"This young lady was helping me with my toilette," she said to the man. "At Mr. Ingram's request, I believe."

Out of the corner of her eye, she could see Ingram push his way through the swinging doors of the saloon and join the others. Clearly, the man had seen him, too.

Ingram moved closer, but made no attempt to intervene.

"You don't mind her helping me, do you?" Eleanor asked, drawing the man's attention back to the situation at hand—but only briefly. He was much more interested in what Ingram might do.

"No," the man said finally, his voice sullen.

"And I'm sure you won't punish her for it later. Will you?"

"No," he said again.

"Do you give your word, sir?"

"My word?" he said incredulously.

"You're not an animal," Eleanor said. "When a *man* gives his word, he keeps it. Especially in front of witnesses. Do I have your word?"

"Yeah. You got my *word*. You can put that damn gun down." He turned to go, roughly pushing his way through the crowd that had gathered.

"Burley," Ingram said quietly as he tried to pass.

"I ain't looking for no trouble with you, Dan."

"Then it's all going to work out fine," Ingram answered.

The man clearly had more to say, but he didn't say it. He shoved the nearest man aside and headed for the saloon. After a moment, the rest of the men followed him—all except Dan

Ingram. He looked at Eleanor and then at the gun that now rested on her lap. Hester still cowered and sobbed on the floor. Eleanor reached out to put her hand on Hester's shoulder, and the girl immediately grabbed her around the knees.

"This is all *your* fault," Eleanor said to Dan. "You should never have put her in a situation where she'd get beaten—and for what? I can do without hot water."

They stared at each other.

"You know," he said after a moment. "You're not going to have near the trouble keeping order in a schoolroom as I thought."

The meager procession of mourners had to climb up the hill to reach the cemetery. The coffin containing the unfortunate Lillyann and her child went first, on a wagon pulled by two fractious horses. Eleanor followed well behind the others, only deciding at the last moment to accept Hester's invitation to attend. She had nothing else to do, and she felt a certain empathy for a young woman who, for whatever reason, had apparently fallen. There was some irony to it all, Eleanor supposed, that *she,* of all people, would be considered a welcome witness to the burial ritual. She could hear Hester still sniffing as she walked along, but she had no idea if it was grief or the altercation with the man called Burley that was responsible for it. Perhaps both, she decided.

The sun was shining brightly and the wind blew as strong as ever. Already the muddiness of yesterday was drying away. They walked past another building—the last structure on the path to the cemetery. A man and woman stood on the lean-to porch, watching, their expressions all too familiar to Eleanor.

Righteous disapproval.

Of the young woman who had died and of every person in the procession who accompanied her on her final journey.

It occurred to Eleanor that she herself was off to a less than stellar beginning in this new life she'd chosen. She hadn't been in Soul Harbor twenty-four hours and already she'd been in a brawl requiring a firearm, and, unless she was very mistaken, she was going to be publicly denounced by the two people on the porch—something not likely to meet Mrs. Selby's approval.

A number of men joined the mourners, but not the man called Burley, thankfully. No singing accompanied the brief interment. Either no one knew "Farewell My Friends," or no one was willing to perform it. Ingram said a few words after all, words that were snatched away by the wind before she could hear them. He removed his hat and stood tall, his face impassive as he spoke. Then, at his signal, the coffin was lowered. Hester stepped forward to drop a clod of dirt into the grave. Each of the women with her did the same, and then two of the men, who had come with shovels, began to fill the gaping hole.

Eleanor was feeling short of breath again, and she turned to walk back toward the exchange alone, nodding purposefully at the man and woman who still stood watching from their porch. The woman gave a short sniff and looked away. The man merely stared.

"Are you ready to go?" a voice asked behind her—Ingram.

"I am," she said without looking at him. As there had been no murders at the graveside, she could only assume that Ingram's intended victim hadn't deigned to put in an appearance.

"A train will be back through in three or four days if you've changed your mind."

"I haven't," she said.

"Why did you come to Lillyann's burial?" he asked bluntly.

"Hester invited me," she said.

"Why would she do that?"

"You'll have to ask her."

"You understand that Mrs. Selby might not like it that you did."

"It occurred to me," Eleanor said. Too late, she thought. "I suppose the couple on the porch will tell her."

"Well, they'll be two of the ones standing in line for the

privilege. You might want to say something to Mrs. Selby before anybody else gets to her."

"No," she said. Even as a child, she had never had the slightest inclination to try to justify her behavior, and she wasn't about to start.

He made a small sound of disapproval or understanding or neutrality. She had no idea which.

"That's a shortcut to the privy," he said of a path to her left. "I'll meet you at the exchange."

She looked at him for a moment, then took the shortcut. It was indelicate of him to mention the proximity of the sanitation facilities—but it was very helpful.

He was indeed waiting for her in front of the exchange—on the same wagon that had just served as a hearse and now held her trunk and her valise and what looked like a basket of food. He sat in the driver's seat, holding the reins to the same cantankerous horses, his own mount tied to the back.

"I can drive a wagon," she said.

"It's a long way. You can spell me after a couple of hours."

She looked around at the sound of running feet—Hester hurrying down the hill. Her eyes were puffy from crying, one more so than the other, thanks to Burley.

She stopped a few feet away, then walked the rest of the distance to where Eleanor stood. "You're going now," she said unnecessarily.

"Yes."

"Well…thank you."

"I didn't do anything," Eleanor said.

"You helped give Lillyann a good send-off. You stood up to Burley."

"And you'll likely be the one to pay for it."

She shrugged. "Burley, he don't need a reason to go and hit somebody. You made him promise he wouldn't—in front of everybody. Maybe he'll keep it," she said wistfully. "I reckon you won't be back in town for a while—but if you do come and there ain't nobody watching, I'd be much obliged if you'd say hello to me—if we was to meet on the street or something like that."

"I'll say hello to you, Hester. Whether anybody's watching or not."

Hester leaned closer. "You got to watch yourself, miss," she whispered. "Colonel Selby and Mrs. Selby—they don't get along. They'll be trying to use you against one another, trying to blame each other for things you do even if you didn't do anything—"

"Miss Hansen," Ingram said.

The girl glanced in Ingram's direction and reached up to touch her swollen face. Then she nodded. "I believe you will say hello to me, miss," she said out loud. "But it's all right if you don't. I ain't wanting to drag you down."

"Hester—"

"Let's go, Miss Hansen," Ingram said, and the girl turned and ran back up the hill.

Eleanor stepped up on the hub of the wagon wheel and climbed in, accepting Ingram's help only as a last resort. Her parasol was strapped to the valise, but she didn't bother with it, in spite of the bright sun. The wind would have snatched it away before they crossed the railroad track. She grabbed on to the side of the seat as the wagon lurched forward, and braced herself for the last leg of the journey to a new life.

She made no attempt at conversation. She already understood that Ingram was no great talker. Their conversations consisted more of the things *he* wanted to know rather than the things she could pull out of him.

She looked out over the land and up at the sky, which seemed to be forever changing. There was nothing else to see. After a time, Ingram drove the wagon off what passed for a road and into the open grassland. She wondered how he could possibly know where he was going, but she didn't ask. She just rode along, mindful of the fact that she was alone in the middle of an unfamiliar and dangerous land—with a man who was a complete stranger. All she knew of him was that he worked for the Selbys and that he was willing to give a dead girl and her baby a decent burial. Thanks to Hester, she also knew that he meant to kill the man responsible for it.

She gave a wavering sigh. She would never understand that kind of dichotomy in men's natures. Killing another man— even with a good reason—was still that.

Killing.

The very idea was abhorrent to her. Rob's willingness to take another person's life, albeit for a so-called noble cause, had cost her dearly, and yet she'd just threatened a man with the very same consequence. She liked to think she wouldn't have actually shot Burley, but she was by no means certain. Clearly, the dichotomy was a part of human nature in general and not just that of the male of the species. In the quest for "civilization," Mrs. Selby surely had her work cut out for her.

They rode for what seemed a long time. Eleanor was comfortable in the silence, so much so that it startled her when Ingram suddenly spoke.

"You were right," he said.

"About what?"

"I put Hester in harm's way—I know what Burley's like."

His admission was unexpected, to say the least. He kept glancing at her. She didn't know what to say.

"It…wasn't my intention to make enemies," she said finally.

"Enemies?"

"That man—Burley—"

"I don't much think you made an enemy of him, miss. He's so impressed, he'll be asking Colonel Selby if he can marry you."

Eleanor looked at him, not knowing whether he had meant it as a joke or whether he had spoken the truth.

"In that case, I…should have brought my hope chest," she said.

To her immense surprise—and his, she figured—Ingram

smiled. It was brief, and, she thought, embarrassingly unwelcome. Ingram, for whatever reason, had clearly given up on finding things to smile about, and he didn't much appreciate her resurrecting his sense of humor.

She looked away, trying not to smile herself. For a time she occupied herself by listening to the creaking and rattle of the wagon and the clink of metal on the horses' harness—what she could hear of it above the wind. It made a constant whistling sound against her ears, one she couldn't escape no matter which way she turned her head.

"I want to ask you something," Eleanor said abruptly. "I want to ask you about Lillyann."

"She was a whore, miss," Ingram said with a bluntness that surprised her. "She was hoping to get herself a better life with a man named Karl Dorsey. She couldn't have picked anybody worse. It was just a matter of time before he killed her."

"She...loved him?"

"I reckon she did. You know what they say, miss. There's not a man so bad that a woman or a dog won't love him. He decided she needed to be put in her place, and he locked her out in the cold the night it snowed. Some say he was drunk. Maybe he was. Maybe he wasn't. Anyway, she died from it and her baby with her. It was a cruel thing for a man to do, drunk or sober."

"And you're planning to kill him for it," Eleanor said. It wasn't quite a question.

"It's more that I'm planning to keep him from killing me. Lillyann had a good heart. She didn't deserve what she got from Karl Dorsey, and she didn't deserve to be tossed into the ground and forgotten like she and her baby were nothing. Karl took offense when I pointed that out."

"I see," Eleanor said. And she did—a little. It was more a matter of perceived insults than justice for Lillyann.

She took a quiet breath and stared at the horizon. "It all depends, you know," she said after a time.

"Miss?"

"On the dog and on the woman."

Eleanor could feel him waiting for her to elaborate, but that was all she wished to say. Instead of talking, she focused her attention on her surroundings.

She was learning as they rode along that there were animals about, small creatures that scurried out of their way. She also realized that the flat land wasn't really all that flat. There were dips and hollows along the way that could keep all manner of things from view until you were right on top of them.

Like trees. She would have sworn there were none beyond the scrubby, bushlike things she had spotted growing here and there, but she could just see the tops of some real trees off to her right, a long zigzagging line of them.

"Cottonwoods," Ingram said, as if he'd read her mind. "When you see them, you know there's water. They don't grow anywhere else."

"Is there a river?" Eleanor asked with a certain amount of dread. Thus far, crossing rivers had been a less than pleasant experience.

"Yes, but you won't think much of it."

"Why not?"

"Not very wide, not very deep."

She might have been more reassured if she'd had at least some idea of what he meant by "very."

"How much longer until we get to Colonel Selby's ranch?"

"After we cross the river, we'll be on it. But it'll be nearly dark by the time we get to the main house."

"What's it like—the main house?"

"Big," he said. "Made of stone. Some think it's like the houses the Colonel and his late brother were used to in England. Some say they brought just about everything on their estate with them, including the pigs and chickens and milk cows."

"What happened to his brother?"

"Got himself killed two winters ago."

"And his wife—widow—stayed?" Eleanor asked, avoiding the obvious but likely unsettling question about the manner of the man's demise.

"She's got controlling interest in the cattle company."

"I see. I don't imagine the colonel is happy about that."

"He doesn't talk to me, miss—but I think he's not as happy as he could be."

"If he owned all of it, you mean."

"Something like that. Some men need to own things. Others don't—"

He stiffened suddenly and reached for the rifle that leaned against the seat between them. She looked around to see what had caught his attention—riders on horseback that had popped up out of nowhere.

"Not Selby men," he said.

"And?" she asked when he didn't elaborate.

"Don't know, miss."

He did know; Eleanor was sure of that, but she didn't press him for answers. She was all too willing to abide in that elusive place where ignorance was bliss.

"What did you do with that revolver?" he asked quietly.

"It's in the valise."

"I want you to reach back and slide the valise where you can open it. Take your time. Get the revolver but don't hold it where they can see it."

She looked at him, and for a brief moment he looked back. He was worried about this and so, then, was she, ignorant of the circumstances or not. She took a quiet breath and reached back for the valise, fumbling to get it open and the revolver out without appearing suspicious. As an afterthought, she got the parasol as well, hiding the gun behind it as she drew it forward. She slipped the weapon under her skirts and opened the parasol, gripping it hard to keep the wind from taking it.

"Now what?" she asked.

"If they kill me, I'd appreciate it if you'd send at least one of them to hell along with me."

"Any particular one?" she asked, because he was being flippant—or as flippant as a man like Ingram could get.

"Here they come," he said, but he made no attempt to raise the rifle or to speed up the horses.

The riders had broken into a gallop, all six of them. They rode straight for the wagon, then began circling it, around and around, all of them showing the grins of grown men about to play the adult version of King of the Hill.

Eleanor glanced at them, then looked straight ahead, ignoring them as Ingram was doing—or seeming to. She slid her free hand under her skirt and let it rest on the handle of the revolver.

"Danny!" one of them said finally. "Who you got there, son?"

Ingram didn't answer.

"She can't be a friend of yourn," the rider said. "Way too high class for the likes of you."

The rider stood in his stirrups, apparently so he could get a better look, and perhaps to test Ingram's resolve. Eleanor had had enough experience in the company of men to have no doubt that this particular one was the kind whose personal bravery depended on how many other scoundrels just like him were along to back him up. Alone, his boldness would completely dissipate.

"You boys coming to the party?" Dan asked mildly. Accosting a Selby wagon on this side of the river was a bold gesture, even for Karl Dorsey. Dan watched him warily, knowing the others would take their lead from him. If the son of a bitch was drunk, he was apt to do anything, whether his boss had approved it or not.

Dan could sense the apprehension in the woman next to him, but she didn't show it. He had no notion of whether she realized how badly they were outnumbered or not. She sat there, aloof and a little disdainful of the intrusion, her hand resting on the revolver under her skrts. Karl might make the mistake of thinking she was helpless like Lillyann, but if he did, Dan suspected that Karl would die a very surprised man.

"What party?" Karl asked.

"I hear you're all invited—Mrs. Selby's doing. She rode over to see your boss herself day before yesterday. I wouldn't want to miss it if I was you. Mrs. Selby sets a fine table. She's not ashamed to have milk cows and chickens on the place— and these are the fancy English kind. Makes for some good eating, I can tell you—cakes and custards and butter bread like you wouldn't believe. Maybe you ought to check with the big man—before you go and do something *he* might regret."

For the first time, Karl looked doubtful. "You boys hear anything about a party?" he asked the others.

None of them had—but they were clearly interested.

"You know what I think?" Karl said. "I think you're a damned liar."

"Suit yourself," Ingram said. "But you might want to remember there's a lady present before you get into any more name-calling. Be seeing you, Karl." He whistled sharply and set the horses to a faster pace.

Karl?

"Is that Lillyann's Karl?" Eleanor asked when she was reasonably sure they were going to be allowed to ride on in peace.

Ingram frowned. And didn't answer.

"Is it?" Eleanor persisted.

"Yes," he said.

"Why didn't you try to kill each other, then?"

"It's not the time."

"Not the time? You have some kind of…schedule?"

"You were here, miss. That made it not the right time."

Eleanor started to say something else, then gave up. The land was sloping downward toward the line of trees. She could just see the river, the *shallow* river.

But shallow or not, one of the horses balked at going into it. It might as well have been a raging torrent. Ingram finally handed the reins to her and got on his mount to lead them across.

On the other side, they stopped under the cottonwood trees. The wind still played havoc with the tree tops, but didn't reach the ground nearly as much. Eleanor found the respite wonderful.

"Does the wind blow all the time?" she asked Ingram as he fiddled with one of the horse harnesses.

"Don't let it scare you, miss," he said, still busy.

"I'm not afraid of it—"

"It gets strange sometimes, miss."

"Strange?"

"Sometimes you think you can hear things."

"Like what?"

"Like…singing. Voices singing—sort of like a choir. I don't know what causes it, but it happens. So don't let it scare you if it does."

Eleanor frowned. "You've heard it?"

"Me and everybody else that stays outside a lot," he said. "Maybe the ones who work inside all the time don't. I don't know. Are you hungry, miss?"

"Yes," she said.

"I'm going to ride off for a bit, look around, give you some privacy. When I come back, we'll open that basket. Don't pack the revolver away again. Keep it handy."

With that, he mounted his horse and rode away. It took all Eleanor could do not to call after him. She stood for a moment, then looked around her. She didn't particularly need "privacy," but she knew to take advantage of the opportunity anyway, carrying the revolver with her in case of heaven knew what.

Afterward, she walked to the river's edge and wet her handkerchief so she could wash her face and hands, all the while listening for Ingram's return.

She didn't hear anything but the quiet rush of the river, the wind in the trees and the occasional blowing of the team of horses. She let her mind pick through the information she'd gathered so far. It was interesting to her that Mrs. Selby had control of the cattle company—and that tidbit had certainly clarified what Hester might have meant about the Selbys using Eleanor to try to get at each other. Just what she needed—to be caught in yet another civil war.

She took a quiet breath and walked toward the wagon, not seeing the Indian women until she had nearly reached it. There were three of them, two very young, one very old. She looked at them, but made no attempt to speak. Neither did they. They simply walked past under the trees and into the river, clearly for a purpose, but Eleanor couldn't imagine what. None of them carried anything. One of the younger ones glanced back over her shoulder at one point, until the old woman apparently chastised her for it.

Eleanor watched them until they disappeared into the tall grass on the other side—grass that she suddenly realized was significantly taller here than it had been around Soul Harbor.

Eleanor walked around under the trees for a time, the revolver still in her hand. She couldn't see anything of Ingram in the direction he'd gone nor hear the sound of his horse. After a time, she sat down on the back of the wagon to wait, leaning against her valise, her legs dangling. Her belly rumbled with hunger and she considered opening the basket, but only briefly. Her eyes were growing heavy in the dappled but warm sunshine. It was so…pleasant to be out of the wind.

She closed her eyes.

After a moment, she moved the valise to find a more comfortable position, and closed her eyes again, only to wake with a start because Ingram was standing next to her.

"Sorry, miss. I was afraid you were going to fall off."

"Then why didn't you just call my name and wake me up? It's too bad it's not fly season. You could have entertained yourself by watching to see if one flew into my mouth. How long have you been back, anyway?" she added crossly. There was no real reason for her to be annoyed beyond the usual fatigue and inconvenience of travel, but she was.

"Long enough to eat. I saved you some," he said.

Nowhere on his face could she see the amusement she heard in his voice.

"We're going to have to go—you can eat what's left on the way. Or you can ride back here, take another nap if you want."

She didn't want. She sat beside him on the seat with the basket on her lap. There was some cheese left, and a cold biscuit and a withered apple. She ate all three. He offered her a drink of water from his canteen, which she took gladly.

"Did you find what you were looking for?" she asked after a time.

"I wasn't looking for anything," he said.

"You were looking for trouble, Mr. Ingram."

He glanced at her, and he didn't deny it. She waited, but there was nothing in the way of conversation forthcoming.

"How many children are on the ranch?" she asked, to prod him into saying something, at least.

"Six or seven," he said. "Unless Mrs. Selby makes the older boys come."

"Do you think she will?"

"I guess she will if she can get them away from the colonel. We'll be busy with the roundup. He's going to need every hand."

"The boys work on the ranch?"

"Yes, miss."

"How old are they?"

"Not sure. The youngest must be about twelve or so. The oldest, sixteen. It doesn't really matter if Mrs. Selby wants them able to read and write. Most of them are as good as any man when it comes to doing their job—except they're not as strong as a grown man yet. But they band together to get things done when they need to. Are you ready to drive the wagon, miss?"

"What? Oh. Yes."

"Good," he said, handing over the reins. He climbed in the back and took the rifle with him.

"Looking for trouble again, Mr. Ingram?" she asked.

"I thought I would, miss," he said, his voice quiet and matter-of-fact. And very alarming.

"And how likely is it that you'll find it?"

He waited too long to answer, and she thought he knew it. She could feel him trying to decide how forthcoming he could be.

"It's not likely. I don't expect him to cross the river."

"Karl, you mean."

"Yes, miss."

"The fact that even Hester knows you mean to kill him has to be some kind of incentive."

"Yes, miss."

"So if he does cross—"

"I'll need my hands free."

She took a deep breath to steady her nerves. "All right. Which way do I go?"

"Just go straight, that's all."

"Straight."

"That's right. I'm not worried. You can do it."

"There are no landmarks—"

"You can do it," he said again.

Clearly, she had little choice in the matter, so she drove the wagon—hopefully, straight. She didn't ask him any more questions, didn't look back to see what he was doing. She just kept going. Her arms began to ache from the strain of it after a time, but she didn't complain.

Their shadows grew longer. For all she knew, Ingram had gone to sleep. Once again the land around her began to change. The grass was not so tall, and she could see little groups of cows and calves grazing here and there.

A dark speck on the horizon caught her attention.

"Is that—?"

"That's the house. You didn't get us lost, after all, miss."

She glanced over her shoulder at him, but he didn't say anything more. It was a new experience for her, to know she was being teased when there was no outward indication whatsoever.

A horse and rider were bearing down on them from their left, a young boy riding a huge roan as if he'd been born in the saddle.

"Dan!" he yelled, more in surprise than in greeting, but he was looking at Eleanor.

"Petey! Go tell Mrs. Selby her schoolteacher has arrived."

"She's out riding!"

"Well, see if you can fetch her in."

"Yes, sir!" the boy said, letting the horse rear, twice, before he turned it sharply and galloped away.

"Showing off for you," Ingram said, and Eleanor laughed softly. This time, when she looked at him, he was smiling as if he no longer minded it.

"Will you take the reins now?" she asked.

"It will be better if you do it, miss—let them see you're not helpless."

She nodded, in spite of her fatigue and the tremor in her arms from the long strain of keeping the horses in check.

"Miss?" he said when they were close enough to see the outbuildings and some fences, and men working in groups and alone. She looked at him again.

"It's good you've got the revolver," he said.

When they reached the house, Dan helped her down and followed a few steps behind as she walked toward what she obviously believed was a new life. She was a pretty woman, he thought, but there was more to her than a fine figure and a pleasing face. Already he was feeling responsible for her, in the way a soldier might feel responsible for a new comrade-in-arms, one who had survived his early trial by fire but who didn't yet realize how much worse things could get.

Eleanor Hansen had done well so far—in town and on the

way out here. She didn't scare easily. Dan had wanted to say more to her just now. He had wanted to tell her to be careful, whether she understood what he meant or not. She had no idea what she was getting herself into. Colonel Selby had no fear of consequences. His word was law, and any man he hired followed his orders without question or found other employment. Only the colonel's sister-in-law, Lavinia, dared to challenge him, and she did it at every turn. Eleanor would become yet another pawn in their struggle for power, a struggle that Dan had managed to avoid until now. He had blundered into the middle of this latest round by making an unplanned trip into Soul Harbor to arrange for Lillyann's funeral. He doubted that Lavinia had known Eleanor's arrival was imminent, and he didn't want to have to worry about these things, about being caught up in the longstanding feud between Selbys or about the young woman who was walking into a situation she couldn't begin to comprehend. He took a little comfort in the fact that he had at least told Eleanor Hansen the truth. It was good that she had the revolver.

Chapter Three

Eleanor realized immediately that, in spite of the letters she carried, Colonel Vandereau Selby wasn't expecting her. He covered his surprise at her appearance quickly, but not quickly enough and not charmingly enough to fool her.

"My dear Miss Hansen—here you are at last," he said, accepting the gloved hand she offered. Her arm still trembled from fatigue, so she supposed that he would think she was nervous about meeting him—which was true enough. Her immediate impression was that he had the potential for being a fearsome entity. He wasn't a big man, but his military bearing and his calculating manner made him a commanding one.

"You were in town?" he said to Ingram, his tone of voice suggesting that he hadn't been advised of that plan and he wouldn't have approved it if he had.

"Personal business, Colonel," Ingram said.

"Ah. Quite." The colonel smiled—but he didn't mean it.

"I regret my sister-in-law isn't on hand to greet you," he said, turning his attention to Eleanor. "She's out for her daily ride—a bit later than usual, unfortunately. Well! Come inside, my dear! You must be exhausted. It's a long way from South Carolina."

"North Carolina, sir," Eleanor said, as she let herself be guided into the huge stone house.

"Ah, yes. *North* Carolina. There is a difference, isn't there? Mary!"

He only had to yell the girl's name once. She came at a run from the back of the house.

"Mary, take Miss Hansen to one of the east wing rooms. See to her every need, give her anything she requires. My dear Miss Hansen, you must make yourself at home—rest, have your supper at your leisure and take your ease. Nothing else will be required of you today. Tomorrow, after you're refreshed and rested, we will introduce you to your new home, yes?"

"Thank you, Colonel," Eleanor said. "You are very kind." She looked around to thank Ingram, as well, expecting him to be behind her. He hadn't come inside, and she could no longer see him in the yard.

"This way, miss," Mary said with a little curtsy. "Follow me, then."

They didn't go up the elaborate main staircase. Mary briskly led the way back in the direction she had come, down one hallway and into another more narrow one, then to a series of steps going upward until they reached what must be the east wing. Eleanor could hear the murmur of voices from time to time as she passed closed doors, but she didn't see anyone.

The girl finally stopped in front of a door and opened it with one of the keys she had on a ring in her apron pocket.

"This is it, miss," she said. "What can I get for you?"

"If I could wash—a basin and a pitcher of water?"

"Oh, yes, miss. I'll bring everything you need for that. And a tray for your supper. What would you like, miss?"

"Anything will be fine. I'm more dirty than hungry."

"And tired, too, I'd guess. I remember how tired I was when I got here. Why, I could hardly put one foot afront the other. One of the boys will be bringing your trunk along. I'd wait for that, if I were you. They're not so good about knocking first. Mrs. Selby and I try to teach them, but they forget. You rest. I'll be back soon."

She hurried out of the room, closing the door quietly behind her. Eleanor stood for a moment, then wearily took off her gloves and her hat. There was something disconcerting about a young woman who felt such a need to…*scurry.*

She looked around the small room, at the brass bed and a somewhat scarred oak dresser. There was a washstand and one chair and a small writing table with a tall lamp. The single window was large, but the sun was going, and already the room was growing dark.

Eleanor walked to the table and lit the lamp. Then she moved to the window to look outside. She was on the back side of the house now, and she could see a number of outbuildings and several barns and enclosures, but nothing she thought might be a school. She wondered if the schoolroom would be somewhere in the house.

After a moment, she could hear heavy scraping and muffled laughter. She walked to the door and opened it. Two young boys were struggling with her trunk and valise, and they grew immediately bashful when they saw her.

"This way," she said to them as they pushed and shoved and half carried the trunk. "Thank you for your help. You are both very kind."

"It weren't nothing," one of them said, and the other one giggled.

"Is this where you want it?" the giggler asked.

"That will be fine."

"We'll be going then," the first one said, then poked his partner to get him to stop staring and come along.

Eleanor closed the door after them, smiling to herself. Someone knocked on it almost immediately. When she opened it again, Mary came in with a large can of hot water and a small tub and towels and soap. Two more girls followed her, one carrying a tray of food, the other a large pillow and blankets.

"You'll need these blankets. It gets cold here at night,

miss," Mary said. "Mrs. Selby is back. She says she'll see you tomorrow and you can sleep as long as you like. There'll be lots of people coming here tomorrow. She wants you all rested for the party. Can I help you with your dress, miss?"

"No, I can manage. What sort of party is it?"

"No sort at all, miss. That's how Mrs. Selby is. Sometimes she wants a party, so we have one. Mr. Warner and his people are invited to this one—he owns the land on the other side of the river. We've been cooking for *days*." She shooed the other two girls out ahead of her. "The stairs at the far end of the hall will take you down to the kitchen if you need anything. There's always somebody there," she added as she closed the door.

Alone again, Eleanor began to undress. She took a long time to bathe, savoring the miracle of hot water and soap. She brushed out her hair and put on the nightdress she had yet to wear, then she ate the biscuits and jam and butter Mary had brought and drank some of the tea. And, for the first time in a long while, she lay down in an actual bed—without a gun in her hand, in spite of Ingram's approval that she had it. And who was she supposed to use it against? Burley and those like him? The Indians? Wild animals? Perhaps, in this place— where men killed each other by appointment—her own pupils.

On the edge of sleep, she ignored for as long as she could the raised voices that suddenly came from outside the window. But her curiosity exceeded her fatigue, and she got up to see. The colonel stood down below with a woman, both of them bathed in the light from an open door.

"You meant to scare her away," the woman said. "Don't think for a moment I don't see what you're about. Unlike my late husband, I am *not* easily fooled."

With that she turned and walked back into the house, leaving the colonel alone. After a moment, he, too, went inside. Eleanor frowned, realizing that she might very well be the person the woman had been talking about. It suddenly occurred to her that the colonel might have meant for her to be left standing when she arrived in Soul Harbor—only Ingram had unexpectedly come into town for his "personal business"—Lillyann's funeral. If that were true, then Hester had been telling the truth about the contention between the colonel and his sister-in-law.

Eleanor gave a sharp sigh. She was too tired to worry about it. She fell back into bed and immediately went to sleep, waking to find the sun was up and the house and grounds full of activity. As she sat up in bed, she could hear all manner of commotion from both places. She noted immediately that the food tray of last night had been taken away and that her travel dress had been pressed and carefully draped over the chair.

Even so, she couldn't bear to put it on again. She took her best dress—a somber gray merino with buff trim—out of the trunk instead. It was somewhat crushed, but it was very…respectable, perfect for a schoolteacher. She would at least look the part.

When she stepped outside the room, she met Mary in the hallway.

"Did you have a good sleep, miss?" she asked, smiling.

"Yes, thank—"

"Will you come with me, miss? Mrs. Selby is waiting. She wanted to see you the minute you were up and about."

She turned and hurried in the direction she had come without waiting for an answer. Eleanor followed, almost having to run to keep up.

"In here, miss," Mary said when they reached a pair of mahogany doors. She knocked softly, then opened one of them and stood back for Eleanor to go inside.

The woman Eleanor had seen last night was seated at a writing desk on the other side of the room. She was impeccably dressed in clothing the quality of which Eleanor hadn't seen since before the war. Even the wives of the officers of the occupation army back home didn't dress so finely. Mrs.

Selby was also quite a bit younger than Eleanor had expected—which made the remark she'd overheard last night all the more significant. Mrs. Lavinia Selby did *not* let herself be intimidated.

"Journey's end, Miss Hansen. Welcome to Wyoming Territory," she said in her perfectly cultured English voice. "Do come and sit for a moment. How did you pass the night? Is there anything you require this morning?"

"No, nothing, thank you," Eleanor said in spite of the persistent rumbling of her empty belly. She sat down in a fragile-looking chair near the desk. "I slept quite well, and Mary has been very kind."

"Yes. Mary is one of my successes. Her living situation was appalling before she came here. I…regret there was no one to meet you when you arrived in Soul Harbor. Were you terribly inconvenienced?"

"No," Eleanor said—unless embroiling herself in a near gun brawl and attending a funeral she ought not to have attended counted. "I should like to get started right away, if that's all right."

"Perfectly all right. We are having a gathering of the warring clans here today, but that won't interfere. They've already begun to arrive, as a matter of fact."

"Warring clans?"

"Livingston Warner and his people from across the river. A rival cattle operation, I'm afraid. I've had enough of our men and their men antagonizing each other, and everyone looking the other way. I intend to see what can be done about it—something I learned in India. One should always keep one's enemies close."

"If he's an enemy, is he likely to listen to…suggestions?" Eleanor asked, even though the question was inappropriate coming from someone in a newly hired position.

"I have something he wants—the stud service of a true Arabian stallion, a magnificent animal. I believe Mr. Warner will like my terms.

"There are people here you should meet today—and the children, of course. Then you're free to go set up the schoolroom however you like. The school isn't as close to the house as I would have wanted, but…we'll make do," she said, the determination apparent in her voice, a determination Eleanor recognized immediately that she was expected to emulate. "You understand that you will be residing there, on the premises, as will some of the children from time to time, when sudden weather changes don't permit their travel back home. Two of them will be coming out from the military post, a good hour's ride on a fast horse. I believe the wife of one of the Indian scouts will deliver and fetch them. I have been led to believe that you are not a fearful person, Miss Hansen, and that will come in very handy to us both. Now…" She got up from the desk with a rustle of heavy taffeta. "You and I shall go and break bread with our esteemed guests. I am most pleased that you're refreshed and ready to begin."

Eleanor followed after her, expecting to be led to a dining room somewhere. But the meal had been set up outside—on long tables placed between two lines of canvas that had been hung on ropes strung post to post, then anchored by more rope and staked into the ground. The canvas shook in the wind, but it did an adequate job of blocking the worst of it. Women young and old either stood expectantly or bustled around the tables, setting platters and bowls of food anywhere they could find room. One manned a huge enameled coffeepot and a stack of tin cups. The serving plates were tin as well, but there were crisply starched napkins and wooden-handled forks and knives and spoons. Children ran and played in the background, and two distinctly separate groups of men—all sizes and ages—seemed to be standing around waiting. Apparently there was no dress standard for ranch workers. They wore all manner of hats, some wide brim, some not. Two even had dandified "city hats." Some wore coats, the kind that had once been part of a man's suit. Others had on what was left of a military uniform, blue and gray. Those not wearing coats had on vests, some made of a kind of furry hide and some the formal kind that seemed, like the odd jackets, to be missing the rest of the suit. She noted immediately that there was only one white shirt among them and Ingram was wearing it.

She could feel the stares and the buzz of interest as she walked along. Apparently, they had been waiting for Mrs. Selby's arrival and her permission to eat—and Eleanor Hansen was considered the entertainment.

Dan Ingram stood back from the others, and on the opposite side, so did Lillyann's Karl. Ingram nodded and touched the brim of his hat as Eleanor passed, something the other men noticed and seemed to find both interesting and humorous.

Lavinia Selby walked toward a tall man with long white hair who stood with the colonel, stopping short of actually greeting him so that he would have to come to her. Eleanor thought for a moment that he wouldn't do it, but after an awkward delay, he abruptly smiled and stepped forward with his hand extended.

"Mrs. Selby," he said graciously.

"Livingston," she answered, shaking his hand. "Welcome—and do please call me Lavinia. We are neighbors, after all, and have been for a long while now. May I present Miss Eleanor Hansen, who has just arrived from North Carolina. She will be teaching at the Selby school."

"Miss Hansen," he said, briefly taking her offered hand. "I reckon we are making real progress out here if the schoolmarms are arriving. Tell me, what do you think of our country so far?"

"I think it's no place for sinners," Eleanor answered, and he laughed out loud.

"And why do you reckon that, Miss Hansen?"

"It's very high and it's very open. There's no place to hide from God's ever watchful eye."

"That is so—but I have to say I never noticed it before. Maybe I better be mending my ways. Did you hear that, Reverend?" he asked a man standing a short distance away.

Eleanor recognized him—and the woman with him—immediately. She gave an inward sigh. Perhaps she should have taken Ingram's advice and told Mrs. Selby that she had attended Lillyann's funeral.

It was too late now, however. The reverend took the remark as his cue to preside. He called the group to order and offered up a lengthy blessing for the food and for the distinguished company. As soon as he'd finished, two lines of hungry men formed, on each side of the tables, more than ready to sit down and partake of the mounds of meat and potatoes, bread, boiled eggs, pies and cakes. The colonel and Mr. Warner went first, followed by Lavinia and the reverend, then his sister and Eleanor.

The reverend's sister made it perfectly clear that she was not receptive to any polite conversation from the likes of Eleanor Hansen, and Eleanor had to fight hard not to annoy her. "Nell" would have done it and gladly. It was too bad she hadn't been invited.

Eleanor was surrounded by unrestrained appetites, but she herself scarcely had the opportunity to eat. After a few random introductions, she took the place Lavinia indicated in the shade and shelter of one of the canvas screens. All the remaining women present and some of the men came to introduce themselves without Lavinia's escort—some to present their reticent children, most just to see the new schoolteacher up close.

"You ain't got a husband, I guess," one of the woman said bluntly. Her face seemed to have sunk into a permanent and suspicious frown.

"No," Eleanor said.

"It's a shame when a woman can't get herself married," the woman said.

"My fiancé was killed at Gettysburg," Eleanor answered quietly. "And yes, I suppose it is—according to some. I always thought a woman should have standards. I have never believed she should marry a man simply because he asked."

The woman moved on—quickly—and went to eat with the

reverend's sister. The two of them began whispering immediately, sharing the tidbit of personal information Eleanor should have had more sense than to give. She didn't want people to know about Rob. Inevitably, it led to the need to offer condolences, and even the most well meaning ones were like a knife in her heart.

She continued to smile and converse with people until her face hurt—then she smiled some more. She had seen Ingram pass through the line to eat, but he was no longer anywhere in view. Not that she was looking for him. It was simply that he was the one person here she felt she actually knew.

Someone began playing a fiddle and someone else joined in with a concertina—perhaps the same one she'd heard in the saloon. The approachable women present were all busy, but that seemed not to deter the kind of men who worked for cattle companies. Soon all the serving girls were engaged in what might, in sheer desperation, be called a waltz, around the dirt space that served as a dance floor.

Eleanor realized suddenly that Karl Dorsey was coming purposefully in her direction. She had seen that expression on a man's face more times than she cared to count, and she looked around for a way to escape. There was none save crawling under the canvas. He was halfway to where she sat when Dan Ingram suddenly intercepted him. She couldn't hear what he said because of the taut flapping of the canvas in the wind. She could only see the change in Dorsey's expression when Ingram said it. Conversations around her stopped. Every eye was on the two men, who stood staring each other down.

Eleanor abruptly got up and headed toward Mrs. Selby, deliberately walking between the two.

"Gentlemen," she said quietly as she passed.

She didn't stop. She simply removed herself as an excuse for an altercation.

"Here you are," Lavinia said, as if nothing was happening among her guests. "I don't know about you, my dear, but I am in desperate need of respite from all this untrammeled male society. Shall we go now, and I'll show you your new home." She made no excuses to anyone. She simply left the group with Eleanor in tow.

Eleanor looked over her shoulder once. Thankfully, the confrontation between Ingram and Karl Dorsey seemed to be over. She walked with Mrs. Selby to the other side of the house, where a horse and buggy stood waiting.

"I understand you don't ride," Mrs. Selby said as she got into the wagon and made room for Eleanor.

"No," Eleanor replied, wondering if anything of her conversations with Ingram had been left unreported. Or if *he* would be the one to mention the incident with Burley and her presence at Lillyann's funeral.

"What would you like to know?" Lavinia said as they left on a narrow road that seemed to go nowhere.

"About…the school?"

"No. About Dan Ingram."

"I don't think—" Eleanor began, startled.

"Don't get attached to him, my dear," Lavinia interrupted. "I'm saying this as your employer and as a…woman. I believe he already sees himself as a champion where you're concerned, so it would be an easy thing for you to do, especially in a strange new place. It isn't wise for you to encourage it, however—for your sake. He's very apt to get himself killed. This thing with Karl Dorsey can't be stopped."

"Why not?"

"Oh, it's become a matter of the Wyoming version of honor. Dorsey does have a long list of sins, and Dan has said he'll kill him for his latest one. So now he has to—or be killed himself."

Eleanor didn't say anything. It made it more ominous somehow, that Mrs. Selby was as matter-of-fact about the situation as Hester had been. Eleanor looked off at the horizon. She didn't know Dan Ingram well enough to be this bothered that someone might kill him, but she was, and it wasn't a happy realization. She couldn't let herself become concerned about yet another man who deliberately put himself into harm's way. Not again.

"It's the way things are done here," Lavinia was saying. "It's the reason we need someone like *you* here. I can't stop the blood feuds once they're started. No one can. But I'm hoping that education—in the long run—will help prevent them."

"This is...it's murder," Eleanor said.

"Yes, it is. But many say Karl Dorsey deserves it."

"Then why doesn't the law take care of it?"

"There isn't any law, Eleanor. I thought you understood that."

Apparently, she hadn't. She had just assumed that there would be military law, at least, the same kind of arbitrary law that ruled the world she'd left behind.

The land began to slope upward, and Lavinia urged the horse to go faster. Eleanor could feel the full force of the wind again, and she could no longer hear the fiddling and the laughter from the house.

"Life is precarious here," Lavinia said. "And that precariousness can break your heart. Believe me, I know."

Eleanor gave a quiet sigh and tried to focus on the passing scenery. "I have no intention of becoming attached to Mr. Ingram," she said after a time.

"Our intentions are sometimes not apparent to us," Lavinia said. "Even if there were no situation with Karl Dorsey, an interest in Dan Ingram would be fraught with...personal risk. He's like so many men who have returned from a war. I know about that, as well—mine is a military family, by birth and by marriage. Dan Ingram survived, and he doesn't understand why. It's almost certain he thinks he didn't deserve to. He knows he's not any better and perhaps a great deal worse than many who didn't. I believe whatever he's seen and done is a heavy burden to him. The sad thing is that I don't believe he'd really mind if Karl Dorsey killed him—ah! Behold! There it is."

Eleanor could see cottonwoods and a small wooden building on the high side of the stream of water that wound its way through them. It was much more than she expected—an actual schoolhouse with two wings, one her residence, she supposed, and one a place for children to stay if need be. Incredibly, the building had a post out front—with a bell.

"I wasn't expecting anything so…grand," Eleanor said. She wasn't expecting it to be so far from the Selby house, either, but she didn't say so.

"I never do things by halves," Lavinia said. "The bell has two purposes, of course. To call the children in and to send out an alarm should the occasion arise. It's a fine bell, if I do say so myself. I bought it from the Union Pacific Railroad—right off the locomotive. It cost a fortune—the colonel had a fit. They didn't want to sell it, of course, but I reminded them that, if their wonderful new tracks across Selby land aren't monitored as well in the future as we do it now, something could go awry and they wouldn't *need* a bell. I dare say you will have far more use for it than the Union Pacific ever will." She threw back her head and laughed.

"You have a good water supply and not too far to carry it. Someone will keep your wood cut for you, so you won't have to bother with that. I expect they'll all be eager to get down here, so you may end up with more sticks and logs than you can ever use. Your trunk has already been moved to your part of the building. And there are plenty of supplies. Food staples. And a box from Chicago with school items—slates and copy books, maps and the like. An actual globe on a stand, I believe. I've also sent down some books for your personal use from my own library, so you don't get too lonesome. When you're done with them, you must feel free to come up to the house for more."

She drove the buggy across the stream and pulled up in front of the school.

"A quick tour and I'm off to bribe Mr. Warner's better nature. Someone will also come by from time to time to see if you need anything. Or you can walk back to the house if it's pressing. I'm sure you can see an urgency for you to learn to ride, but we'll attend to that later. I understand you have your own firearm."

"I—yes."

"Please don't shoot at any of the native peoples unless you're absolutely certain your life is threatened. Firing at a good-for-nothing layabout like that Burley is one thing. Members of a peaceful tribe are something else again. I don't want my treaty with them broken unless it's utterly necessary. One last thing—children will present themselves for schooling in two days' time. They should arrive by eight or nine in the morning and the school day will continue until two-thirty in the afternoon—that will give them time enough to get home before dark. Any questions?"

"No," Eleanor said. "None."

The tour of the school and the immediate surroundings was whirlwind at best, and she was suddenly left on her own. She walked around trying to take everything in, trying to assess if indeed there was anything she needed. The place smelled of new wood and sawdust. There was a potbellied stove in the center of the schoolroom. Three long tables, each with backless benches, had been provided for the children. There was a very large desk for her. The desk exuded authority, and she was grateful for that. There were shelves and cupboards, pegs for coats and hats, lanterns and plenty of oil, copy books and slates, ink and inkwells, a water bucket and a dipper. A path out back led to the privies, one for the girls and one for the boys.

The windows in the schoolroom were small; they would likely need a lantern lit even on sunny days. Each window had a hinged shutter on the inside, which could be swung shut and barred. She didn't want to dwell on the reason for them.

The walls in her living quarters had been whitewashed. The kitchen itself wasn't large, but incredibly, she had a brand new cookstove. There was a small fireplace in the room where she would sleep, and a rocking chair, and a chamber pot, and an iron bed with a large pillow and a stack of brown blankets folded and placed neatly at the foot. There was a small alcove where she could hang her clothes and a single window near the bed. When she looked out, she could see the stream and the cottonwoods through the wavy glass. This window, too, could be shuttered from the inside.

She liked the idea of the rocking chair. Already she could imagine herself seated by the fire on cold winter nights with one of the blankets over her knees, reading or sewing or whatever content schoolmarms did after the children had gone.

She crossed the shoolroom to the other wing—one large room half full of stacked wooden boxes—enough provisions and school supplies to last for a long time. There was a fireplace at the far end, but no windows. She made a mental note of what the boxes contained, then walked back to her quarters, still trying to ascertain if there was some necessary item missing.

There was nothing. On the surface, Lavinia Selby seemed as straightforward as they come, and she had thought of everything—even protecting Eleanor from a broken heart.

She spent the rest of the day unpacking her trunk and the boxes from Chicago. She carried a bucket of water from the stream up to her small kitchen, rearranged the food supplies to her own liking and convenience, made up the bed with all the blankets left for her. Then she built a fire in the stove and ultimately ate a late supper of fried bacon and toasted bread.

Once or twice, she thought she heard a horse galloping, but when she went to the window to look, she didn't see anyone. The sound of hoofbeats came again when she was about to retire for the night. This time there was no mistaking that someone had arrived. She stood for a moment, then picked up the revolver before she went to answer the knock on the door.

"Miss," Dan Ingram said when she opened it. He glanced in the direction of the gun she held hidden behind her skirts. "You ought not open the door if you don't know who it is, miss."

"Thank you," she said. "I'll try to remember that."

"This is a dangerous country, miss—"

"Have you killed Karl Dorsey yet?"

He looked into her eyes for before he answered. "No, miss, not yet. I came to see if you wanted anything."

"No, nothing."

"You can find yourself lonesome in this country—"

"I haven't had the time to be lonesome as yet."

"If you say so, miss. Tomorrow or the next day, I need to fix up a place for you to have a horse."

"I don't want a horse."

"Yes, miss, you do."

"I think not. I can walk to the Selby house if—"

"It might come that you'll need to get there faster than a walk, miss. Me and maybe a couple of the boys will be fixing up a place for it—I've got a good, gentle mare in mind for you. Then you can set about learning to take care of it and ride it. I just wanted you to know ahead of time what the noise is all about."

He stood looking at her. "I'll say good-night to you then, miss," he said finally.

"Good night, Mr. Ingram."

He touched the brim of his hat, and she closed the door and leaned against it. It seemed to take him awhile to ride away, and she impulsively opened the door again.

He was nowhere in sight, but there was something wrapped in brown paper and tied with string lying on the porch in front of her. She fetched it inside, and she couldn't keep from smiling when she opened it.

Peppermint candy.

He had left her three sticks of peppermint candy.

Chapter Four

More children showed up for the first day of school than Eleanor expected—and most of them *were* children. The colonel had only been able to spare one of the older boys—Petey, the one who liked to show off.

He wasn't showing off now, however. Eleanor didn't know when she'd seen a face that reflected more abject misery. She fervently hoped he never gave in to the temptation to gamble at cards.

The day was overcast, but there was no threat of rain, as far as Eleanor could tell. The children—five girls and four boys, not counting Petey—had arrived as predicted. She had done all the preliminary registration of names and ages, and they now sat on their benches staring at her, their clean faces showing a mixture of apprehension and a certain degree of…relief, she decided, probably at being exempted from their usual chores. Two of the boys she recognized as the ones who had carried her trunk to her room. The biggest surprise had been a girl named Annie, who had a baby boy on her lap. Annie's mother filled a vital position in the Selby's household staff, and carting her little brother along to school was the only way Annie would be able to attend, according to the note Lavinia Selby had sent with her. Clearly, there was a limit to how much Mrs. Selby was willing to be inconvenienced, civilization or no civilization. The note also advised Eleanor that Annie was one of three in the group who were already able to read and write a few words.

That settled, there was nothing left for Eleanor to do but begin. She took a deep breath and decided to be devious and logical. Petey's was a particularly delicate situation, she thought, because there was a matter of his male pride to consider. So she started with him first, hoping, if nothing else, to end his suffering as quickly as possible.

"Mr. Watson," she said to him, causing the little boys who sat in front of him to giggle and Petey's ears to go red. She quelled the gigglers with a look, but they were having to work hard not to start up again.

"*Mr.* Watson does a man's job," she said to them. "And I understand he does it well—much better than any of you or I could do. For that reason, *we* will show him a certain respect, until such time as he proves he is not worthy of it or until he says we may address him otherwise. Now, Mr. Watson…" She motioned for Petey to come sit across the desk from her, then she opened the Bible and placed it on the desktop.

After a moment, he walked forward—but he looked as if he expected to be hanged.

"This is what I want you to do," she said, quietly enough not to be overheard, when he'd finally mastered his sudden awkwardness and managed to sit down. "I want you to look at the page here, and I want you to keep looking at it while you answer my questions. Do you understand?"

"No, miss," he said, glancing up at her.

"Do it anyway, Mr. Watson."

"Yes, miss."

He obediently dropped his head and stared at the page.

"Your full name, please, where you were born, your parents' names, first and last, your favorite food and drink. And speak softly so that only I can hear you."

He gave her another brief, doubtful look, then did as she asked, lifting his head only when he was done.

"One more question," she said. "Look at the page, please. Can you read, Mr. Watson?"

"No, miss," he said, his voice barely audible. This time he didn't look at her.

"Do you know your letters?"

He shook his head.

"Does anyone else in this room know that?"

"I don't reckon so, miss."

"Then I expect to keep it that way—if you're agreeable."

He glanced up at her, then immediately looked down again.

"Are you agreeable?" she asked.

"Yes, miss. But I don't see how—"

"The 'how' is basically up to you. You will have to work hard away from the schoolroom and you will have to be…cunning here. I think it can be done, Mr. Watson. Now. Take your seat again, please." She looked at her list. "Jimmy Gallagher. Please come forward."

Eleanor continued with each of the pupils, verifying their degree of expertise or the lack thereof. Then she gave the seating assignments.

"Mr. Watson, I would like you to share a desk with Jimmy Gallagher. Jimmy, I want you to take your slate and write the first three letters of the alphabet very carefully so that Mr. Watson can watch for mistakes. Then I want you to tell him the sound each of the letters makes and give him a word with that sound. After that, you will write the word until he is satisfied."

"Yes, miss," he said, clearly in the throes of hero worship. Young Jimmy Gallagher would have no problem showing Petey Watson the respect his position on the ranch afforded him.

Eleanor put the others to work, as well, giving the older children an assignment to be completed independently and the younger ones her undivided attention. At one point, she carried the now fretful baby boy, Theodore, on her hip so his sister could write on her slate in peace.

They didn't stop for their midday meal until early afternoon, when she sent them all out to eat and run and play, while the baby slept peacefully on a folded blanket on the schoolroom floor.

She sat at her desk in the stunned aftermath of a high-stakes situation where the need for success was imperative. The stress of it all was intensified by the fact that all morning she had expected to see Dan Ingram again. Thus far, no one with a mind to construct an enclosure for a horse had appeared.

It occurred to her suddenly that she had had no discipline problems this morning. None. Perhaps word of her confrontation with Burley had reached the ears of her pupils. If an orderly classroom was the result, she decided that she was glad.

She looked up to find Petey standing in front of her desk with Jimmy's slate in his hand. He didn't say anything. He placed the slate where she could see it, then carefully scratched out an upper- and lowercase *A,* then a *B,* then a *C.*

"Good progress, Mr. Watson," she said.

He continued to stand there, clearly with something on his mind.

"What is it?"

"I need to get back now, miss—if I'm going to keep Dan out of trouble."

"I see," she said, when actually she didn't see at all. "What about tomorrow?"

"I can't say, miss. Dan, he'll try to make it so's I can come. He said…"

"What did he say, Mr. Watson?" she asked when the boy didn't continue.

"He said a man ought never waste the chance at something that can make his life better. He said I ought not pay any attention to what the others say about it."

"I expect he is quite right about that."

"If you'll give me leave to go then," he said. "I'm not to walk off without you knowing about it."

"Yes. You may go. Tomorrow then—or so we hope."

He gave her a nod and left.

Ingram. He was such a...puzzle to her. The things she knew firsthand and the things people said about him left no clear picture in her mind as to what he was really like. His being a war veteran would explain the melancholy in him— perhaps even his willingness to do murder. She wondered suddenly if Rob would have been the same man if he'd survived the war.

She abruptly opened the desk drawer and removed the velvet case that contained his photograph. She looked at his handsome young face, then closed the case and put it away. Most of the time the sense of loss was dim, like a distant bad dream, and sometimes, inexplicably, like this very moment, it was strong and aching and raw, as she realized she was never, ever going to see him again. Kindly Verillia Douglas, a woman from back home, had told her once that her heart had gone into its winter because of the pain and the loss, but it would come out again, when Eleanor least expected it. She didn't want it to come out again. A winter heart was...safe.

She took a deep breath and went outside to call the children back to their lessons. The short afternoon session went swiftly, and somehow, the first day of school was over. The Selby children began their walk back to the big house, with one of the boys carrying Theodore. The three children from the army post climbed on the one horse the Indian scout's wife had brought them, and trotted away. Eleanor felt uneasy about letting them go, but they seemed to be used to such traveling and much more comfortable about the ride than she would have been.

She walked down to the stream to fill a bucket of water, and when she returned, Dan Ingram and another man waited on horseback by the porch.

"I was just coming to hunt for you, miss," Dan said, glancing at the other man.

"Why?"

"This is Mick Landry," he announced, instead of answering.

"Mr. Landry," Eleanor said. She thought she recognized him. He was the man who'd lain weeping on the sidewalk the day she arrived.

"Miss Hansen," Landry said, smiling mischievously. "In case you're wondering, Dan here, he took a bath before we rode over."

"Did he?" Eleanor said, enjoying Ingram's obvious discomfort at the revelation. "I'm sure we both appreciate it."

"Well, I do, miss. He really did stink."

"Where's the revolver?" Ingram abruptly asked. Clearly, he was in no mood to be teased by anyone.

She waited before she answered, because of the tone of his voice as much as anything.

"Where is it?" he asked again.

"It's…handy," she said, when the truth was she hadn't given it a thought.

"You don't go anywhere—not down to the water, not to the outhouse, not *anywhere*—without taking it with you."

He turned his horse and rode off, leaving her with a considerable amount of annoyance and nowhere to put it. She frowned and watched him head toward the stream and disappear among the cottonwoods.

"Don't mind him none, miss," Mick said. "He likes you and he don't want to, that's all. It scared him when we couldn't find you."

"He hasn't known me long enough to like or dislike me," Eleanor said.

"Maybe so. But I reckon whoever made that rule don't know much about people. Especially when the people are a man and a woman. Good day to you, miss." He touched the brim of his hat, then spurred his horse and followed after Ingram.

Dan waited just beyond the cottonwoods for Mick to catch up.

"What did she say?" he asked as soon as Mick was close enough to hear him.

"Nothing," Mick answered. "I think she was still addled from hearing you took a bath."

Dan ignored Mick's heavy-handed attempt at wittiness. "What did you say to her?"

"Nothing. *Nothing,*" Mick assured him. "Does the colonel know you keep riding over here to see about her?"

Dan didn't answer him.

"That's what I thought," Mick said. "Son, just how much trouble do you want to be in, anyway?"

"I'm not worried about me," Dan said, spurring his horse to end the conversation.

"Well, maybe you ought to. If you want my advice—"

"I don't!" Dan called over his shoulder, urging his horse into a gallop so he could get to where he was supposed to be.

He likes you and he don't want to, that's all.

Eleanor didn't want to think about what *that* meant. She set about making the schoolroom ready for the next session, and, in spite of her annoyance, she made sure the revolver actually was within her reach if she needed it. It had been reckless of her not to have taken it with her down to the stream. She had been living in a town occupied by enemy soldiers. She knew about the dangers that might befall a woman caught alone. She realized, too, that her annoyance came as much from Ingram seeing her lack of good sense as the fact that he'd presumed to chastise her about it.

She made sure the door to the schoolroom was locked, then went to her own side of the building. There was still daylight left when she heard a wagon. She picked up the revolver and looked out to see who was coming.

Ingram was back, driving a load of fence posts. He made

no attempt to come to the door, and she made no effort to speak to him. She left him to whatever it was he intended to do in the remaining light, and set about cooking herself some supper. When it was nearly done, she opened the door and stepped outside. He didn't stop working when he saw her. She stood and waited, anyway.

"I have some supper nearly cooked," she said when he finally looked at her. "I'm willing to share it."

It wasn't the most gracious of invitations, but it was the best she could do—in return for the peppermint candy, if nothing else.

He stopped what he was doing. "I'd appreciate it," he said. "After the light goes, if that's all right."

"Perfectly all right," she said. "I'll set you a place."

She turned and walked back into her quarters. She actually had extra plates, thanks to Mrs. Selby's preparations for the times when the children couldn't get home from school. Eleanor set two of them on the small table in the kitchen. The meal was nothing fancy—fried potatoes and onions, bacon and coffee, some hard cheese.

She lost sight of Dan Ingram for a time, until he knocked softly at the kitchen door. When she let him in, his hair and the front of his shirt were wet. She supposed that he must have gone to the stream to wash up.

"It smells good," he said of the food she was about to set on the table.

He stood awkwardly—in the way. The kitchen had grown small suddenly, with him in it. He had taken off his hat, but he didn't know where to put it.

"Peg," she said. "By the door. Sit down. Either chair."

He hung his hat and sat in the chair facing the window. She got the coffeepot and poured two cups. He was looking at his surroundings as if he'd lost something.

"What is it?" she asked.

"Nothing, miss."

"You expected something…different?"

"I was just seeing where you live."

"Why?"

"Can't say, miss. It's of interest to me, I guess."

"I'll show you the school if you want."

"No, miss. I'm not much for schoolrooms, even if I'm just passing through."

"But you made sure Petey got here."

"Yes, miss. Petey's smarter than I am."

"Please. Serve yourself, Mr. Ingram."

She brought the bacon to the table and sat down across from him, handing him the bowl of potatoes. They ate in silence. If he felt the need to make conversation, it didn't show.

"I know how to take care of a horse," she said at one point, surprising herself and him. "You said I needed to learn to take care of the horse. I can do that. I know how to feed and brush and water. I can catch and harness. I can clean out stalls. I just can't saddle and ride."

Dan looked at her while she recited her accomplishments and shortcomings, but he didn't say anything.

He was trying to memorize her face without seeming to do so, the same way he'd been memorizing her surroundings. He had never dared to think he might actually sit down and share a meal with her—alone—especially at her invitation. But, as much as he wanted to be here, he should have said no. He should have let one of the other hands build the fence. He should have—

I think about you all the time.

The thought came so abruptly into his mind that he was afraid for a moment he had said it out loud. When exactly had he crossed the line from benevolent concern to such a relentless, aching *need?* He spent every day uneasy and dissatisfied until he'd seen her, even if it was only at a distance. He told himself that he just wanted to know she was all right. He liked her. He liked to tease her, liked to see if he could get her all flustered, liked to try to make her smile. Sitting here now, looking at her across the table, he knew there was more to it than that.

"I don't have any riding clothes," Eleanor said abruptly, without really knowing why. No. That wasn't true. She did know. In spite of all she could do, she was becoming more and more disconcerted by his scrutiny.

"Don't need them, miss. Mrs. Selby wears her husband's britches when she goes out."

"She does not!" Eleanor said.

"She does, miss. First time the reverend's sister saw her, she nearly fainted in the dirt."

Eleanor frowned. "I never know if you're serious or not."

"I'm always serious, miss. Anybody that knows me will tell you that."

"Then I think they don't know you very well."

He smiled suddenly, then stood. "Thanks for the meal, miss."

"Thanks for the candy," she countered.

"I thought you might need the peppermint."

"I thought you might need a supper. We're even now."

"Until I can come up with something else to make you beholden," he said, putting on his hat. "Be careful, will you, miss?"

Now he was serious.

"Yes. I'll be careful."

He nodded and left, closing the door quietly and firmly behind him.

"Don't worry about not seeing me again, miss," he called from the other side of it.

She tried not to smile at his audaciousness and reached to draw the bolt. She saw the hole suddenly appear in the wood of the door and the splinters fly a split second before she heard the faraway report of the rifle that fired the bullet. The door flew open and Ingram flung her onto the floor. Another bullet glanced off the door facing and still another hit the far wall.

"Stay down," he hissed into her ear. He crouched over

her, then moved to the doorway. "Damn it! My rifle is on my saddle…"

It was so quiet suddenly. She could hear the wind buffeting the house, but nothing else save Ingram's breathing.

Her cheek began to sting, and she reached up to touch it. Her fingers came away wet and sticky with blood.

"I think he's gone," Ingram said. He looked in her direction and swore. "You're hurt!" he said, immediately coming to her.

"I'm all right," she murmured, moving to sit up.

"Let me see."

"I'm all right," she insisted.

"It needs tending," he said, holding her face where he could look at the wound. "There's a wood splinter. Stay down…"

He moved to get the piece of flannel hanging by the water bucket, dipped a corner to wet it and came back to her, all the while avoiding the window.

He sat down on the floor beside her and carefully removed the small slivers of wood that were apparently imbedded in her cheek. It hurt. She stared into his face as he worked, measured the intensity of his expression and the concern. He didn't seem to notice.

"I've let this go on too long," he said, cleaning her cheek with the wet corner of the flannel.

"What do you mean?" she asked, reaching up to touch the place that stung so. He intercepted her hand and put it firmly in her lap.

"Karl Dorsey."

"How do you know it was him?"

"I know."

"No, you don't. Mrs. Selby told me there's no law here. It could be anybody. You have no proof, no reason to do anything to him because of this—"

"I don't want to see you hurt!"

"And I don't want to see you dead. Please. Don't do anything to him on my account. I can't bear it. I'm not—"

Worth it, she was going to say. But she didn't. She gave a wavering sigh instead, surprised at how close to tears she felt.

Incredibly, Mrs. Selby had been too late with the warning not to let herself become attached to this man.

"Please," she said again. He was looking into her eyes, but she could tell by the closed expression on his face that it was useless. She had seen the same look when she'd begged Rob not to go off to war.

"I'll take you up to the house. We'll have to ride double."

"No. I'm staying here. I'm not afraid."

"Damn it, you should be!"

"Why? If *you're* the target?"

"You don't understand the way things are out here—"

"I understand the willingness to do whatever it takes to further a cause. Sometimes the cause is all wrapped up in fine sentiments like honor and freedom, family and home. And sometimes it's personal—like this thing between you and Karl Dorsey. Lillyann, and now me—we're just…handy reasons for something you intend to do anyway."

"That isn't the way it is. Some things have to be done."

"Yes. And when a blood feud starts, it can't be stopped—until the right person is dead."

"I know this is strange for you—" he began, and she gave a bitter laugh.

"No. Not strange. It's not the first time I've listened to a man explain how he *has* to go kill or be killed."

"Is that what *he* did? The man in the tintype?"

She looked into Ingram's eyes. "Yes," she said evenly. "He wasted his life—and mine, too."

"I don't reckon he saw it that way."

"No," she said. She was so tired suddenly. "None of you ever do."

He reached out and took her hand, and he didn't let go when she would have pulled free of his grasp. After a moment, she gave up, and they simply sat there on the floor, her small hand lost in his big one. Such a small gesture and, incredibly, she found comfort in it.

"I don't intend for Karl Dorsey to kill me," he said after a time.

"Don't you?" she asked, and the moment she said it she realized that Lavinia Selby had been right about him and his not minding if he lost his duel with death.

She took her hand out of his and got to her feet without his restraint or his help. He immediately stood with her.

"Eleanor—"

"What is it you want from me, Mr. Ingram? Tell me."

"I want…" He stopped and gave a sharp sigh. "All the way out here to Selby's I could see how hard you were trying—it was plain to me."

"I don't know what you mean."

"You were looking for something—anything—in this place you could like. That's what I want. I want you to look for something you can like—in me."

The room was filled now with the soft darkness that had come as the last rays of sunlight disappeared. His horse whinnied and blew where it waited, tied to the wagon.

"Go away, Mr. Ingram. Do what you have to do and leave me be. I don't want to know about any of it."

She began clearing the table. She heard him walk to the door, and when she turned around he had gone.

She thought that she wouldn't see him the next day, that he would give her what she'd asked for. She was only half-right. He didn't stay away, but, clearly, he intended to leave her alone.

He went immediately to work on the fence, saying nothing. She might have believed she was glad of it, if she hadn't found herself looking in his direction at every opportunity. After a time, even the children noted it and would look at Ingram in unison every time she did. She was hardly setting the example for proper social decorum, especially for the girls, and all she needed was Lavinia Selby to witness it, when Eleanor had already been warned that Dan Ingram—or his whereabouts—should not be her concern. Her only comfort was that if he was building a fence and a shed, he wasn't hunting for Karl Dorsey.

By the end of the week there was significant progress in the fence-building for the horse she didn't yet have. The children gave up their recess play to help. Clearly, *they* thought she needed the animal. Or perhaps it was a sad reflection on her teaching. In the evenings after school, she began to try to fashion a riding habit of sorts—britches with a skirt over them. If she was going to have to do this, she intended to do it astride. She wasn't going to ride half a horse.

The arrival of the mare when both the fence and the habit were finished was a gala occasion indeed. Dan brought it saddled, but immediately unsaddled it and put it inside the enclosure.

"It's my job," he said before she could offer any further protests about a situation—and perhaps a man—she didn't want.

She gave a resigned sigh. Learning to ride in theory wasn't the same as the actuality.

"Let's see what you can do," he said—in front of the children.

"Not now," she said pointedly.

"Yes, now, miss. I've got other things to do. I want you to be able to get a saddle on her at least. Then Annie is going to teach you how to ride."

"Annie," Eleanor said, thinking she'd misunderstood.

"That's right," he said.

"Annie *who?*"

The children giggled.

"Me, miss," Annie said. "I'm the best rider there is. Rain taught me—he's the scout at the fort. He says I'm good enough to teach anybody. Nobody else here knows how as good as I do, except Dan and Petey, and they ain't got—I mean, don't have—the time."

"I…see," Eleanor said. She glanced at Ingram. He was enjoying this, she was almost positive. "What are we going to do with Theodore while all this is going on?"

"We'll watch him, miss," Jimmy Gallagher piped up to say.

"And who's going to watch you, Jimmy Gallagher?"

"Aw, miss," he said, grinning.

She looked at Ingram. "All right. What do you want me to do?"

"Catch her—if you can."

"I can only try," she said, very humbly. And she set about using the same technique she'd used on the docile horse—her namesake—that she and Maria Markham had played with as children. Bribery. She went and pulled up two fistfuls of grass and then stood inside the fence until the horse realized what she had, and came to her.

She fed it the grass and stroked its neck. The mare was beautiful, she had to admit—a bay with a black mane and tail.

"Well, that will work as long as you're not in a hurry," Dan said.

"I'm not done yet, Mr. Ingram."

She left the fence, and this time she went to the kitchen in her quarters and brought back three small chunks of brown sugar. When she went inside the fence this time, the mare was interested, but it didn't come. Eleanor whistled and held out her hand. The mare gave a soft rumble and stretched her neck toward the sugar Eleanor had lying on her open palm. Eleanor stayed out of reach, and when the mare ultimately came to her, she fed it one lump. Then she left again and came back to repeat the process two more times. The horse came at her soft whistle immediately both times.

The next time, Eleanor didn't have anything to offer, except pats and soft words, but after an inspection of her person for hidden sugar lumps, the mare didn't seem to mind.

Eleanor reached for the bridle and put it on without difficulty. The saddle was something else again. It was much heavier than she expected, and she made the horse nervous trying to heave it upward. The saddle blanket fell off. The air rang with pointers from her audience, but none of them made her any stronger.

"You need a lighter saddle," Ingram observed mildly after a time. She gave him a look.

"Or that one will do," he amended, scratching the side of his nose with his forefinger.

Finally—*finally*—she was able to get the saddle on, and, with a myriad of instructions from the onlookers, she managed to get it buckled tightly enough so that it stayed put. More or less.

She looked around at the others for some indication of their delight and approval—and met a sea of pained and somewhat incredulous expressions.

"I think you better learn to ride bareback, miss," Annie said.

By the end of the day, she had gotten better at saddling and more guilty about not having regular lessons. Ultimately, Ingram was satisfied with her new ability. He left without a word before the children did, and neither he nor Petey returned the next morning.

She was now in Annie's hands. The girl's unorthodox approach to riding instruction included her insistence that Eleanor know how to fall on the ground—not an easy task, because Eleanor felt obliged to monitor a singsong chorus of multiplication tables from the assembled spectators at the same time. Both she and the children practiced until Annie was satisfied that Eleanor would make every attempt to roll instead of plunk when she was thrown. As school days went, a good time was had by all—even Theodore.

By the next day, Eleanor was considered ready for an actual ride—bareback. She put on her makeshift riding apparel and set forth. The children had enough sense not to remark upon the outfit, and, incredibly, riding the docile "Nell" when Eleanor was a little girl had left a certain residual skill when it came to sitting a horse. She didn't fall off, and she found the whole experience not unpleasant.

Her confidence grew, and by the end of the next week she had graduated to riding with a saddle. There had been no sign of Dan Ingram since the day he'd satisfied himself that she could get a saddle cinched. Petey made it to school two days, and she could have asked him about Ingram's whereabouts, but she didn't.

After Petey had gone the way of Dan Ingram, she continued the lessons with the other children and tried not to think about…anything.

One afternoon, when she had opened the schoolroom door and was about to dismiss her pupils for the weekend, she found a small package wrapped up in brown paper and tied with string. She knew immediately what it had to be—and was. Three sticks of peppermint candy.

"Where did this come from?" she asked them.

They looked at each other.

"Well?" she insisted. "Jimmy?"

"It weren't any of us, miss," Jimmy said with a certain alarm, apparently at being thought guilty of something that for once he didn't actually do. "It weren't there when I closed the door after recess."

"'Wasn't any of us.' 'Wasn't there,'" she corrected absently. "Does anybody know anything about it, then?"

"No, miss," they said in unison, and she sighed.

"Your pocket knife, please," she said to Jimmy. He brought it forward, wiping it on his pant leg along the way. She cut the candy into smaller pieces and distributed them among the group.

"Run along home now, and I'll see you Monday morning," she said, sending them off smiling. And she sat for a long time at her desk—eating the last small piece of candy.

As the weather grew warmer, there were days when none of the children came to school. Every pair of hands was needed to make ready for the long winter, which, she was assured, would come much more quickly than she could imagine. Even so, she saw riders from time to time, passing on their way to some other part of the ranch, or sometimes actually riding into the schoolyard, if she happened not to be visible outside or at a window where they could see her when they passed. She was grateful for the monitoring, she supposed—if, indeed, that was what it was. And she was more than a little annoyed with herself for always looking for a white shirt among them or for the white-footed sorrel Dan Ingram always rode. There had been no more incidents, and she could only suppose that he had been the target and not she—which lent more credence to the theory that Karl Dorsey had been behind it than she would have liked.

She missed the children when they didn't come to school, for when they did, she was so occupied with them she didn't have the opportunity to think of Dan Ingram. It was all too familiar to her, this dread she had that something was going to happen to him, and no amount of mental reasoning on her part could take it away. Her concern, her worry, simply *was,* whether it should be or not.

Every now and then she saw him—when she went to the house because Lavinia Selby invited her to dinner so she could satisfy herself that Eleanor had indeed mastered at least some aspects of horsemanship. Once, she encountered him on what passed for the streets of Soul Harbor. And always, *always,* it caught her off guard, before she could steel herself against the relief and the elation the chance meeting gave her. He never presumed to speak to her. He merely touched the brim of his hat and moved on.

In the middle of August, the children could be spared long enough for half days in the afternoon. She worked hard to give them the lessons she thought they needed in the limited time she had. The hurry of it all left her feeling restless and ineffective. One afternoon, she abandoned the tidying she always did at the end of the day and went to sit in the sunshine on the porch steps. Dan Ingram was there ahead of her. She was startled, but she made no attempt to run him off with the broom she still had in her hands. Instead, she put it aside and sat down beside him.

"Is warming my porch part of your job, too?" she asked.

He glanced at her. "No."

He looked so tired—physically exhausted and deprived of sleep. He didn't say anything else, and the silence between them lengthened.

"Nobody's shot at me lately," she said to end it.

He nodded. Then he drew a quiet breath. Then he looked at her.

"Come walk with me, Eleanor."

It was in her to refuse, but she didn't. She didn't even ask where he wanted to go. She stood, and he with her. They walked in the direction he chose—down toward the stream and the cottonwoods. There was a slight chill in the air. Already she could feel the summer going.

"It's all tangled up in my mind," he said.

"What is?"

He smiled slightly. "You and the cottonwoods. I don't ever see one without remembering how glad they made you. You thought you'd never see a real tree again."

She smiled in return. "So I did—but I didn't think you knew it."

"It shows on your face when something makes you happy."

She looked at him, then away, concentrating on the sound of the water and the leaves rustling in the trees.

"Sometimes it's me," he said quietly. He moved to where he could see her face.

"Sometimes it's me," he said again.

She didn't object to the truth of his observation. She didn't say anything.

"Petey's dead," he said in the same quiet way.

She gave a sharp exhalation of breath. "Oh—oh—Petey."

"We found him in the high meadow yesterday."

"What happened to him?"

"He was too good a rider, too good with cows to have ended up the way he did. I think he was deliberately dragged and trampled."

"Who would do that?"

Dan didn't answer the question. "I'm…going to be gone for a while. I just wanted you to know. It's one thing for me not to come here because that's the way you say it has to be. I wanted you to know I'm not coming now because I can't." He picked up a small pebble and tossed it into the stream. "I think about you. It's—"

"Don't," she said.

"Don't think about you? Or don't tell you I do?"

"Both."

"If the thinking could be stopped, I would have done it. Eleanor—"

He reached out for her, and she meant to move away from him. She meant to—but she didn't. She stepped into his arms instead, her face pressed hard into his shoulder. He held her tightly, his head bent so that his stubbled cheek rested against hers. In her agitation, she struck his arm with her fist, once, then clung to the back of his shirt with both hands. It had been so long since she'd felt these things, things she'd never wanted to feel again. Love and fear and desperation. She was caught, and she couldn't escape.

She lifted her face to his.

It's the sadness. Because of Petey. That's all.

He kissed her eyes with such tenderness that she wanted to weep. She could feel the tremor of desire in his body, and when his mouth found hers, she gave a soft moan. The kiss was deep and needy, and with the last ounce of will she had, she pushed herself free of his embrace.

"No," she said. "I can't—"

"You need to know—" he began.

"I already know all I need to."

"Eleanor, wait…"

She backed away from him and all but ran in the direction they had come. Yes, she knew. She *knew*.

Dan Ingram was going to break her heart.

Chapter Five

"Did you see her?"

"I saw her," Dan said.

"What did she say?"

He glanced at Mick as they rode along, but he didn't answer.

"So what do you think?" Mick persisted.

"I think we wouldn't be looking for whoever killed Petey if they hadn't taken twenty-five cows with them," he said, choosing to pretend that Mick had moved on from Eleanor Hansen to the job at hand.

"Did you tell her where we was going? What we was going to be doing?"

"Mick—"

"Well, I got to ask, don't I? If I wait for you to come out and tell me, I'll be too damn old and deaf to hear it."

They rode for a time in silence, mostly because Dan urged his mount on until he was riding a little ahead.

"I reckon some of the boys will watch out for her while we're gone," Mick said, catching up.

"If the Selbys don't go trying to spite each other."

"Yeah, there's that all right. I reckon we'd best find the sons of bitches that killed Petey pretty quick then. You reckon it's Karl and his bunch or not?"

"It's Karl."

"I never figured him to take up rustling. He'll cheat you at cards if he gets the chance and there's that thing with Lilly-ann—but stealing the colonel's cows? By damn, that's like asking to be a dead man."

"He'd do it if Livingston Warner set him to it."

"You know, she sure is pretty, Dan—your Miss Eleanor."

"She's not mine."

"Sure she is—she just don't know it yet. Did you get a lit-tle kiss from her or anything—?"

"Oh, shut up! I'm not listening to you all the way to Montana."

He spurred his horse hard.

"Canada's more like it—and I don't know how you're going to help it!" Mick called after him.

"I could shoot you and blame it on the rustlers," Dan yelled back.

Mick laughed, and for once, he stayed behind, leaving Dan to his own thoughts.

Eleanor.

He was worried about her, damn it, and had been from the first day he'd met her. The school was too far from the house, thanks to the colonel's spite against his sister-in-law. Dan had been certain Lavinia Selby would relocate it, but thus far she hadn't. He knew Eleanor was strong, stronger than the colo-nel had bargained for and stronger than Lavinia had dared hope. He had to believe she'd be all right.

He could still feel her, still taste her. And he could still see the look in her eyes. It would never work out for them. He knew that. He might have gotten past the fact that she deserved a better man than he was. He could have worked hard to give her a good life, to be worthy of her.

But he couldn't get the blood off his hands. Even if the colonel hadn't ordered it, something had to be done about Karl Dorsey. And Dan Ingram was the one with the skill to do it.

He'd killed men for four long years, and he still remembered how. He had Mick with him. Mick would watch his back, and he was the best marksman Ingram had ever seen. Surely, between the two of them and the men who had gone on the hunt ahead of them, they could get this done.

Once and for all. Until the next time.

"She'll be all right," Mick called.

"Somebody shot into the schoolhouse, Mick!"

"I don't think you got to worry about that!"

He didn't justify the remark with a response.

"You going to mope the whole damn way?" Mick called.

"Yeah," Ingram said, and urged his horse into a gallop.

"I like having Petey here," Annie said, looking out at the new grave just visible from the schoolhouse window. "He liked coming to school. He liked us calling him 'Mister.'"

"Did he?" Eleanor said. She had been surprised at first by the plan to bury Petey nearby, but she liked having him close, too. As long as there were children in the school, his grave would be tended.

"Are you worried, miss?"

"No, Annie," Eleanor said. It was a lie, so much so that she couldn't look Annie in the eye. She handed Theodore over and drew the slates the girl had collected for her closer.

"The Selby men have been gone a long time, miss. I'm worried whoever killed Petey might kill Dan, too. Will they, do you think?"

"I don't know, Annie. I hope not."

"Dan and the rest of them, they won't give up. They'll chase whoever did it all the way to Canada if they have to. I know they will. I heard one of the men at the exchange say they'll just chase them until they get somebody's cows, but I know better."

"Cows?"

"Those men took the ones Petey was watching. People say

they killed him for the cows, miss. And it weren't—wasn't—the Indians, either. They liked Petey. Everybody liked Petey."

Theodore began to fret, and Annie went to find the cloth with the lump of sugar tied in the corner to give him to suck on. She popped the sugar teat into Theodore's mouth and looked out the window again. "Rain says the snow is coming early this year. You reckon Petey will know it, miss?"

"He might know—but it won't bother him," Eleanor said, trying to get to the crux of the question. "He'll see the beauty of it and that's all."

"Like he sees us when we come to visit him."

"Exactly like that."

Eleanor went back to the slates, calling the children in when she'd finished, essentially so she could send them home. The days were growing shorter, and she didn't want them out in the dark.

She had her school routine well established now, the lessons passing exactly according to plan. She went riding nearly every afternoon after the children had departed, looking, always looking, for some sign that the men from Selby's had returned.

She never saw anyone on her lonely jaunts over the grassland. She made certain to keep the cottonwoods in sight on these excursions, and she always returned feeling better somehow. Perhaps there was something to be said for being under God's ever-watchful eye, after all.

In the evenings after her supper, she read or sewed or crocheted or made small prizes to award the children for their scholastic accomplishments. Nothing elaborate—sheets of writing paper she'd decorated with watercolor flowers or ribbons or laurel leaves, and a carefully copied inspirational verse. At the end of the school year she would present each one of them with a little something—even Theodore. His was empty wooden spools tied together in a circle for him to bite on when his budding teeth made him restless.

But no matter what she was doing, she thought about Dan Ingram. It was like living Rob's farewell all over again. She couldn't muster any hope that Dan would be all right. Experience had left her with no room for any emotion except fear.

She was afraid for him, every waking moment. Lavinia Selby had said it: life was precarious here. Lavinia was a widow too young, and Petey slept in his quiet grave in the schoolyard. Eleanor didn't want to think about Lillyann and her baby.

The last day of September the snow Annie's Indian scout had predicted arrived. Eleanor woke to find the ground covered, and it was still falling. She got several buckets of water in and enough wood to keep the fire lit during the coming night.

She kept moving restlessly from window to window. There was nothing to see but the blowing white flakes. It was so different from the snows at home. There, it coated everything and stayed put. Here, it swirled endlessly in the wind. Part of the ground covered one moment might be all but uncovered the next.

She baked bread to have something to do. Boiled coffee. Paced. She didn't want to be at the Selby house for the duration, but she missed the prospect of human contact. She had no expectation of seeing anyone for days.

Once, she thought she heard a noise coming from the schoolroom, but when she went to look, there was nothing but the endless sound of the wind.

She gave a heavy sigh and returned to watching out the kitchen window, and after a time she pulled on her heavy shawl and made her way out to the enclosure to make sure the mare was all right. She pitched some hay into the crib and satisfied herself that there was enough water in the trough. The mare gave a soft, rumbled greeting at her appearance, but then its attention was taken by something in the distance, toward the cottonwoods. Eleanor looked in that direction, but could see nothing except swirling snow.

But then she saw movement—a riderless horse approaching. It was saddled, and it trotted up to the enclosure and stopped, its reins trailing on the ground.

The horse was a white-footed sorrel. *The* white-footed sorrel.

Eleanor walked toward it carefully, catching the reins before it shied away. She patted its neck, searched the saddle for some clue as to what it was doing here.

She gave a sharp intake of breath. There was a dark stain on the horse's shoulder and down the saddle—blood. She stood for a moment, trying to decide what to do, knowing immediately that if the horse was here, then Dan must be somewhere around, too.

She didn't let her mind go beyond that. She wasn't going to waste time. She brought the horse around to the porch so she could stand on the bottom step to get on, and she managed easily enough in spite of her dress and petticoats. The stirrups were too long for her, but she kicked the horse in the sides to make it go, reining it in the direction it had come. She could go down to the cottonwoods and not get lost, but beyond that…

She gave a sharp sigh and tried to see through the swirling snow, tried to find footprints or hoofprints—anything. The horse was in her control, but it was fretful and kept wanting to sidle and toss its head. She had to hold on to the sticky saddle horn with one hand to keep from falling. As they approached the stream, she stopped, listening hard. She could hear the water rushing and the cottonwoods creaking in the wind, but nothing else.

She looked around. It would be dark soon; she should have brought a lantern with her.

"Dan," she called softly. "Dan!"

She kept listening and listening, but heard nothing. She rode on, crossing the stream. She would zigzag back and forth as far as she could to cover more ground.

"Dan!"

The horse shied suddenly, and she pulled hard on the reins, making it prance. And then she saw it—something. A log half buried in the snow.

Except that there were no logs here. The hands from Selby's had gathered them all and sawed them into firewood for the schoolhouse stoves.

She urged the sorrel forward. It picked its way carefully and stopped a short distance from the half-buried object.

"No," she whispered. "No. No…"

She slid off the animal and, still holding the reins, walked forward. It wasn't a log. It was a man.

"Oh, no—Dan!"

She hooked the reins onto the nearest branch and ran to him, pushing the snow away, pulling on his coat to turn him over.

"Dan! Dan!"

She managed to raise him up, and his head lolled against her shoulder. He made a small moaning sound.

Not dead, then. Not dead—

"Dan, can you hear me? You have to help me. You have to *help* me! I can't—"

He made a feeble gesture with one hand and said something.

"What?" she asked, pressing closer to hear.

"I…could smell…the bread," she thought he said. She frowned. If he meant her baking, then he had been in the cold a long time. Why hadn't she heard the shot? Or perhaps she had—the noise she thought came from the schoolroom.

"Come on—come on. Can you stand up? Stand up!"

She pulled and dragged him closer to the sorrel, then dragged some more, until she had him on his knees. She wrapped her arms around him, nearly buckling under his weight.

"Stand up, Dan. You can do it. You have to do it! Please!"

He finally made it to his feet. She realized she was crying, but she couldn't stop it.

"Now—across the horse. Put your foot in the stirrup…"

Incredibly, between the two of them, he managed to heave himself upward. In one mighty effort, he flung himself across the saddle and stayed there, hanging head down, and he gave such an agonized cry of pain she could only guess at how much the effort hurt him.

Still weeping, she began the slow trip back to the school-house, leading the horse, trying to keep him from sliding off. She had no idea if he was conscious. All she knew was that she had to get him inside out of the cold.

She led the sorrel around to the back door of her quarters and as close to the small porch as she could get. Then she pulled Dan off, causing them both to land hard on the wooden planks. The horse shied and ran away, but she had no time to worry about it. She managed to drag Dan the rest of the way inside, smearing fresh blood across the floor.

She made no effort to get him any farther; the relative warmth of the kitchen would have to do. She turned him to pull his coat off so she could see where the injury was, finding it high on his shoulder just under his collarbone. It was oozing bright red blood—not pouring, thankfully. Maybe, just maybe, being in the cold had saved him.

She let her fingers search along his back, and gave a sigh of relief when she found the exit wound. The bullet had passed completely through, and that was good. She had helped for many long hours in the town's wayside hospital during the war. She had seen hundreds, thousands of wounded men being sent back to the hospitals along the railroad line after the battles in Virginia. Her experience told her that this wound would mean a quick end for Dan Ingram or it would mean a long recovery, and what she did now could make the difference.

She hurried to drag the mattress from her narrow bed into the kitchen. Then she began cutting away the rest of his clothes so she could make sure there were no other wounds. His body was…beautiful, lean and strong.

She rolled him onto the mattress and covered him with

blankets. Then she collected a bowl of snow and put wet cloths into it to make icy compresses to stanch the bleeding. He moaned from time to time, writhed in pain when she touched the wounds, but he didn't say anything.

The bleeding slowed, but he was cold and began to shiver. She moved to the stove and built up the fire to heat the coffee she'd boiled earlier. She put her heavy shawl over him. As soon as the coffee was warm enough, she began to spoon-feed it to him, as much as he would take. He was still cold, and she slid around behind him, lifting him up so that he rested against her and she could put her arms around him.

"Don't die," she whispered against his ear. "Please—please!"

She held him tightly, as if she could physically keep Death from snatching him away. It was like losing Rob all over again, except this time she was experiencing it all firsthand.

The bell, she thought suddenly. She could ring the bell, except that she didn't know who was responsible for this and whether they could still be around somewhere. Perhaps it was Karl Dorsey. Perhaps it was whoever had killed Petey. Ringing the bell could bring the wrong person, the gunman who, hearing it, would know his quarry was still alive.

Dan grew quieter, and she gently moved away from him. She placed her pillow under his head and added more wood to the fire. The wind was sweeping snow in under the door. She went to get the revolver, and to roll up a small rag rug, stuffing it in the wide crack between the door and the floor. She tore up a petticoat to use for bandages, cleaned the blood off the floor, all the while listening for some sound outside.

And she heard something—a small thud on the porch she couldn't attribute to anything normal.

She moved carefully, gun in hand, to the window to peer out. The sorrel stood, head lowered in the blowing snow, at the edge of the porch.

She looked at Dan; he was still quiet, so she pulled the rug away and stepped outside, catching the sorrel easily and leading it inside the enclosure. She put the revolver down long enough to unsaddle it and pitch some more hay. Then she grabbed up the gun, along with Dan's saddlebags and his rifle, and ran back to the house.

He was just as she'd left him. She got down on her knees to check the bandage. He was bleeding still, but not badly.

She licked her lips and tried to think. There was nothing to do but keep a vigil so that she could stop the bleeding when the fits of fever and agitation came. She would have to stay right here, away from the window, and whatever he needed, she would do.

"Oh, Dan," she whispered, but he was past hearing anything.

Chapter Six

*"H*e ought not be moved. You've done a good job stopping
the bleeding, but a rough wagon ride could undo it all."

"He can stay here."

"Mrs. Selby might not approve."

"Then she can disapprove. I thought you were a lawyer."

"Former lawyer. Former physician. Alas, my fondness for
the Oh, Be Joyful has served me ill in both those chosen pro-
fessions. Undertaking suits me better—but I can still write a
contract when the Selbys need it and I still remember the fine
points of the healing arts—my medical skills were tempered
in the fires of war. Give him this for the pain. Sleep when you
can. I'll stop by and speak to Mrs. Selby, tell her how things
are here...."

Dan couldn't hear any more. He wanted to turn his head
to see where they had gone, but it hurt so—a different kind
of hurt from the deep relentless burning in his chest and shoulder. He didn't quite know where he was. He was no longer on
the floor—he knew that. But Eleanor was in the room night
and day, and how could that be? He wasn't even sure what
had happened to him. He had come back from the search for
Karl Dorsey. It was snowing. He'd wanted to see Eleanor
first thing, and he...

He couldn't remember, and he was too weary to try. It was a dream—or was it?

Karl Dorsey. Karl…yelling from his hiding place.

"Blame me for Lillyann and the baby. I was drunk. And, yeah, I locked her out in the cold. But I never shot at your schoolteacher. Look to your *friends* for that, goddamn you!"

Dan closed his eyes again and slept.

"Is it still snowing?" he asked, making her jump.

"What?" she said. Her voice sounded strange to him, husky, trembling.

"Is it still…snowing?" he asked again.

"Not still," she said. "Again."

He thought about this. "How…long have I been here?"

"Two weeks. Give or take a day or two."

"Who…else is here?"

"No one. Just you and me."

"Good," he said.

"You…don't ask me…anything," he said.

"Because you don't often say anything that makes sense."

"I think I've…always been that way," he said, and she smiled.

"You…don't ask if I killed Karl Dorsey."

"If you didn't, you will," she said, gazing into his eyes until he looked away. A man had no defense against a woman who understood.

"I was in an Illinois…regiment. Eighth Cavalry."

"I know."

"How? Who told you?"

"*You* did. I've been on the campaign with you for days."

"What did I say?"

"Nothing I could understand."

"What else did I tell you?"

"You said you had no family."

"They…died. From the typhoid. All of them. All…of them…"

"You're supposed to rest, not talk."

"You…talk then. Tell me about…North Carolina."

"Nothing to tell. It's been ruined by the war—and probably an Illinois regiment."

"Tell me about…Miss Eleanor Hansen, then."

"Nothing to tell about her, either."

"Your family, then. I want to know."

"I was the only one in the house who wasn't left-handed. It wasn't easy to do housework in tandem."

"Like what?"

"Like carrying the mattresses out to sun. My sisters and I would always get into a fight over which way the ends went."

"Will you go back there again? To see your family?"

"Not without a good reason. My sisters and my father are dead. My mother…has her own life."

"I'm going to get up and…go walking tomorrow. Outside, twice around the schoolhouse. I mean it."

"Oh, good. I always delight in the prospect of having you keel over and scare me out of my wits."

"Be careful, miss. I might get to thinking I matter to you."

He did matter to her. More than Eleanor would ever have believed possible. And he likely knew it, as must everyone at the Selby house and in Soul Harbor by now. He was much better, stronger every day, but she was not convinced yet that he would survive. Bouts of fever and nightmares still came unannounced, times when he didn't know her or that the war was over.

She was grateful for the unlikely help she'd received from people here. Annie had come on horseback as soon as the snow stopped, to see if all was well. It wasn't well and, thanks to her, the alarm had been raised and Hapwell, the doctor-lawyer turned-undertaker, arrived. Later, Hester came and stayed for a time to relieve Eleanor so she could eat and sleep and bathe.

"That preacher's sister," Hester told her. "She don't like you looking after Dan the way you are. She says it ain't decent. She's been writing letters to North Carolina."

"Let her," Eleanor said, even knowing that it was likely just a matter of time before the reverend's sister found somebody who knew somebody who knew Eleanor Hansen or her kin.

But she didn't worry about it. She had too many other things to dwell upon. Nearly four weeks had passed, and in all that time there had been no personal visits from Colonel Selby—until today. The wind blew cold and the sky was gray and heavy. A light snow had begun to fall, but the buggy from the Selby house arrived anyway—with Mick riding escort. Colonel Selby clearly expected to find Dan stronger than he was, but it didn't stop him from sitting down with him—and Mick—and having a private conversation Eleanor wasn't allowed to hear.

She thanked the colonel for the stream of food baskets that had come from his kitchen, wondering all the while if he even knew about them. Then she brought them all coffee and left them to make their plans, plans for a renewed manhunt in the spring, she thought. It was no hardship for her to see to the horses; she didn't want to eavesdrop on their conversation. What she did hear made her realize how much Colonel Selby and his operation relied on the steadfast loyalty of Dan Ingram. Unfortunately for Dan, vengeance hadn't been served nor had the stolen cows been returned, and the colonel was here to make certain Dan would still do his part, that he understood he was still obliged to take Karl Dorsey's life, now more so than ever.

But she no longer sat in judgment; she only knew that she couldn't live through the fear and the waiting yet another time.

I cannot bear it. The thought repeated over and over in her mind as she fed and watered the horses. The reverend's sister was writing letters, and there was only one thing to do.

Dan was so quiet after the colonel left. She didn't ask him anything, and she thought he was glad of it. They were strangers suddenly, as distant as they had been the day she arrived in Soul Harbor. It was as if the kiss they had shared the day he told her about Petey had never happened, and they had not spent all these days together, learning about each other, while she struggled to save his life.

She could feel him watching her as she put some of her things into her trunk, but he, too, asked no questions. He sat by the window, looking out. The daylight was fading. The snow had begun to fall more heavily.

When he finally looked at her, it was if he had called her name, the way he did sometimes in the middle of the night, when the fever woke him and he didn't know where he was. She went to him, kneeling down by his chair, hiding her face against his knees. His hand stroked her hair.

After a moment, she lifted her head and looked up at him. "This place—"

"It's not the place, Eleanor."

"These people, then. The Selbys. Livingston Warner. They're going to be the death of you. They're going to kill you, as surely as if they'd done it with their own hands, and you're going to let them."

"It's the way—"

"Yes. The way things are here." She gave a quiet sigh. "And there's no help for it."

"I think it's likely you know me better now than anybody else on this earth," he said. "I am what I am, Eleanor."

So am I, she thought.

"When are you going back to Selby's?" she asked, because it suddenly occurred to her that the colonel might have wanted him to return to his other life today, invalid or not.

"Tomorrow," he said. "Mrs. Selby wants it. There's too much talk. I can't cost you your reputation—"

"Take me to bed," she interrupted. She had no reputation

to protect, and she could feel the end of everything bearing down on them. She stared into his eyes.

"I…love you," he said, as if that was an argument for not doing as she asked.

"I know."

"There are a lot of things against us."

"I know," she said again.

She stood and waited, her mouth trembling despite all she did to try and stop it.

He got to his feet without her help and made his way to her narrow bed, his hand resting on her shoulder as they walked. He sat down on the edge of the bed, and she sat beside him.

"I want you—like this—more than anything I've ever wanted in my life. But if you—"

She pressed her fingers against his lips to stop whatever he meant to say, then began to undo the buttons on her dress, letting him take over the task when he wanted to. She sat passively, watching his face as he slowly removed her clothes, one garment at a time. She had the feeling that he was doing what she was doing—committing it all to memory, trying to make it last. She could feel his hands trembling, not from his illness but from his desire. He was strong enough for this; it was she who was weak.

At one point, when she looked down, a tear dropped onto the back of his hand. He looked up sharply, and she lost her passiveness. She reached for him to stop the question she saw in his eyes, pressing her face into his good shoulder, clinging to him hard.

"The first day," he said. "Even then I loved you."

She moved out of his embrace and lay down on the narrow bed, making room for him. When he came to her, they lay face to face, breath to breath, skin to skin, and once again he kissed her eyes.

So gently.

As if she were the lady he believed she was.

His hands began to stroke her and her body responded. She meant to have and keep this memory until the day she died.

He kissed her mouth, and she returned the kiss.

"Are you sure?" he whispered against her ear. "Eleanor…"

"I'm sure," she answered. She could hear the fire burning in the stove, the wind against the walls.

He no longer held back. She closed her eyes to savor the sensation of urgency, his hands and his mouth on her, leading her until her body rose to receive his.

And how good he felt, inside her. The storm in her grew and grew until finally she cried out in release, awash in the pure pleasure of him. His movements quickened, until he suddenly stiffened and groaned against her neck. Then he slumped against her and rolled away, his breathing heavy, both of them bathed in sweat.

After a time, he lifted his head to look into her eyes. "Are you…all right?"

"I'm not the one shot," she answered. She gave him a mischievous smile, not because she wanted to tease him but because she didn't want to weep. "Have I done you in, Ingram?"

"If you have, I don't mind," he said. He put his arms around her. "I intend to marry you, Eleanor Hansen. You might as well know. I decided it a long time ago."

"I've…never had much luck with making plans," she said. He looked into her eyes, then moved away, stretching out beside her. The remark had brought the ghost of Rob Markham into the room—as she intended.

Dan had said he loved her, and he was waiting for her to say it, too. She knew that.

But she closed her eyes and turned to him, not yet done with the goodbye.

Chapter Seven

Ten days.

Ten days was far too long to wait. Dan rode in past Petey's grave, taking his time, testing his ability not to cause the all-but-healed wound in his shoulder to stab with pain. He was doing surprisingly well, he thought, but pain or no pain, he was determined to see Eleanor today, regardless of what Hapwell said about him staying off horses. He couldn't stand the bunkhouse any longer. He had been in Eleanor's care and presence for weeks, and if he hadn't already known it, he knew now that the company of men would never be the same for him. He was tired of hearing about cows and the weather and Karl Dorsey.

Dan missed her. He lived in the memory of their last night together. There was no doubt that he'd had to leave her house: how could he have stayed and not taken her to bed again? He was still amazed that it had happened. He had no idea what he might have said and done during the worst of his recovery, but whatever it was, it clearly hadn't mattered to her. She had seen past the ravings, and she had given him everything a woman had to give.

He didn't see any smoke coming from the schoolhouse chimneys, nor did he see the mare in the enclosure. He frowned and urged his mount forward, touching the brim of his hat as he passed by Petey's marker. The wind was strong enough to make the clapper in the Union Pacific bell peal softly from time to time, and it gave the place an eerie and empty feeling, one he had to shake off before he could dismount.

The door to the schoolroom stood slightly ajar. Everything inside seemed to be in its place, ready for the next lesson. He walked through to her part of the building. That door was closed. He rapped on it softly, then pushed it inward.

Anyone else might not have noticed, but he did. He couldn't sense her presence, nor did he see any of the few personal belongings she'd brought with her. The stove was cold.

He walked to the bedroom and pushed the door open. The bed had been stripped, the mattress rolled. The room had been stripped, as well. She might never have even been here.

"Eleanor?" he called, still not ready to believe it. "Eleanor!" And he listened hard for some reply, already knowing it was useless.

He went back outside to look around. There was no snow on the ground now. He could see hoofprints and wagon tracks. And a single small footprint in the mud that must be hers.

After a moment, he got back on his horse and began to ride toward the Selby house, picking up speed as he went, as the sense of dread began to well up in him.

Men working in one of the enclosures near the house hailed him when he rode by, but he ignored them. He caught a glimpse of Mick coming out of the bunkhouse.

"Dan!" Mick yelled after him. "Wait! I got to talk to you! Dan—!"

He abruptly reined the horse and wheeled it around. "What do you know, Mick?" he asked when he reached him.

"I know it ain't no use to go bothering Mrs. Selby about this."

"About what, Mick?" he asked, his voice deadly.

"Ah, damn it all, Danny. Eleanor…she's gone—"

"Gone where? By God, tell me what you know!"

"I don't—she got on the eastbound train."

"She wouldn't do that. Not without…" He didn't believe for a minute she would just leave and not say a word. "I'm going to see Mrs. Selby—"

"Wait, now, damn it." Mick grabbed the bridle and gave a sharp sigh. "She left you a letter."

"Where is it?"

"Hester's got it. She told me when I went to see her last night. Eleanor left letters for Mrs. Selby and the young-uns at the school. And there's one for you."

"Why didn't you bring it?"

"She wouldn't give it to me—and me her best customer, too. She said Eleanor made her promise she wouldn't give it to nobody but you—her hand to your hand—and if she couldn't, she was to burn it—"

Dan swore and spurred his horse, jerking the bridle out of Mick's grasp.

"The colonel's looking for you!" Mick yelled after him. "You're going to tear that bullet hole open—see if you don't!"

Dan's shoulder was killing him by the time he got to the river. He stopped long enough to water the horse, then took off again, riding straight to the exchange when he finally reached Soul Harbor.

"Where's Hester?" he asked one of the men leaning on the bar.

The man grinned. "In a big hurry, are you?"

"Where is she!"

"Here I am, Danny," she said from the stairs. "Look at you! I never thought I'd see you looking this good again. I thought we'd be planting you up there with Lillyann."

"Where's the letter?"

"I got it. Come on up. I'll give it to you."

He followed her up the stairs, holding on to the banister to stave off a sudden wave of dizziness that washed over him.

"Come on, Danny," Hester said, slipping an arm around him. "You done got too big for your britches, is what."

"I want the letter, Hester."

"Well, we got to get there, don't we?"

"Did…she say anything?"

"Not much. She just told me what to do with the letters she wrote. I wish I could write a fine hand like hers—so pretty."

"Did she say where she was going?"

"No. She missed her mail. The west train brought her a letter last week."

They reached a door and Hester opened it.

"Here's yours," she said, stepping just inside. She handed him the envelope, and he stared at his name in the fine handwriting Hester admired so.

"If she said anything about me in there, you tell me, Danny," Hester said as he made his way back downstairs.

"Here," the bartender said, shoving a shot glass of whiskey at him when he passed. "You look like you need it."

"I'll have to owe you."

"Yeah, yeah," the bartender said.

He took the whiskey and sat down at the nearest table, laying the letter in front of him for a moment before he opened it and began to read.

Goodbye, Dan. I couldn't say it to your face. It would have been too hard for me. You will think you know how it is with me. You will think that I can't bear being a witness to the terrible danger you court. It is true. I can't. What you don't know is that that is not the only reason I have gone. You are a good person, a decent person. I knew it the very first day we met. The truth is I am not. I am not speaking of what happened between you and me. That was beautiful, and I will remember it always. It's the life I lived before I came to Soul Harbor that shames me. I was a woman of the town, someone not fit to teach children—

He abruptly stopped reading and looked up. Then he began reading again.

>   —not fit to teach children. I was "Nell" Hansen then, and I have no explanations for the things I have done nor any excuses. I had hoped to start a new life in Wyoming. I just didn't count on finding you, loving you. There. I have said it now. I do love you, Dan, and that is the true reason I am gone. One last thing. On the wagon ride here to catch the train, I heard it. I heard the singing in the wind. Eleanor.

He sat for a long time, but he didn't reread the letter. He was aware that the bartender was watching him. Eventually, he drank the whiskey.

Mick didn't ask him anything when he returned. No one did. Not then and not in the weeks that followed. After a series of noisy arguments with Mrs. Selby, the colonel unexpectedly left for England. The schoolhouse sat empty.

Dan knew that he must seem to be all right to Mick and the rest of them. He ate when he was supposed to eat. Slept when he was supposed to sleep. His strength returned.

But he wasn't all right. He knew it for certain the afternoon he saw the reverend's sister and one of the church women arrive at the Selbys' front door. They disembarked from their buggy and went bustling into the house—and came right back out again, both of them clearly agitated.

"Ladies," he said when they stomped past him to their buggy.

The reverend's sister immediately turned on him. "Well, I see *you're* up and around again," she said.

"Yes, ma'am."

"That woman—no *decent* woman would have put herself in that situation."

"What situation is that, ma'am?"

"You lived with her—for weeks!"

"If you mean Miss Hansen, she saved a life, ma'am," he said. "*Mine.* Nothing you say will make me think hard of her."

He walked away, leaving them both in a huff. And he delayed his departure into town for a time, not because he hadn't made up his mind, but because he needed to work out a feasible plan. Eventually, he went to see Mrs. Selby and got an advance on his wages, and then he rode to Soul Harbor.

He went to the exchange, looking for the man who sold train tickets and handled the mail.

"You still got that letter for Eleanor Hansen?" he asked.

"Yeah, but you can't have it."

"I don't want it. I just want to see it."

"Why?"

He reached across the counter and caught the man by his shirtfront. "Are you going to show it to me or am I going to hurt you?"

"All right! You cattle people are damn touchy, you know that?"

"Living with cows all the time will do that to you," Dan said. "The letter?"

The man sighed and hunted until he found it, holding it up so Dan could see—everything except what he wanted to see.

"Get your thumb off the return address," Dan said.

The man started to argue but thought better of it.

Dan read the name and the town. *Mrs. Maxwell Woodard. Salisbury, North Carolina.*

He had to start somewhere.

"Where you off to?" Hester asked when she saw him waiting on the platform as the train going east pulled in.

He didn't answer her.

"You going to bring Eleanor back?"

"Maybe," he said.

"You know, I…don't think I told you two letters from North Carolina came that day. One was for Eleanor. And somebody said the other one was for the reverend's sister. I stole that one."

"You what?"

Hester shrugged instead of elaborating.

"Bring her back, Danny," she said, giving him a little grin. "If she won't come, tell her the sad news—tell her a letter to the reverend's sister got itself dropped down the outhouse hole."

"Hester, what are you—?"

"She'll know what it means. Get on the train, Danny, and quit bothering me."

He boarded the train, but he stood watching Hester make her way back up the slope to the exchange. After a moment he shook his head and smiled to himself. Help sometimes came in strange guises.

February was no time to be traveling across the plains. It took him a lot longer than he anticipated to reach St. Louis. He passed the time thinking about everything except the thing that troubled him most. *What if?*

What if she wasn't there? What if she wouldn't come back with him? What if she—?

He traveled the length of Tennessee to Knoxville and eventually made it into North Carolina. He got on the train again at the railhead in Morganton, assured that it would take him into the town where Eleanor was at least known.

He arrived to find the place like what he expected; he'd passed through hundreds of Southern towns just like it during the war. Some had been left far worse off. The military presence was apparent the minute he stepped off the train, but the boredom of occupation duty had taken its toll. The soldiers barely glanced at him. He asked a man stacking boxes where he could find a meal, and was directed to a restaurant near the depot. He ordered fried eggs and biscuits, and he ate slowly, listening to the conversations around him, surprised at how quickly he heard the name "Woodard."

"Is that Maxwell Woodard they're talking about?" he asked the nearest man.

"Yeah. Occupation commander. If you got business here,

you best see him about it first. Save yourself a lot of grief. The
Yankees run everything."

Dan got directions to the army headquarters and went there
as soon as he'd finished eating. He found the place busier than
he expected, and he sat down on a barrel outside to wait,
watching the passersby. Looking for Eleanor.

It was cold and threatening to rain, and, after a time, he decided to take a chance.

"You know where Mrs. Maxwell Woodard is this time of
day?" he asked a young soldier standing guard by the doorway.

"She'll be here directly," he said. "Always brings Colonel
Woodard his vittles around noon."

"Is that her?" he asked, because he could see a young
woman walking in their direction with a basket on her arm.

"That's her."

Dan waited until she reached the front entrance of the
headquarters. "Mrs. Woodard, ma'am, I wonder if I could
trouble you for a minute."

She stopped and looked at him inquisitively.

"I'm looking for Miss Eleanor Hansen—"

"Why?" she interrupted, and her tone of voice suggested
that she had better like the answer. She reminded him a great
deal of Eleanor at that moment, and he tried not to smile.

"I've come a long way to find her, ma'am."

She looked at him steadily, clearly not convinced that he
was worthy of any information she might have.

"From Wyoming…" he said, blundering on.

"Are you Dan Ingram?" she asked.

"Yes, ma'am," he said, taken aback.

"Then you stay right where you are. I'll return directly.
Don't let him go anywhere," she said to the young soldier
guarding the door. She hurried into the building, and he could
hear her making her way up the wooden stairs to the second
floor. She was gone longer than he expected, and he eventually sat back down on the barrel again, glancing up at the over-

cast sky occasionally. By the time she returned, it had started to rain, something that seemed not to trouble her in the least.

"Walk with me, sir," she said. She led the way to the middle of the street, where she stopped and turned to look at the upstairs window of the building she'd just vacated. Two men in uniform stood watching. "My husband and his sergeant. They want to see you," she said. "Just in case."

Dan didn't ask "just in case" what. "Is Eleanor here, ma'am?" he asked, walking with her when she crossed the street and stepped up on the sidewalk.

"If she is, what are your intentions?"

"I've come to get her, ma'am. I want her to come back to Wyoming Territory with me."

She made a small noise, one he couldn't necessarily interpret as approval.

"She knows I want to marry her," he said as they walked along.

"Well, you took your own good time getting here."

"Some of that was my stupidity."

"And a gunshot wound. How is your shoulder?"

"My—it's…well."

"That's good to hear. My husband was shot not too long ago. Weather like this bothers him."

Dan didn't know what to say to that. He just kept walking. They passed a burned out house.

"Our best friend—Nell's and mine—used to live there."

He didn't know what to say to that, either.

She stopped walking. "Nell—Eleanor—is in there," she said, pointing to the last house on the street. "She's living with her mother again. I trust you understand that neither Mrs. Hansen nor I wish to see our Eleanor hurt. Good luck, Mr. Ingram. You will need it."

She continued on her way, leaving the entire matter of approaching the woman he'd come so far to find in his nervous hands. He stood for a moment, then continued to the house she'd indicated, and opened the gate. When he knocked on the door, he didn't really expect Eleanor to open it, but she did. She gave a small cry of surprise, but recovered quickly.

They stared at each other.

"I'm…sorry you've come all this way," she said finally. "I wrote you a letter. Hester—I guess she didn't give it to you." He thought she was about to cry.

"She gave it to me," he said.

"You should have read it."

"I did read it."

"Then why—?"

"Eleanor, it's cold and wet out here. Do you think I could come in?"

She stood back to let him inside, but she clearly didn't want to.

"Who is that, Nellie?" a woman's voice called from the back of the house. "Tell the rent man he'll get his money." The woman stepped into the hall. She had flour on her hands.

"It's not the rent man, Mama. It's Dan Ingram," Eleanor said, her voice quiet and strained.

"Well, I swan! Dan Ingram!" she said. "Stay and eat with us, Dan—take his coat and hat, Nellie. Let him go and get warm by the stove." She went back into the kitchen.

"Does everybody here know who I am?"

"Just Maria and my mother."

"Maria…Woodard?"

Eleanor nodded and took his coat, but she didn't do anything with it. She stood in the middle of the hall, holding it tightly to her breast, her head bowed.

"Eleanor," he said.

She looked up at him. "I never expected to see you again. Never."

"You are so beautiful…" He wanted to touch her, but he didn't dare.

"What are you doing here?"

"I came to get you—"

"No, you didn't."

"Yes, I did. I told you I intend to marry you."

"That was before. When you didn't know…anything."

"Then I'll ask you again. Will you marry me, Eleanor Hansen? I'll go and speak to your mother right now. What do you think?"

"I think you're crazy—and I can't marry a crazy man."

"I'd be pleased if you made an exception in my case," he said, but she wouldn't smile.

"Nothing's changed."

"Everything's changed," he said. "I'll do my best to make you happy. I've already talked to Mrs. Selby."

"Why? To get her permission?"

"To get a better paying job."

"She let you stop looking for Karl Dorsey to come here?"

"She's not worried about Karl Dorsey—and neither am I."

"The colonel is."

"He's gone back to England. Mrs. Selby says it's permanent. She sold the Arabian, and she mortgaged enough land to buy him out. Karl left the territory. Last I heard he was in Mexico. Marry me, Eleanor. You like Wyoming—I know you do. And you like me."

"I *love* you," she said, as if it were the worst thing in the world. "You're going to make me cry."

He put her arms around her then, and she let him, resting her head on his good shoulder.

"I can't go with you. You know I can't."

"The past is the past, Eleanor. Yours *and* mine. It's not going to matter—"

"It will matter. Sooner or later."

"Not to you and not to me. And we're the only ones that count. Mrs. Selby wants me to tell you the job is still yours."

"Dan…" She lifted her head to look at him. "I want to believe it can be done. Oh, I'm afraid!" She hid her face in his shirt.

"Do you love me, Eleanor? Tell me again."

She nodded.

"Then trust me—and I'd kind of like to hear you say it."

She looked at him again. "I just did."

"I'd like for it to sound a little less like an affliction."

"It is an affliction."

"Say it anyway."

She smiled suddenly. And it was at that moment he knew he had won.

"I love you, Dan Ingram. I do," she said.

"Then come with me. Come *home*."

He kissed her then, her forehead, her cheek.

"We'll get married there—so they can all see it. Hester, Annie and Theodore—everybody. A spring wedding because we're both starting new. Don't cry." He kissed her eyes, her mouth. "Say yes. Go on. Say it!"

"Dan—"

"Say it," he whispered against her ear.

"Yes," she managed to gasp between kisses. "Yes!"

Epilogue

Soul Harbour, Wyoming
June 1870

It was a beautiful day for a wedding.

Eleanor held on to her new husband's arm and walked with him among the guests, greeting each and every one who had come to witness their marriage. So many people. All of Soul Harbor was here, including Hester and most of the army garrison. And passengers—strangers all—from the west-bound train, who had wanted to share in the festivities before they traveled on. The out-of-doors was the only place in Soul Harbor big enough to hold them all.

She looked into their smiling faces, wondering as she always did about where they had come from—and what they might have done. It troubled her still that no one knew who had shot Dan that snowy afternoon. Some said rustlers, coming back for more cows. Some said Karl Dorsey, following his boss's orders. But if Livingston Warner was guilty of any machination in the event that had nearly cost Dan his life, he certainly didn't show it. She could see him now, laughing and talking with Lavinia Selby and the few men here he considered important enough for his time and attention.

Thanks to Hester, Eleanor did know who had shot into the schoolhouse—Mick. The colonel hadn't given up on trying to scare Lavinia's schoolteacher away, and Mick had done the scaring, because he was the only one of the Selby hands who was a marksman with a rifle. The colonel had given yet another of his irrevocable orders, and Mick, believing that he was the only one who could keep her safe, had secretly carried it out. He hadn't wanted to see Dan's schoolmarm get hurt in the Selby war—or so he said. The incredible part was that Eleanor believed him. Clearly, she had been in Wyoming Territory long enough for his reasoning to make perfect sense, and she smiled at the thought of how far she had come.

"What is it?" Dan asked, putting his hand over hers.

"I'm happy," she said, and he kissed her on the lips—much to the delight of the guests.

"I've made another promise," he said, looking into her eyes as if they were alone. "Besides the wedding one."

"What promise is that?"

"I made a promise to…Rob. I've promised him I'll do the best I can for you. Always."

She could feel the tears welling. "Dan…"

The music for the first waltz began to play.

"Will you waltz with your husband, Mrs. Ingram?"

"I will, sir," she said.

Smiling now, she accepted his hand—and with it his love and their new life together.

It was a beautiful day for a wedding. Winter had gone from the land. Winter had gone from her heart.

* * * * *

McCORD'S DESTINY

Pam Crooks

To my editor, Melissa Endlich,
who honored me by asking for this story.

Chapter One

A lone eagle soared over the breadth of the small oxbow-shaped lake, its wings spread in graceful flight. Beneath it, the water shimmered and sparkled, kissed by the midday sun. Lazy waves lapped against the shoreline, which stretched toward hills crowned with trees and teeming with wildlife. Here, nature pulsed with springtime abandon. Fragile sprouts had burst into color, and vibrant hues of green painted the land as far as the eye could see.

Juliette Blanchard stared and stared. The place was even more beautiful than she remembered.

"It's perfect, isn't it?" she breathed, her eyes riveted to the three hundred acres sprawled out before her. "The water. The trees. The gentle slope of the land. It's all so perfect."

"Indeed." Stephen Dunn, the entrepreneur who intended to purchase the acres, nodded. He was clearly pleased.

"There isn't a finer place to build the hotel," she added, more convinced than ever of her choice. "None this side of the Missouri."

"I suspect not east of it, either, Miss Blanchard."

"No." She'd done the research, had painstakingly investigated every suitable body of water in the Midwest and beyond.

But this, *this* had always been her favorite. And now her dream would come true.

"I've designed the hotel so the guests will be spared the morning sun when they have breakfast on the patio. On the other hand, the outdoor pool will soak up the heat from the hottest part of a summer's day. Families can lounge to their hearts' content."

From the time she'd been ten years old, the serenity of this little patch of Nebraska had captivated her. Even after moving to New York three years ago to continue her studies in architecture, she'd not forgotten it.

"The land, of course, will make a fabulous golf course, don't you think?" Her mind envisioned the well-manicured greens, the bunkers, even the tiny balls being lobbed about. "Gentlemen will come from all over the country to play here."

"Your enthusiasm is most catching." Dunn beamed. "I can hardly wait to break ground." He turned to Charles Hatman, the Omaha land developer in charge of the project. "I trust the building contractor is prepared to begin as soon as we give him a date?"

"Yes, sir." Hatman puffed on a cigar. "The bids are in. Construction crews are assigned. Materials are ready to be ordered."

"Good. Very good," Dunn said.

Excitement spiraled through Juliette. Only one detail remained, a formality at this point, and the deal would be final. She glanced at her watch and noted the time. "The bankers are waiting for us, gentlemen. We have papers to sign, and I don't want to be late."

Dunn chuckled. "No grass will grow under her feet, will it, Charles?"

She smiled at his teasing. He was highly recommended by her aunt Louise, a renowned architect in her own right; indeed, the man had financed many of her famous designs. Juliette was honored by his interest in her hotel.

In the time she'd been conferring with him, they'd fallen into a comfortable business relationship. Still, until the project was complete, Juliette intended to remain professional and attuned to every detail.

Oddly enough, Hatman made no response to Dunn's comment. Just puffed vigorously on his cigar and stared at the land beyond the lake.

He looked inexplicably grim. She exchanged a quick glance with Dunn. She'd arrived in Omaha only a few hours ago, with her younger sister, Camille. Hatman and Dunn had met them at the train, and they'd driven directly out here. While she knew Dunn well enough, she hadn't met Hatman before today, though they'd corresponded many times via her aunt's office in Buffalo. Perhaps the man was always this tense.

"Shall we go?" she asked, and pivoted toward the carriage, where Camille waited for her.

"Certainly." Dunn extended his hand, indicating she was to precede him.

But Hatman didn't move.

"He won't sell," he said suddenly.

Juliette blinked in puzzlement and turned back toward him. "Who won't sell?"

"The son of a gun who owns these acres."

Horror coursed through her. *"What?"*

Dunn's chest puffed in indignation. "I thought everything was set, Charles."

"Everything was—except the land." Cigar smoke billowed in frustrated swirls. "He won't budge, damn him."

"But he must sell!" Juliette gasped. "This entire project depends on it."

"You think I don't know that, Miss Blanchard?" Hatman jerked the cigar out of his mouth and faced her. "He's been stringing me along for weeks. I've done everything I could to convince him."

"Why weren't we informed of this problem?" Dunn demanded. "You led us to believe the sale was proceeding as planned."

"Because I was sure it would."

"You offered him the price we discussed?" Juliette asked.

"More." Again, Hatman puffed furiously on his cigar.

The entrepreneur's brow arched. "And he didn't take it?"

"No."

"Why not?"

"Claims he's not interested."

Juliette pressed trembling fingers to her lips. "Perhaps you should speak to him again. Offer him more money or—or something."

"I'm telling you, it won't do any good, Miss Blanchard," Hatman said. "I rode out to his place just this morning. Figured it was my last chance to deal with him before you got into town. Didn't do me a damn bit of good."

"A stubborn cuss, isn't he?" Dunn muttered.

"Thickheaded like his pa was. Everyone knows the Mc-Cord boys are down on their luck. We've offered Tru the sweetest deal around. Why he won't sell is beyond me."

"Tru?" Juliette's world tilted alarmingly. "Tru McCord owns this land?"

"He does."

"But that's impossible," she said, her heart pounding. "His father lost it. In a card game several years ago. He—"

Memories crashed in on her, stifling the words on her tongue. She hadn't known, never dreamed…

"Don't know how he came to own it, Miss Blanchard. But he's had these acres for as long as I've been acquainted with him, which has been a good long while."

Dunn frowned. "Doesn't matter how he came to own them, just that he does. And he won't sell."

Juliette squared her shoulders. The entrepreneur's brisk tone was a sober reminder of the seriousness of their dilemma. "Of course. That's the crux of the problem, isn't it?"

She would do well to hide her past relationship with Tru from these men. They had little interest in it, especially since a luxury resort hotel was at stake—as well as the enormous profits they would stand to lose.

But, oh God. Why Tru? Of all the landowners in the state of Nebraska, why did *he* have to own the acres she needed?

"Well, Miss Blanchard. There's no use in meeting with the bank now, I'm afraid. Can't buy land that's not for sale, can we?" Dunn heaved a heavy sigh.

"I'm sorry," Hatman said, genuine regret in his expression. "I did all I could. There are other sites available, however. I'll draw up a list—"

"No." Juliette shook her head emphatically. "There's no other location that would be as well-suited for my hotel as this one. I've designed it *specifically* for this very spot."

Both Dunn and Hatman studied her, then shook their heads in unison.

"A damn shame," Dunn said.

With Hatman beside him, he strode toward the carriage, and Juliette could feel the deal slipping through her fingers.

"Wait!" she called.

They halted, and she hurried toward them.

"I'll talk to Tru," she said, and swallowed hard.

Hatman frowned. "Won't do any good, Miss Blanchard. He won't listen."

"I can try." God, she had to.

"But—"

"What harm can it do, Charles?" Dunn asked. "We don't have anything to lose at this point." He gave her a faint smile. "Would you like me to accompany you, Miss Blanchard? Perhaps between the two of us we might convince him to sell."

The weak side of her wanted to say yes, that she couldn't face Tru again, alone, after all these years. But the proud side didn't want the entrepreneur to see her beg.

Because if that's what it took to get Tru McCord to give up his land, that's what she'd do.

Get down on her knees and beg.

"No," she said. "I'll see him myself."

"Very well, then." Dunn patted her shoulder, a grandfatherly gesture of encouragement. Or perhaps it was one of sympathy for a lost cause, she couldn't be sure. "You know where to find me. Do inform me how this meeting transpires, won't you?"

Juliette managed a confident nod. "Of course."

The businessmen climbed into the carriage, and after a long, troubled moment, Juliette joined them.

The Next Day

Juliette ignored Camille's concerned gaze upon her. For the second time in as many days, she and her younger sister were in a carriage, riding toward the McCord ranch. Yesterday's scheduled appointment with the bankers had come and gone. Today, Stephen Dunn and Charles Hatman were somewhere in Omaha, free to see to their own matters.

Matters that no longer pertained to her and her beloved hotel.

Juliette alone had to keep her dream alive. What if she failed? What if Tru tossed her on a train back to New York empty-handed and defeated?

The worst of it would be explaining to Aunt Louise that three years of study, planning and hope were wasted. That the demise of this project had doomed her career before it started.

A career she urgently needed to support herself and Camille. The salary she'd earn from the hotel project would replenish her bank account, alarmingly drained from the high costs of their education and the Blanchard family medical bills.

"I suspect he's not the monster you think he is, Juliette," Camille said quietly.

Juliette's thoughts scattered. Her gaze flew to her sister's.

There was no need to ask who "he" was. "He's being deliberately defiant about selling."

"I'm sure he has his reasons for refusing."

"He's in dire need of money. The McCords always are."

"Tru is entitled to his land. It's all he has."

Why was Camille defending him? Juliette leaned forward, desperate to make her understand. "With the money we want to pay him, he could have so much more. Don't you see, Camille? He could put a down payment on a nice house in town. Or buy more land someplace else."

"Juliette." Camille sighed. "Listen to yourself."

Her sister's softly reproving words pulled Juliette up short. Her mouth dipped in a wry grimace. "I'm sounding like Father again, aren't I?"

"Yes, you are. He was driven to make money, any way he could. And he didn't care who he stepped on along the way."

Juliette shifted her stare back out the carriage window. She was like her father in some ways, she supposed. She had the same need to succeed. The same intelligence. The same creativity.

But was she as ruthless?

She'd never been tested before now. Had never had so much at stake.

She was fast learning why her father had become successful in the business world. He'd done what he had to to make a name for himself, even if it meant resorting to tactics that were…ruthless.

If only he were still alive. He'd tell her exactly how to get those acres for her hotel.

"You're a Blanchard, Julie-girl. Don't ever forget it. Your name will open a lot of doors in this part of the country. Do what you have to to keep them open and don't look back."

The words he'd instilled in her over and over again came alive, as if it were him sitting across from her in the carriage instead of Camille. They gave her courage to face Tru again and refreshed her resolve to fight for what she wanted.

"I don't think I like the look on your face, Juliette."

She shifted away from the window and considered her frowning sibling. The scarlet fever that took their parents' lives had almost claimed Camille's, too. The disease had left her forever frail, but what she lacked in strength, she made up for in her outspoken opinions.

"This is a business matter, Camille. You needn't have bothered coming with me this morning."

"I didn't want to sit in a hotel room by myself while you rode out here and tangled horns with Tru McCord."

"'Tangled horns'?" The term amused Juliette. She adored her sister and took no offense at her scolding. Camille was almost nineteen and the only family she had left except for Aunt Louise. They were as close as sisters could be. "You're talking like a ranch hand, not an educated young woman from New York."

"You make it sound as if being a ranch hand is demeaning."

Juliette's smile faded, and she puzzled over the defensiveness in Camille's tone. "I didn't mean to. It's just a phrase I've never heard you say before."

"It doesn't matter. Oh, Juliette, why do you have to have *this* land?" Her slender arm swept outward, indicating the McCord acres they were riding on.

She stiffened. "You know why. We've discussed it many times."

"But there are other places in Nebraska where you could buy three hundred acres. In Iowa, too. Can't you just—just change your vision a little?"

Juliette gaped at her.

"You don't have to prove yourself like this," Camille said. "Aunt Louise already favors you. She wants you to be a partner in her agency. Why isn't that good enough for you?"

"Because it's a man's world, Camille," Juliette shot back. "I want to earn my own place in it."

"With Waite and Caulkings." Camille rolled her eyes.

The most prominent architectural and building firm in the state of New York.

And completely male.

Juliette's dream to become their only female partner made even Aunt Louise salivate. Richard Waite and F. W. Caulkings had followed the development of her luxury resort hotel with great interest. They intended to expand their firm on an international level and were considering adding another partner to aid them in the process.

Juliette intended to be that partner. And she really needed Tru's land, no matter what Camille said.

She leaned back in the carriage seat and sought a different topic of conversation. One far safer and less likely to stir Camille's ire. "Why don't you call on Sarah Evans this afternoon? Perhaps you can go shopping together."

Camille blinked. "Sarah?"

"Yes. Your very best friend in the whole world. Remember?"

Camille fidgeted with the folds of her skirt. "That was before we moved to New York. Sarah has new friends now. I doubt she has time for me anymore."

Juliette's heart squeezed. The move from their comfortable life in Nebraska to the bustling city of Buffalo had been hard on them both. Still reeling from the deaths of their parents, Juliette had found solace in her studies. Camille, however, experienced difficulty finding a social circle that suited her.

Yet Sarah had corresponded often, especially of late, and Camille always looked forward to her letters with eager delight.

"Nonsense. We'll call on her as soon as we're finished with Tru," Juliette said.

His name slipped from her lips easily, and her stomach did a funny flip at the reminder of what lay ahead. She'd be seeing him again. Talking to him.

Pleading with him to sell his land.

As if she, too, suddenly recalled where they were and why, Camille turned her gaze toward the window and the cabin that loomed ahead. The sight of it seemed to startle her, and she reached for the crocheted handbag in her lap.

"Oh, Juliette. We're almost there." She opened the bag, withdrew a small mirror and patted the dark curls at her nape with fingers, Juliette noted, that weren't quite steady.

"Yes. We are." She drew in a slow breath, tried to calm the incessant fluttering in her belly.

She'd stayed up until the early hours of the morning studying the construction costs of her hotel yet again. She knew the margin of profit. She knew the potential for loss. She knew exactly how much she could offer Tru before the project dropped into red ink.

Red ink the bankers could never see. Tru had to accept her best offer. He had to!

The carriage rolled to a stop, and the driver opened the door.

"Shall I wait, Miss Blanchard?" he asked.

"Please." She took his hand and descended the step. "I won't be long."

"Tru's a reasonable man," Camille said, her voice low so it wouldn't carry. "Try not to worry."

There she was, defending him again. How would she know if Tru was reasonable or not? Juliette hid her annoyance and lifted her chin. "If it's the last thing I do, I'll convince him to sell."

"But it's not the end of the world if he doesn't," Camille persisted. "It's *his* land. He's entitled to keep it if he wants."

Juliette bit back a retort and turned toward the cabin. This wasn't the time or place to challenge her sister's stubbornness. She had to concentrate, remain composed.

She had to succeed.

"You're a Blanchard, Julie-girl. Don't ever forget it."

Her father's words inspired her, as they always did, and bracing herself for the confrontation ahead, she went in search of Tru.

Chapter Two

It was only a matter of time before she came.

Tru knew it. He could feel it.

He didn't like it.

Having Juliette Blanchard in his life again was a distraction he could ill afford. The woman was trouble, had been from the moment she first rested those violet-blue eyes on him more than four years ago, bewitching him, seducing him with her innocent female wiles.

Hell, she was all-woman back then, even at seventeen years of age. She had the ability to knock the wind out of him with a demure sweep of her lashes or a shy smile. And her kisses...

But that was four years ago. And now was now. He'd grown up plenty since she was in Nebraska last. Had to, considering her old man was responsible for taking what little the McCords owned.

Everything but these three hundred acres.

Not surprising Juliette wanted those, too. To build a damn fool fancy hotel on. For the love of Pete, wasn't that just like a Blanchard?

Grimly, Tru shook his head. He refilled his coffee cup, left the cabin's kitchen and strode outside. His younger brother, Ryan, was waiting for him, but thoughts of Juliette left Tru distracted this morning. His routine was off. He'd spent more time on her than he should have.

He blocked her from his mind. If it was the last thing he did, Tru intended to see she never got his land. Nothing she could do would make him sell. He'd done enough thinking on it.

He found Ryan at the stock pen, one foot propped on a low rail. Inside the fence, a dozen cows lingered at their feed, but one in particular, a black Angus heavy with calf, had separated herself from the rest.

"Looks like we got trouble coming, Tru," Ryan said without greeting. "She's acting real anxious. Won't eat."

"I noticed as much last night." He'd checked her twice after midnight, but she appeared worse now. He studied her swollen abdomen, the extended tail, her listless movements around the pen. He suspected her little critter was complicating matters. "I hoped we'd find her calf bawling his lungs out this morning."

"No such luck."

"Seen the water bag yet?"

"It burst not long ago."

"Let's get her in the chute."

He tossed aside his coffee cup, his taste for the brew gone. The as-yet-unborn calf represented his dream of developing a brand-new breed of cattle, one more suited to the weather extremes common to this part of the West, providing high quality beef at the same time. If he succeeded, stockmen from all over the country would clamor to add the breed to their herds—and pay well for the privilege.

He couldn't lose the animal. His future—and Ryan's—depended on it.

Once the cow was secured, Tru examined her. Labor was in full swing, and though she strained, she couldn't expel the calf from the womb.

"Going to have to pull it." Concern built inside him. If the fetus was already in the birth passage, the risk increased with

every minute that ticked by. He strode toward the barn, un-
buttoning his shirt as he went. "Keep an eye on her. I'll be
right back."

He returned in moments, carrying a pair of ropes. He removed his shirt and threw it over the top rail, then oiled his
right hand and entire arm with petrolatum. Ryan took one of
the ropes and formed a small noose, handed it to Tru, then
did the same with the second. The cow tensed with a contraction, and the effort presented one foreleg and a glimpse
of the nose.

"Can't see the other leg," Tru said. "It's in the wrong position, damn it."

He looped the rope above the fetlock joint to keep the leg
from passing back down into the womb, and figured the contractions were a couple of minutes apart. He wouldn't have
much time to find the errant limb.

He waited until the labor pain ended before he went in for
the search. He found what he was hunting for, tucked behind
the calf's ears. Working between contractions, he manipulated
the foreleg back into place beside the head, then managed to
loop the second noose above the leg's joint like the first.

He withdrew and tugged on the rope, a gentle test to ensure the nooses held. They did. He braced his feet and Ryan
did the same.

"Next contraction, you pull first, and I'll alternate with you.
Go easy. We can't lose this little fella," he ordered.

Ryan had pulled calves before, but none as important as
this one. Tru trusted him implicitly, and Ryan didn't fail him.
They worked in tandem, walking the shoulders out, using
their combined strength firmly but cautiously. Several inches
at a time, the calf squeezed through the birth passage. Once
the head and shoulders were out, they pulled the calf downward, nearly parallel with the rear legs of its mother.

Tru held his breath. The next maneuver was crucial. The animal was out to its midsection, and should the hipbone become

lodged against his mother's pelvis, they could lose him. He wasn't yet breathing on his own, and seconds were precious.

Tru and Ryan kept pulling, and finally, after a great gurgling, sucking sound, the calf dropped to the ground, the navel string broke and his lungs filled.

Ryan broke into a grin. "Look at him, will you? He's a beauty!"

"That he is," Tru breathed. "That he is."

He hunkered down and stared at the wet, wriggling creature before him. The miracle of nature amazed him.

A miracle he'd helped create.

The knowledge humbled him. Exhilarated him. The calf would look nothing like his Angus mother; instead, he'd be a strong replica of his sire—Tru's prize Romagnola bull he had shipped all the way from Italy. The bull he'd signed his life away to buy.

The bull that'd give the McCord name respectability again.

His gaze lifted to the other cows in the pen. They'd all been impregnated by the bull and were due to calve at any time. He murmured a fervent prayer that their offspring arrived healthy and strong. If they did, his herd would increase in size and superiority. There'd be no other stock like them in America. Maybe even the entire world.

His mind envisioned the pen a month from now, crowded with scampering calves and watchful cows. He'd have to move them—

"We've got company, Tru."

—give them room to graze, get a feel for Nebraska weather—

Ryan gave him an impatient shove. "Tru, did you hear me? We've got a caller."

Tru dropped back to reality with a jolt. He rose. Turned. And drew in a stunned breath.

Juliette.

Sweet Jesus.

He'd known she'd come, of course. Had expected her to yesterday. Last night. Today, for sure.

But to have her arrive now, when he was dirty and smelled like a cow's birthing…

Damn.

Just his luck she'd come when he looked his worst. She stood outside the pen, watching them in all her high-society perfection. He wasn't a vain man, but it'd been so long since he'd seen her and—

If anything, she'd gotten more beautiful. More female. The gown she wore absorbed the morning sun, the dark navy fabric looking more expensive than anything he'd ever paid for in his entire life, except his bull, and maybe not even then. The color leaped to her eyes, making them appear more blue than violet. She held him transfixed and unable to form a coherent string of words to save his pathetic soul.

"Hello, Tru," she said quietly.

Hearing his name roll off her lips in that soft, cultured way of hers broke the spell she held over him. He turned away, his gaze raking the pen for something—anything—to clean himself with. He found his shirt and snatched it from the rail.

By the time he faced her again, her chin had hiked up an inch. She'd clearly dismissed his lack of response as something not to be concerned with. Instead, she lavished his brother with a bright smile.

"Why, it's Ryan, isn't it? You've grown up since I saw you last."

Ryan whipped off his Stetson and clutched it to his chest with both hands. "Yes, ma'am, I have. It's been a good while since you've been back to these parts."

"Three years." Her head cocked slightly. "How old were you then? Twelve? Thirteen?"

"Sixteen, Juliette," Tru said, impatient with her line of thinking. She needed to know those days were gone, that the

McCords could hold their own in life, no matter what she thought. "He's nineteen now. A man."

"Yes." She swiveled her heavy-lashed gaze on Tru again. "I see that. Could you excuse us, Ryan? There's a matter I need to discuss with your brother."

Ryan's uncertain glance bounced between them. Tru jerked his chin toward the cabin, a silent command to do as she asked. Ryan nodded, still holding his hat in a death grip, and began backing toward the fence.

But he halted and cleared his throat. "You come alone in that rig, Miss Blanchard?"

A slight frown puckered her brows, as if she'd had to reshuffle her thoughts. She considered the carriage waiting in the yard. "No. My sister, Camille, accompanied me. You remember her, don't you?"

"Yes, ma'am. I do. I sure do." Ryan's cheeks flushed, and he threw another quick look in Tru's direction.

Tru knew the meaning of that look.

"Go on," he murmured.

Ryan looked relieved. Did he think Tru would deny him? He ducked between the fence rails, pushed his hat back onto his head and headed straight toward the Blanchard rig.

Juliette faced Tru squarely. "Before we have another word between us, just let me say I hope we can discuss this without resorting to fisticuffs."

"Fisticuffs?" The term amused him. "As I recall, the last time we saw each other, a hand fight was the last thing on our minds."

Twin dots of color bloomed on her cheeks.

Seeing it, a corner of Tru's mouth lifted. Seemed she recalled it, too. "My hands were more intent on pleasuring you than—"

"That's enough, Tru," she snapped.

He shut the memories down, as he always did when they crept in to haunt him.

"You're starting on me already, aren't you?" she accused.

"We haven't even begun to discuss this—obstacle between us before you accost me with your cynical innuendos, which are highly improper, not to say downright rude!"

The memories surged forth all over again. "Nothing rude about what we were doing that night, Juliette. Only thing rude was your father and the way he handled the situation."

"My father had every right to act the way he did given the fact that *your* father—"

"Leave my father out of this," Tru snarled.

"He's a factor in this discussion."

Tru bristled as the ugly memories cut through him. "Not anymore, is he, Juliette? The high-and-mighty Avery Blanchard saw to it my old man would never be a factor again, in our discussion or anyone else's. Ever."

Moisture sprang to her eyes, and she angled her head away, hiding it from him. "You're being hateful, Tru."

"That's right, I am."

He'd been consumed by hate for anything that had to do with Juliette's father, or the fact that she'd abandoned Tru when he needed her most. Still *was* consumed, and he didn't intend to apologize for it. Avery Blanchard had been responsible for Pa's death, and a whole hell of a lot of heartache besides that, whether Juliette believed it or not.

The one good thing Blanchard managed to accomplish was his daughters. Camille was as innocent of the feud between their families as Ryan. And Juliette—

Would she resort to her father's way of doing business to get the three hundred acres she wanted?

She'd always respected Avery Blanchard. Admired his accomplishments. His blood ran in her veins.

Hell, yes, she would.

Yet she'd been sweet and vulnerable in Tru's arms four years ago. Untouched by the harsh ways of the world. She looked vulnerable now, too, as if he'd hurt her feelings with the slur against her old man.

Unexpected regret shot through him. Moments like these, it was hard to remain convinced she'd be as underhanded as Avery Blanchard was.

Tru turned away. The feeling unsettled him, and he let himself be distracted by the bull calf up on all four legs and making a wobbly attempt at walking. Tru maneuvered the cow from the chute so she could get acquainted with her baby.

"He's cute," Juliette ventured.

Tru grunted. The calf was far from it—not when he was just-born scrawny and hadn't been cleaned yet by his mother—but Tru refrained from disagreeing with her. The little critter rooted eagerly for his first taste at the udder, acting starved for it.

Tru feasted his eyes on them. An appetite like that was a good sign. Hungry calves grew into swarthy bulls with a healthy sexual drive. In a few years, his herd of prime stock would be increasing in leaps and bounds. Before long his three hundred acres wouldn't be big enough to feed them all.

"You can't ignore me forever, Tru McCord," Juliette said stiffly.

His thoughts scattered, and he faced her again. "Nothing you can say will make me give up my land."

"You won't be giving it up in the strictest sense of the word." Tru figured she had to work to keep the desperation out of her voice. "You'll have made a business decision, a very profitable one, I might add, which will allow you a variety of different options."

"Such as?"

He'd thought the situation through inside and out. There wasn't anything she could offer him that he hadn't thought of first, but he figured she had a right to talk now that she was here.

"You could lease your stock to another rancher," she said. "Live in town and conduct your business from there."

Let someone else have his prize bull? He nearly choked on the idea.

"No," he said roughly.

"Or you could rent someone's land," she continued, talking a little faster. "Live there and take care of your cattle, just like you're doing here."

"No." He'd have to *pay* to rent someone else's land, and what would he do when the money ran out? Right now, he didn't have a margin of profit to work from. Eventually he would, but not now. It was all he could do to pay his bills.

"Or you could take your money and—and go back to school." She hesitated. "I understand you left your studies at Creighton University after your father died."

"No thanks to yours," he growled.

"You wanted to be a veterinarian back then, didn't you?" She went on as if he'd never spoken. "Why, you still can, Tru. The money I'm prepared to pay you for this land will easily cover the tuition fees."

It had been his dream once, to become a respectable veterinarian. He had a way with animals. Always had. He'd wanted to open his own practice and help the area ranchers care for their stock with the latest techniques and medicines.

He didn't think about it much anymore. His dream was gone forever, replaced with the burning desire to develop a new breed of cattle. With the little bull calf, he succeeded. To keep the dream alive, to build and soar with it, he needed his land.

She just had to accept that.

"'No' to all your suggestions, Miss Blanchard. Discussion closed."

He left the pen and headed toward the water pump. He had a strong hankering for a bar of soap. His shirt was soiled beyond wearing, and smelling like he did, he doubted Juliette would follow too closely.

He was wrong.

Her fingers gripped his wrist and pulled with more strength than he expected. She moved damn quick, considering he was determined to put distance between them, and when he faced her, her nearness yanked the breath right out of his lungs.

He'd forgotten that the top of her head just reached his chin. But he hadn't forgotten how finely sculpted her features were, the elegant cheekbones, the full mouth. In spite of his own foul smell, the flowery scent of her perfume surrounded him, reminded him yet again just how female Juliette Blanchard was.

"Tru. Please. I'm convinced we can reach a compromise," she said.

He pulled from her grasp. "I'm not."

He turned, resumed his trek toward the pump, heard the rustle of her skirts as she followed him again.

"But you don't understand," she said.

"I understand plenty."

"My hotel would be *perfect* here."

"My cattle already are."

"But they don't care where they live!"

He gripped the pump handle to keep from throttling her. "*I* care."

Her bosom heaved, and Tru could almost taste the panic coursing through her. He swore under his breath, worked the handle with fierce motions and thrust his arms under the gushing water. He scrubbed himself clean, then because Juliette fired up his blood, he bent down and pushed his head into the stream. Icy cold water poured over his scalp and the back of his neck.

He felt better for it. He straightened, shoved the pump handle down with one hand, raked his fingers through his hair with the other.

He glared at her. Dared her to continue arguing with him.

But she seemed distracted with the water spilling over his shoulders and disappearing into the hair on his chest. He suspected she wasn't used to seeing a man naked from the waist up.

Tru thought her cheeks looked pinker than normal, but he couldn't be sure. She angled her face away, and her throat moved in a hard swallow.

"You're being infuriatingly stubborn, aren't you?" she said, her voice hardly more than a whisper.

"That's what the McCords have always done, isn't it, Juliette?" he taunted. "Infuriated the Blanchards?"

Her mouth tightened, and she swung back to face him. "Is that your final answer, then? You refuse to sell to me?"

"Yes."

"No matter what price I offer you?"

He made no response. He didn't need to.

Her breath quickened, as if his silence terrified her. "I'll do anything, Tru. I swear it."

His brow arched. His mind entertained a variety of ways she could entice him to sell, none of them very honorable. Did she intend to prostitute herself for her precious hotel?

"Anything?" he murmured.

He knew it cost her plenty to lower herself to him like this. It amused him, a Blanchard falling to the level of a McCord.

"Anything," she said.

An idea bloomed in his brain, one so far-fetched she would never in their combined lifetimes agree. But she'd tossed down the glove and was waiting to see if he accepted the challenge.

"Come to think of it, there is one thing you could do," he said.

Hope sprang into the deep violet-blue of her eyes. "Name it."

"If you want my land, you'll have to marry me for it."

Chapter Three

The shock of his words left Juliette speechless.

Marry him?

Tru's mouth quirked, as if he took pleasure in seeing her stunned reaction. But as the absurdity of what he'd suggested sank in, it was all Juliette could do to cling to her composure and keep from banging her fists against his stubborn skull in frustration.

"Is that your idea of a joke, Tru?" she demanded hoarsely. "Because if it is, it's most inappropriate!"

"I've never been more serious."

"I'm trying to conduct a business deal with you, not an offer of *marriage!*"

"In this instance, they're one and the same."

She gaped at him. "They're not!"

"You know the terms, Juliette. Take 'em or leave 'em."

He had the audacity to walk away from her then. Just left her standing there, staring after him, without another word to say.

Because he'd said it all.

Of course she wouldn't marry him. He *knew* she wouldn't. Marry him for his land? What kind of ridiculous proposition was that?

She'd done everything but fall at his feet and beg. If she

thought it'd do any good, she'd beg the whole day long. But Tru wasn't going to budge, no matter what she said or did, with one ridiculous exception.

Marriage.

Damn him.

She watched him stroll toward the cabin. He carelessly slung his shirt over his shoulder, as if he knew the power he held over her—and it suited him. His broad back, tanned a deep golden-brown, rippled with muscle. Even his buttocks were tight beneath the denim of his Levi's. He walked with the lithe, unhurried gait of a man who was in control.

Which, of course, he was.

She swallowed down the stir of sexual heat that slid through her blood, and pulled her stare away. It rankled that he could affect her so when he didn't care one whit about her resort or the potential of its success, not only to her career and her pathetic financial situation, but to the eastern part of the state of Nebraska.

She rubbed her forehead. What would Father do in a situation like this one?

She had to get away from Tru and think. Go back to her room at the hotel and replan her strategy. Find Tru's weak spot. Something, anything, she could use to convince him to sell.

He disappeared through the cabin's back door. She'd clearly been dismissed from the conversation, and with a resolute squaring of her shoulders, she headed back to the rig.

Tru McCord hadn't seen the last of her, she vowed. Not by a long shot.

In the front yard, Juliette discovered the interior of the carriage was empty. Exasperated, she scanned the premises, even the road leading back to Omaha. Camille was supposed to be waiting for her. Where had she gone?

"Over there," the rig's driver said in a loud whisper and, grinning, he pointed toward the barn.

Juliette frowned. She couldn't see her sister there or anywhere else in the vicinity, but she strode closer to have a better look. Her trek took her past the front of the cabin, around the corner and down the side. By the time she reached the back, the stock pen loomed just ahead. Her puzzlement increased tenfold.

She'd come full circle, and Camille was nowhere to be found. Juliette set her hands on her hips and endured the first bite of worry.

It wasn't like her sister to wander off, and where would she go, anyway? Juliette scrutinized the area around the barn. The cottonwood and elm trees that grew thick beyond it. If the carriage driver saw her heading this way, then she must be here somewhere.

Determined to find her, Juliette stepped away from the cabin to investigate the perimeter of the barn, but movement in the trees stopped her. She spotted Camille among the shadows, with Ryan McCord, and they were—

Juliette's eyes widened. She emitted a shocked squeak and leaped backward, pressing herself against the rough-hewn side of the cabin, hiding from their detection. Surely she'd been mistaken. What she saw wasn't what she *thought* she saw. Camille and Ryan weren't…oh, God.

She drew in a long breath and ventured another cautious peek, but the second look confirmed the first. Her eyes squeezed shut, and she flattened herself against the cabin again, her chest heaving.

In her obsession to talk to Tru, she'd forgotten all about Ryan. But there he was, holding her sister in his arms and engaging her in the most passionate of kisses, as if he was positively *starved* for the taste of her.

This couldn't be happening. Ryan…and Camille?

Oh, God.

"They're entitled to a little privacy, don't you think?"

Tru's voice cut through her dismay, and her eyes flew open. He stood directly in front of her, dressed in a fresh shirt that he'd only had time to button part way. The breadth of his shoulders blocked her view, as if he was protecting them from her discovery.

Or maybe he was protecting *her*.

She strained to peer around him, driven by some crazy need to see Camille locked in Ryan's embrace once again. "You know about this?"

He gripped her elbow, pulled her away from the cabin. "Have for a while now."

"Why didn't you tell me?"

"Wasn't my place."

"Not your place?" Juliette sputtered, her steps quickening to keep up with his as he herded her toward the front yard and the waiting carriage. "Just how long did the three of you intend to keep this…this relationship from me?"

"Reckon that's something you'll have to take up with your sister."

They reached the rig, and Juliette spun toward him. "It's not like Camille to do this. We're very close. She must have been coerced somehow."

Tru's eye narrowed. "What are you saying, Juliette? That it was *Ryan's* fault Camille deceived you?"

Her mouth opened to blurt that it was typical of a McCord to be unscrupulous when it suited him, that a McCord would resort to less than honorable measures to get what he wanted.

But Ryan wasn't acting alone in that kiss. Camille was an active and willing participant.

Juliette's mouth closed again. "No, I'm not saying that."

Tru unlatched the carriage door. "Then it's best to be open-minded about this. Camille's old enough to make her own decisions."

"She's young, Tru." Troubled, Juliette peered up at him. She saw no condemnation or worry in his features. How could he be so calm? "They both are."

"She's the same age you were before things fell apart between us. We'd shared plenty of kisses by then. Neither of us were thinking of age when the passion was running hot, were we?"

His low-voiced challenge sent the past crashing in on her, vivid memories she still refused to think about. She'd reconciled herself to the fact that getting involved with Tru had been a big mistake, one she intended Camille would never make with Ryan.

It would hurt too much.

"They've never even courted, Tru. They hardly know each other. Besides, New York is our home. We'll be returning there as soon as plans for my hotel are finalized. Camille has no room for Ryan in her life."

Tru caught Juliette by the waist to lift her into the carriage. Startled, she grasped his biceps, and the bulge of hard muscle warmed her palms. He settled her in the seat, then released her, but the strong, capable feel of his hands against her lingered through the fabric of her dress.

"You can't keep doing her thinking for her," he said.

"Camille already knows my thinking."

"Going to have to cut the apron strings with her. Hard as it is to accept that, it's for your own good. And hers."

Juliette chafed at his persistence. "Perhaps Ryan is ignorant of the implications of what he's doing. I would appreciate it if you would speak to him of my disapproval. As I intend to do with Camille."

"The hell I will," Tru growled.

She arched a haughty brow. "Then I'll speak to him myself. This affair must stop immediately."

He stepped closer, and barely suppressed anger emanated from him. "You're on McCord land, Juliette. There'll be no confrontation from a Blanchard here. Ryan is free to make his own decisions about the woman he wants in his life. Damned if you'll tell him otherwise."

Though it rankled, Juliette knew to hold her tongue. Tru's wrath was a formidable thing. She'd do well not to anger him further, not when she needed his land so desperately.

She swung her head, letting her defiance show, but not acting on it. Ryan and Camille were approaching from the barn, a respectable distance between them, as if they were out for a leisurely stroll.

As if their kisses had never happened.

But they had, and Juliette intended to give Camille a good piece of her mind as soon as they returned to Omaha.

Camille's happy chattering on the way back to the hotel wilted Juliette's resolve.

She pondered the glow in her sister's cheeks. The sparkle in her eyes. The way her voice sang with gaiety with every word she spoke.

Ryan McCord had done that to her.

Juliette couldn't recall seeing Camille this exuberant, not in a very long time, anyway, and certainly not since they'd moved East. Her sister had been slow to recover from the scarlet fever, and reluctant to enter New York society. If not for her studies to occupy her time and mind, Camille would've become a recluse, Juliette was sure, and she had worried about her constantly.

How Ryan entered her sister's life, she had no idea. Camille had a great deal of explaining to do, but Juliette was oddly reluctant to demand it of her just yet.

Clearly, she was in love with the young man. Juliette's surreptitious gaze lingered on the rosy fullness of her sister's lips. Ryan had kissed her most thoroughly, she mused, and an unexpected jolt of hot memories rushed through her.

Tru had kissed her the same way. Fierce, possessive kisses that always left her on fire and hungry for more. An addiction that begged for quelling.

A *need*.

Sharp dismay coursed through her, and she yanked herself back to reality. She had to stop *remembering*. Her plans for herself and Camille were spiraling out of control, and if she wasn't very careful, she'd lose everything she'd worked three long years for.

Camille couldn't continue her relationship with Ryan. Absolutely not. She had to overcome the power he held over her. She didn't yet know Juliette had seen them in the shadows beyond the barn. Tru had acted as if nothing unusual had happened, and Juliette followed his lead in not saying anything.

But by the time they reached the privacy of their hotel room, she could wait no longer.

Humming softly, Camille sat at the vanity and began removing the pins from her hair.

"What's this?" Juliette asked, forcing a teasing lilt into her voice. "Getting ready for bed already? It's barely noon."

Beaming, Camille met her gaze in the mirror. "Ryan has asked me to dinner tonight. I'm going to spend the afternoon getting ready."

"Oh?" She managed to act nonchalant. "We agreed you'd call on Sarah today. So the two of you could go shopping."

Camille shook her head slowly. "No, Juliette. *You* said I was going shopping with Sarah today. I never agreed to the outing."

Had that been the way the conversation went? Juliette blew out a breath. "I don't think dinner with Ryan is a good idea."

Camille whirled toward her. "Because he's a McCord."

Juliette hesitated. "Among other things."

"I *knew* you'd be narrow-minded about him."

The accusation stung. Juliette had always prided herself on her liberal point of view. The McCords, it seemed, were an exception to her thinking. "You're wrong to accuse me so rashly, Camille, when it is *you* who has been deceitful. And I'm not talking about dinner, either."

The color faded from Camille's cheeks, taking her happiness right along with it. Juliette regretted seeing it go. "You saw us, didn't you?"

"Yes."

"And now you're going to forbid me from ever seeing him again."

"Camille." Juliette softened her voice, implored her sister to listen to reason. "Your affair with him has no place in our lives."

"That's not true."

"Our home is in New York. Not Nebraska."

"I want to stay here."

Juliette blinked. "In Omaha?"

"I'm not going back East." Camille lifted her chin, the rebellion building in her features. "I've made up my mind."

Juliette had never seen her so adamant. "I'm sure you're caught up with the novelty of seeing Ryan and all, but, truly, you must distance yourself from it. It's not fair to lead him on."

"I'm doing no such thing!" Camille gasped.

"Nothing can come from your relationship with him."

"I'm in love with him! And he's in love with me."

Love? *Love?* Juliette strove for calm. "What you're feeling is a good dose of infatuation, that's all." She refrained from reminding Camille of her lack of interaction with the male gender in New York, that her social life was virtually nonexistent. Surely Ryan's attentions seemed more exciting because of it. "Once we're back in New York, you'll forget him. We'll expand our circle of friends. You'll meet someone new in no time."

"I don't want to meet anyone else."

Juliette gritted her teeth in frustration. "You're talking nonsense, Camille. We've begun new lives in New York since Father and Mama died. Your doctors are there—some of the best in the country. I have my career there. Besides, where would we be without Aunt Louise? She's helped us immensely. She loves us like we're her own daughters."

Camille's mouth curved into a pout. "Aunt Louise doesn't care one whit about me."

"Of course she does."

"She only cares about you and all the fancy buildings you can design. I bore her."

"That's not true." Sympathy poured through Juliette. She didn't know Camille felt like this, alone and hurt and inferior, and she reached out to draw her into an embrace.

But Camille jerked back, preventing her from touching her at all. "I'm a woman, fully grown, Juliette. I can make my own decisions about the man I want."

Tru had said the same thing earlier this morning, but Juliette rejected the words now as she had then. "With Father and Mama gone, we have only each other. I'm responsible for you. I want what's best for you."

Camille's fists clenched. "I'm tired of you coddling me all the time. You may as well know Ryan has asked me to marry him—"

Juliette sucked in a breath.

"—and I said yes!"

She staggered back. "What?"

"I refuse to deny myself Ryan's love the way you've denied yourself Tru's. And I won't allow you to dictate my life like Father did yours, either. He ruined your happiness, Juliette, whether you believe it or not. If it wasn't for him, you'd still be in love with Tru, probably even married to him, and then we wouldn't be having this horrid argument *now!*"

Juliette's world rocked, and she grasped the edge of the vanity for support. "Camille, please. Let's start over, shall we? We'll talk—"

"I've said all that needs saying." Camille spun around, a slender tornado of rebellion when she'd always been so levelheaded and agreeable. She grabbed her coat and handbag and hurried to the door. "I'm leaving for a while, and it'll do no good for you to come after me. I'm not coming back until I'm darn ready!"

"Wait!"

Though Juliette bolted after her, Camille was too quick, and the door slammed shut behind her.

Every instinct screamed with the need to give chase. But Juliette's feet refused to move.

Going to have to cut the apron strings with her.

Tru's words kept her frozen in place, her stare riveted on the closed door, her heart pounding with fear that the life she led with her sister had changed forever.

Chapter Four

Juliette removed her gold-rimmed eyeglasses and set them on top of the ledger. The numbers on the page had blurred together. Her brain was numb. She couldn't think anymore.

She had to face the possibility that Tru might never sell his land to her, no matter how hard she tried to convince him otherwise. The resort hotel project would have to be postponed. Possibly scrapped altogether. The time and expense of finding a new location, of redesigning the structure to fit the topography of the new site, to say nothing of losing the opportunity to become a partner with the Waite and Caulkings architectural agency and stabilizing her very precarious financial situation...

The whole thing was most depressing.

Of course, marrying Tru would ensure her dreams would come true.

Her refusal would destroy them.

She pinched the bridge of her nose and groaned.

And then there was Camille. Her dear, sweet sister fancied herself in love with Ryan McCord, and was taken with the foolish notion of marrying him. The idea of leaving Camille behind in Nebraska while Juliette returned to New York was unthinkable.

For the hundredth time, she checked the diamond watch piece that had once been their mother's. Camille had been gone more than two hours.

Feeling miserable, Juliette snapped the case closed, rose from her chair and strode to the window. She parted the drapes wide and stared into the street below with a heavy sigh.

What if she failed in preventing Camille and Ryan from marrying? Did she have a right to try? Should she heed Tru's advice—cut the apron strings and let Camille make her own decision about whom she wanted to marry?

For the first time, Juliette began to see herself living alone in New York with only her career to occupy her life. She had Aunt Louise, of course, but her aunt was getting on in years, and what was the success of Juliette's career worth if she didn't have Camille to share it with?

Her sister was the only close family she had left. Juliette must figure out a way to keep Camille with her in New York, and already too much time had passed. She must find her before she did anything rash. They would talk. Compromise. Together, they'd discover a way to smooth over their differences.

The afternoon was nearly half gone, and she had no idea where Camille might be. Feeling rushed, a little frantic, but greatly determined, Juliette dashed from the room.

No one had seen her. Not the hotel clerk who thought he remembered someone of Camille's age and description in the lobby earlier, but couldn't be sure. Not the dress shop owner down the street who rather haughtily declared young women entered her establishment all day long, and how was she supposed to remember a certain one? Not the flirtatious delicatessen owner who specialized in Camille's favorite smoked sausages, but would Juliette mind having a glass of wine with him when he closed for the day?

Up and down the streets Juliette walked, hoping to find Camille on one of them. Even a hasty call on Sarah in the hopes that Camille had spent the afternoon with her, after all, failed to produce any news.

The sun showed signs of setting alarmingly soon, and Juliette debated contacting the Omaha Police Department for help. How could she possibly find her sister in the dark by herself?

Juliette fought tears of frustration and panic. She was exhausted and cold—she hadn't thought to bring a coat in her haste—and it was a long walk back to the hotel. She clung to the hope that Camille had returned and was waiting for her in their room. If she wasn't, Juliette thought in despair, what would she do next?

With every step she took, finding her sister seemed more and more hopeless. Time ticked on, block after block, and as she approached a small, nondescript dining hall, a group of men and women on the boardwalk blocked her way. She veered toward the street to avoid them.

But there was something about one of the men that snagged her attention. The way he carried himself, his hip slightly cocked as he waited his turn to go inside. The breadth of his shoulders, the slight curl to the coffee-colored hair hanging past his collar...

"Tru," she breathed, her heart squeezing with relief at the sight of him. He would help her. Surely he would. She lifted her skirts and rushed forward. "Tru!"

At her call, he turned. Beneath the brim of his Stetson, something flickered in his expression, and it was all she could do to keep from throwing herself into his arms.

"Juliette."

The low timbre of his voice wrapped around her, the tone rough with wary surprise and concern. She swallowed down a sudden welling of emotion. She'd never been so glad to see him in her life.

"Oh, Tru. It's Camille." She stopped short, her gaze clinging to his. "I can't find her anywhere, and I've been looking for *hours*."

"Camille? What happened?"

"We argued, and—and she left in the worst huff. I've never seen her so upset. Then when she didn't come back, I went out looking for her, but it's been so long, and—"

Juliette halted. She was babbling like an idiot, and she needed a minute to compose herself. Was she making any sense at all?

Someone moved beside Tru—a woman about Juliette's age dressed in a prim shirtwaist and navy-blue skirt. She was strikingly pretty in a clean, wholesome way, and she stared at Juliette with unabashed curiosity.

Her hand was tucked inside Tru's elbow, and, mortified, Juliette took a hasty step backward.

"Oh, I'm sorry, Tru," she said. "I'm intruding upon w-whatever you were doing, and I didn't mean to—to bother you about Camille."

"You're not bothering me." He turned toward the woman. "Gaylene, go on in without me. I'll join you when I can."

"Of course," she said softly, dragging her gaze from Juliette and smiling brightly up at him. Patting his arm with gentle affection, she pulled free while he said something to another couple, obviously explaining the situation and making arrangements for her in his absence.

Juliette's dismay deepened, and she turned away guiltily. It'd been selfish of her to barge in on his plans for the evening. Of course he would have plans. With friends.

Female friends.

She shivered suddenly and crossed her arms under her breasts. It shouldn't matter that he was with the woman named Gaylene, but it did, and Juliette would give her last dollar to be on any Omaha street but this one.

"You're cold."

Tru stepped closer, and before she realized his intent, he'd draped his jacket across her shoulders. A delicious warmth seeped into her, and her fingers automatically moved to pull it closer. His scent enveloped her—a sensual blend of tobacco and leather. Pure male. In the times she'd been with him, she'd never known him to wear cologne like the smooth-skinned men she associated with in New York. He had no need of the frivolity.

"Thank you," she murmured.

"You look like you could use a drink." He took her elbow and steered her away from the dining hall.

Juliette tossed an uncertain glance behind her. "But the hotel is the opposite direction."

"You staying at the Paxton?"

"Yes."

"Most expensive hotel in the city. I expected as much," he muttered.

Juliette declined to tell him the Paxton was Aunt Louise's idea, that it was important to make a good impression on Stephen Dunn and Charles Hatman, and that her aunt had insisted on paying the hotel costs herself. In light of Juliette's worry about Camille, Tru's opinion of her accommodations held little relevance.

He slowed, reached around her, pulled the door open to a small eatery. Lettering on the door's window proclaimed the place Stan's Restaurant. Resting a hand at the small of her back, Tru nudged her inside.

"We'll stop in here. We need to talk," he said.

The place was almost deserted, and after traipsing along crowded boardwalks all afternoon, Juliette welcomed the serenity. Enticing aromas of seasoned beef and baking bread filled the air. A mahogany-topped bar occupied a corner of the room. Rows of shining glasses and bottles of assorted wines, whiskeys and brandies lined the wall behind it. Wooden tables were scattered throughout, not one boasting a starched tablecloth, vase of flowers or burning candle. The simplicity of the place appealed to her.

"Be right with you, Tru," a white-aproned man said, peering out from behind the kitchen door. "Seat yourself."

Tru lifted a hand in agreement. "Take your time, Stan."

He pulled out a chair, and Juliette sat, keeping his jacket about her. She wasn't ready to relinquish the garment just yet, not when wearing it gave her comfort, no matter how silly the notion sounded.

"You still favor claret?" Tru asked.

A curious warmth spread through her that he remembered her favorite wine. "Yes, but I shouldn't stay. I have to keep looking for Camille."

"It'll be easier to find her when you're not wound so tight. A glass will relax you."

She didn't have the energy to argue. "All right. But I'll only stay a few minutes."

He left her sitting and made his way to the bar. In only a moment, he returned, a tall beer bottle in one hand, a glass of red wine in the other.

Juliette eyed him dubiously as she accepted the libation. "You certainly know your way around here. The proprietor doesn't mind you helping yourself like this?"

"What you're really wondering is how can Stan trust a McCord alone in his restaurant while his back is turned."

She stiffened at his sarcasm. Was that what she'd been thinking, deep down?

"I'm good for what I take, Juliette. Stan knows it. I've never given him reason to think otherwise."

She lowered her lashes. She deserved the rebuke, she supposed. Her opinion of the McCords had been less than complimentary for a long time, yet would she be here with Tru now if she didn't trust him to help her find Camille?

Confusion warred within her, and she sought refuge in a good-size sip of the claret.

"So you've been walking the streets looking for your sister," Tru said, settling into his chair. He removed his Stetson and tossed it onto the tabletop.

"Yes." Juliette sighed. "All afternoon."

"You aren't dressed for it. Which leads me to believe you left in one hell of a hurry."

"I did."

He reached under the table. His lean fingers grasped her calf and lifted. Before she knew it, he had her shoe off and her foot cradled in his lap.

She tensed. "Tru! What are you *doing?*"

"Damn shoes of yours are worthless. Bet your feet hurt, don't they?" The warmth of his hand soaked through her silk stockings as he massaged the sole of her foot with slow, heavenly strokes. "They're cold, too."

There were no linens on the table to hide what he was doing, but Juliette didn't care. She almost purred aloud from the massage, and she sank a little lower in her chair to allow him easier access. "I paid a fortune for these shoes, I'll have you know."

"Doesn't matter. They're still worthless," he grunted.

She couldn't help a smile. Tru had always been forthright in his opinions. In this instance, she conceded he might be right.

"You and Camille had a spat, then," he said.

"The worst."

"Did Ryan figure into it?"

She met his gaze squarely. "He did."

"Want to tell me about it?"

"They're planning to be married."

"I know."

"We have to stop them."

Tru's brow shot up. "We?"

"Of course. He won't listen to *me.*"

"I'd warrant Camille isn't listening to you, either. Which is why you two argued."

"Very perceptive," she muttered, and sipped again from the claret. Clearly, Ryan was quite frank about his relationship with Camille. If only Camille had been the same with her. "I gather you have no qualms about them as husband and wife?"

"None."

So she stood alone against the three of them. "But you should. They hardly know each other. How can Ryan provide for her? And she doesn't belong on a ranch in Nebraska. She's not suited to it."

Tru's mouth tightened. The massaging ended, but he kept a firm hold on her foot. "What you're saying is Ryan's not good enough for her."

Juliette hesitated, her mind working to find the right words. "I'm saying their worlds are very different."

"A Blanchard doesn't belong in a McCord's world?"

She refused to back down. "Not in this case. No."

He released her foot, reached for the other. "You're a female version of your father."

"So I've been told."

"Stubborn. Narrow-minded. Egotistical as hell."

"Call me every name you can think of, Tru. It won't change the way I feel." But his words hurt. Camille had called her narrow-minded, too. "Please try to understand my side of it. Perhaps you've heard how ill Camille had been with the scarlet fever?"

He scowled, but his fingers moved soothingly over her foot again. "Yes."

"She's accustomed to living in the city. Being a rancher's wife is vastly different. I don't know that she can adapt."

"There you go. Making decisions for her without hearing her side of it. Obviously, she *wants* to be a rancher's wife."

"She knows nothing of being one."

"She'll learn."

"She's accustomed to the comforts and benefits a large city can provide."

"Not a thing wrong with clean, fresh Nebraska air, Juliette. It's peaceful in the country. No crowds. No noise. Wide-open spaces. I'd say those are damn nice benefits for a rancher's wife."

"Oh, Tru." He made things sound so logical and simple. Was she really as narrow-minded as he claimed?

"Juliette. Look at me."

She did, and her heart gave a funny flip. The collar of his crisp white shirt—his Sunday best, she guessed, and donned for his intended evening out with Gaylene—provided a stark contrast against the tanned column of his throat. The room's gaslight glinted off his dark hair, thick and shining and carelessly swept back from his forehead. He looked incredibly strong sitting there across from her. Handsome and masculine. Juliette wondered how she'd been able to walk away from him all those years ago.

"I know you're worried about Camille," Tru said quietly. His fingers curled loosely around her ankle, as if he'd forgotten about her tired feet. "Try not to. I have a strong suspicion she's with Ryan somewhere. He'll take care of her."

"But Ryan wasn't to meet with her until dinner. She ran out of the hotel hours before that."

"He left our place in the early afternoon. He was heading to town. Didn't say why, and I didn't ask. Not too hard to figure out Camille was on his mind."

"What if you're wrong, Tru? She could be lost or hurt."

He released her ankle and sat back in his chair. He reached for the bottle of beer. "Since it concerns you so much, I'll help you look for her. Finish your wine, and we'll go."

Gratitude sprang to life inside her, but on its heels, an image of Gaylene. "You've made plans for the evening. I can't ask you to give them up on my account."

"You're not asking. I'm offering. Besides, Gaylene will understand."

"I see."

The woman sounded insufferably *nice,* and Juliette endured a twinge of jealousy over it. She took a healthy swig of wine.

"Hey, Tru! How the hell are you? Haven't seen you in a spell."

She started at the booming voice from the kitchen and hastily pulled her foot from Tru's lap. Still shoeless, she adjusted her skirts and assumed a ladylike posture in her seat.

The door swung shut behind Stan as he approached their table with a bowlegged swagger. His white apron stretched across his ample belly, and a broad smile creased his cheeks. He grabbed a chair from a nearby table, plopped it next to theirs and straddled it.

"Good to see you, Stan." Tru extended his arm and shook the restaurant proprietor's beefy hand.

"So who's the pretty lady?" Stan asked, grinning and eyeing her with flagrant male curiosity. Though he was probably old enough to be her grandfather, there was appreciation, too. "Haven't seen this one on your arm before."

"Name's Juliette Blanchard."

"Blanchard." Stan's grin faltered. His glance jerked to Tru. "Avery Blanchard's kin?"

Tru finished off the beer in one long swallow. He set the bottle down before responding with a curt nod. "His daughter."

"Yeah?"

Stan stared at Juliette, as if seeing her in a different light now that he knew who she was, and a not particularly favorable light at that.

The man's behavior was both unexpected and puzzling. She'd never seen him before in her life. Juliette managed a cool smile and extended her hand in greeting. "You knew my father, then, Mr.—?"

"Parsons. Stan Parsons." He took her hand in a firm handshake. "Yeah, I knew him."

"Oh? How so?"

Again, Stan looked at Tru, as if seeking permission to reply.

"Stan used to own the Antler Saloon." Tru spoke for him, his tone grim. "He was there the night my father was killed."

The Antler Saloon. Juliette recognized the name, and a prickle of unease skidded down her spine.

"If you want to know of his association with your father, you'd best be prepared for what he has to say," Tru added. "If you're not, we'll leave right now."

In growing trepidation, she studied the restaurant owner's serious expression. "Perhaps this is something I need to know, Tru."

Father had forbidden her to speak of that terrible night so long ago, the night when James McCord had died a violent death.

The night that had ended her love affair with Tru.

Why would Father forbid it?

Suddenly, she had to know what happened.

"Reckon you're not going to like what you hear," Tru warned grimly.

Juliette swallowed. As much as she worried over her sister's whereabouts, removing the veil of ominous secrecy from that night was more important.

"I want to know the truth about what happened," she said. "Tell me everything."

Chapter Five

The restaurant owner hooked an arm over the back of the chair. "Your father had a reputation for being a hard man, Miss Blanchard. There's some that say a good businessman has to know how to hit below the belt to succeed. Your daddy knew all the ways."

She arched a brow. "How so, Mr. Parsons?"

"He knew people. He had men who worked under him to help get what he wanted."

"My father was an ambitious man, yes," she said carefully. What was Stan insinuating? That her father was less than honorable?

"'Course, money'll get a man to do most anything. Money or a woman. In your daddy's case, it was both."

"A woman!" Juliette was instantly incensed. "My parents were deeply in love. If you're claiming he took a mistress, I'll refuse to believe—"

Stan held up a hand. "Hold on, Miss Blanchard. I ain't claiming that at all. No, ma'am. He loved your mama, all right."

"More than anything," she said fiercely, flooded with a rush of happy memories of them together.

"Yes. Your mama loved him, too, but maybe not as much as he loved her."

Juliette's eyes widened. "What do you mean?"

"Her heart belonged to another man," Stan said. "Even after she married Avery, she couldn't get her first love off her mind."

"I don't believe it," said Juliette, aghast.

"She had an affair with my father, Juliette," Tru said. "After she married yours."

Shock rolled through her. Mama and *James McCord?*

"They'd known each other since they were kids. Pa even proposed when they were of age, but she spurned him and went off to school in St. Louis. Eventually, she married Avery and bore his daughters. Pa and Elizabeth didn't see one another again until Avery brought you all back to Omaha."

"When he took the job as bank president."

"Yes."

"I remember James and Mama meeting." It'd been purely by chance, outside a grocer's store. Mama had been flustered, a little giddy. Juliette had seen the flush to her cheeks, the brightness in her eyes. The pair had visited an extraordinarily long time, but Juliette hadn't minded.

Tru had been there, too.

"You were wearing a pink dress," he murmured now, watching her. "And a hat to match."

"Yes." *And you stole my heart that day.*

"He was never good enough for her," Tru went on matter-of-factly, as if he'd accepted it long ago. "After all, he was just a two-bit gambler with a couple of sons he'd fathered with a prostitute, and a run-down ranch he managed to scratch a living on. He couldn't give her the life she was accustomed to. Or the respect. Society meant everything to Elizabeth. She intended to keep her place in it."

Yes, Juliette thought, with a pang of dismay. Mama thrived on dinner parties, the theater, expensive trips abroad with friends. All the things a wealthy man like Father could give her.

"Avery found out about the affair and held James responsible," Stan said. "Your mama decided she wanted to stay married and keep the good life Avery had given her, so she ended the trysts with James. But James refused to give her up. He made a real nuisance of himself, slandering your daddy every chance he got. Long about the same time, Tru started to court you. It was Avery's worst nightmare to realize the two of you were smitten."

"Oh, God." Father had been furious, she recalled. He'd forbidden her from seeing Tru ever again, but it'd been Mama who'd soothed her and found a way....

"Avery decided to take matters into his own hands. One night, back when I still owned the Antler, he paid me a visit. Came late at night, after my last customer left, so we were alone in the place. Said he knew I had a loan at his bank, but he'd make sure the account was paid off if I'd find him the best professional gambler I knew." Stan hesitated. "If I didn't, he'd call the loan in."

"He blackmailed you?" Juliette whispered.

"Yes, ma'am, he did. Now, I've owned saloons all my life. Only natural that I'd meet quite a few cardsharps, and none of them could play better than Roger Stillman. Folks called him 'Ace' because he always seemed to have a spare when he needed it the most." Stan shrugged. "Hell, what would it matter if I introduced them? Wasn't my place to ask why your daddy needed a cardsharp. All I wanted was to get out of debt, so I sent word to Ace. He took the next train out here."

"Why did Father need Mr. Stillman's expertise?" Juliette asked, half-afraid to find out.

"Justice," Tru murmured.

She swung her gaze toward him in horror. "For Mama's affair?"

Tru nodded. "Stillman invited my father to join him for a private game in the back room of the Antler. Pa jumped at the chance. Stillman was a high roller. Pa figured he had as good a chance of winning against him as anyone else. He had a few debts of his own to pay off. I suppose he thought he could make himself look good to your mother, too." A corner of Tru's mouth lifted. "Pa was an optimist. Always thought he could beat out his opponents. Got him into more trouble than he could stay out of, I'm afraid."

"James had no idea he was being set up." Stan took up the story thread while Tru strode to the bar. "I'd seen enough card games in my day that I could tell he didn't know. Ace let him win for a few hours. The chips began to pile up. 'Course, the riper the pot, the greedier James got."

Tru returned with the wine bottle and refilled Juliette's glass. "Then he started to lose. Again and again. Wasn't long before Pa got suspicious about his sudden turn of bad luck."

"Desperate, too," Stan added.

Tru nodded. "Came down to the last hand. Pa was almost out of chips. He had only one thing left to bet."

"McCord land," Juliette whispered.

"Don't know what the hell he was thinking," Tru muttered.

Stan raked a hand through his thinning hair. "When he lost that, too, he jumped up from the table and accused Ace of cheating. Now, both men had been drinking heavily. Hell, we'd all had our share of whiskey that night. But looking back, I can't help thinking Ace was more sober than we knew. When James started yelling, Ace whipped out a sawed-off Remington .44. He only fired once, but that's all it took."

Juliette pressed her fingers to her lips and stifled a sob.

"I never figured him for a killer, Miss Blanchard," Stan said. "Never knew Avery had an ulterior motive in hiring him, either."

"You can't prove any of this," she choked out.

Tru's hard gaze held hers. "No. We can't."

"Your daddy made sure of that," Stan agreed with a grim nod.

"You're wrong about him. You're wrong about all this," she cried desperately.

"I was at the saloon, Juliette," Tru said. "I saw everything."

"But maybe Father *didn't* have an ulterior motive that night," Juliette said. "Maybe it was all a horrible mistake, a misconception on your part."

"Stillman skipped town afterward," Tru said roughly. "No one's heard from him since. We tried to get the police to file charges and issue a warrant for his arrest, but the chief was a personal friend of your father's. His wife was your godmother. Not a damn thing was done about Pa's murder."

"Didn't even get reported in the *Omaha Bee* or the *Herald*." Stan shook his head. "Reckon your daddy had a part in that, too. Most folks never knew about the murder, and those that did acted like it never happened."

Juliette threw back a quick swallow of wine. The next day, Father had sent them all to Europe for the summer. He didn't go with them due to business commitments.

Or so he claimed.

Was it to ensure that the scandal remained out of the public's eye? Did he hope to spare Mama and Juliette the certainty of ugly rumors? Did he expect them to simply *forget* about the McCords by the time they returned to the States?

If so, he was a fool. Juliette had never forgotten Tru. And how dare Father remove him from her life.

She would never know Mama's feelings about losing the man who had first stolen her heart. If her marriage had suffered, if she'd suspected Father's part in the killing, she'd never let on. Her parents had appeared as happy as they'd ever been.

The terrible scarlet fever set in soon after that, and the Blanchard sisters' lives changed forever.

"I've had my share of guilt over it," Stan was saying as Juliette dragged herself back to the conversation. "Since then, I've made my peace with Tru and Ryan." He sighed heavily. "After that night, the Antler left a sour taste in my mouth. I sold the place. Opened this here little eatery instead."

Juliette needed a moment to allow the shock to settle. She'd known of her father's contempt for James McCord, of course, but the depth of his hatred mortified her. Did Father have any idea how many lives he'd hurt because of it?

Humbled, saddened, confused, she lifted an unsteady hand and rubbed her brow. An ache had begun to form at her temples. "I don't know what to say."

"No need to say anything. But whatever you're thinking, I hope you know everything we've told you is the truth. I've never lied to you," Tru said.

Feeling miserable, Juliette dropped her gaze to her empty glass. "No."

He'd done nothing to deserve the heartache and pain of what Father had done to him or Ryan. No wonder the McCords despised the Blanchards.

The restaurant had begun to fill with patrons, and Stan rose from his chair. "I'd best head back into the kitchen. It was real nice meeting you, Miss Blanchard. Hope the next time we see each other, we'll have something more pleasant to talk about."

She frowned. "I doubt there'd be anything worse."

"I'm sure you'll find your sister in no time." Concern furrowed his bushy brow as he turned to Tru. "Anything I can do to help?"

Tru withdrew a few coins from his hip pocket and dropped them on the table. "Not at this point, but thanks. We'll head to the hotel first to see if she's there."

Camille. Oh, Lord. Juliette pushed her feet back into her shoes. Tru took her elbow and helped her from the chair. He acknowledged Stan's sympathetic look with a curt nod and ushered her to the door.

"I suppose you hate me all over again," he said in a low voice.

"I need some time to think this through."

"Anyone would."

"And I don't hate you. But if I find out what you're saying is pure slander against Father—"

"You won't." He seemed impatient she would think so.

"—then I shall *never* forgive you."

A matronly woman and a tall, sunburned cowboy with graying sideburns entered the restaurant and prevented his response. Seeing Tru, a wide grin appeared on the man's face, and they shook hands. Tru introduced the couple to Juliette as Cal and Esther Workman, local ranchers.

"How the hell are you, Tru?" he asked. "Been meaning to pay a call on you."

"I'm good, Cal. Real good." Tru glanced at the woman. "Esther, don't tell me he's giving you a night away from the kitchen."

"He is," she said, smiling. "My birthday. He knows better than to forget."

"Got lucky this year. Early enough in calving season to spare the time to take her to town." Cal winked at his wife, then turned back to Tru. "Been thinking of your cows. Have any calved yet?"

Pride shone in Tru's expression. "One so far. Just this morning. Born perfect, too."

"You know I'm interested in building up my stock with your bull's bloodline. Mind if I stop out sometime this week? I'm hoping we can do some business."

"Anytime. You know that."

"I'll do it. See you soon, then."

After a round of goodbyes, Juliette and Tru left. She could see Tru was well-liked in Omaha, had made friends and survived the scandal her father had caused. He was a different man than his father. Honest and hardworking. It seemed Tru had begun to build a name for himself as a respected stockman, as well.

No wonder his land was so important to him.

Deeply troubled, Juliette brooded about the day's events in silence. She didn't realize they'd reached the Paxton Hotel until Tru guided her into the lobby.

"Let's check with the desk clerk. Maybe he's seen Camille," he said, and she agreed.

After hearing a quick description of her sister, the young clerk nodded. "Yes, she was here, oh, about an hour ago." He smiled. "Guess she'd left without her room key earlier this afternoon. She stopped at the desk to get another."

Juliette pressed a hand to her breast in relief. "Thank God. She looked well, then?"

"Very well. The gentleman with her seemed quite smitten, if you know what I mean." The clerk grinned.

"Ryan." Juliette exchanged a glance with Tru, and he nodded.

"Yes, I believe that's what she called him," the clerk said.

"She's probably in the room then."

"I'm afraid not. I saw them leave again, shortly after they stopped by the desk. Of course, I don't know where they went. They had no reason to tell me."

"No," she concurred, but wished they had.

While Juliette was disappointed Camille wouldn't be in the room waiting for her, at least she was with Ryan. They were most likely at dinner now, as they'd planned. Juliette would just have to wait a little longer to see her.

Knowing she was safe took the sting off the fact that Ryan was obviously courting her. Were they discussing marriage at this very moment?

"I told you Ryan would take care of her," Tru said, his tone gently chiding as he led her to the hotel's stairway. "They're fine. They're happy. Let them have their time together."

"Maybe you're right." Pausing at the foot of the stairs, she pulled his jacket from her shoulders and handed it to him.

He hooked the garment over his shoulder with a finger and eyed her ruefully. "Hearing about your father was tough. Maybe I should've spared you."

"No. It was important for me to know. The past is past. I can't change the way he was or all that he did." Strangely reluctant to have her time with Tru end for the evening, she reached up and touched his cheek. "Thanks for the wine. And thanks for staying with me when I was tired and worried about Camille. You escorted me back here when you could have gone back to Gaylene."

Tru's mouth pursed. "First I thought of her until now."

"Is it?" Somehow, that pleased her.

"I'll walk you up to your room."

"There's no need. I'll be fine."

"Juliette…"

She halted at the husky rumble in his voice. His heated gaze clung to her, as if he, too, was reluctant for the night to end. She sensed the churning of emotions inside him, the clashing of the past with the present, the old yearning, the ugly hurts, the fiery passion that still smoldered between them.

The want.

Juliette had no right to want anything from Tru, not after all Father had done, after all *she'd* done, but tonight, this moment, she wanted him to kiss her again. Just one little kiss she could keep tucked inside her heart forever.

To savor when she missed him most.

His head lowered. He felt it, too, this want, and Juliette rose slightly on tiptoe to meet him, her pulse quickening in anticipation of the feel of his lips touching hers.

And then they were. Soft, incredibly gentle, they stirred the longings she'd worked so hard to dismiss over the years, set them free, made her forget to breathe. To think.

She melted into him. Right there, in the hotel lobby. The kiss deepened. His arm snaked around her waist, pulling her to him, keeping her against his hard body. It was one of the things that always excited her about him—the barely restrained wildness that shucked the bindings of polite society and spurred him to take what he wanted, when he wanted it.

"Juliette," he murmured again, her name rough and hungry against her mouth. "Juliette, Juliette."

She knew his need, for it matched her own. Her lips parted, and his tongue plunged inside to sweep with hers. She tasted his beer. She had only to take his hand, lead him up the stairs to her room, the bed that stood empty and ready for them... They'd be alone. God, this fire between them. They could sate it before Camille and Ryan came back—

Someone coughed, and the distant sound shattered her lust with a rude reminder of where they were. She pushed against him to end the kiss, though her fingers clung to his shirt and his arm still banded her waist. She had to let him go, but she couldn't.

What if she never got another chance to be held in his arms? What if Tru never kissed her again?

His head lifted, and for several long, pulse-pounding seconds, he gazed down at her, those dark eyes of his smoldering with the passion he fought to keep in check.

"Go on up, Juliette," he said. "With what I'm feeling, I could take you right here in the lobby if you don't."

"Tru, I—"

"Go on." He released her, gave her a gentle nudge toward the stairs. "We're both wanting some things that neither of us can give just yet."

Bemused, her ardor cooling, Juliette stepped away. Maybe he was right. Things were happening too fast. The differences between them—the land she needed, but he refused to sell; the discord between their families; Ryan and Camille—how would they be resolved?

Would they ever?

Juliette didn't know. But their kiss proved that one thing hadn't changed and most likely never would.

She was still in love with Tru.

Chapter Six

From her window, she watched him head down the street with that lazy, graceful stride she'd always admired. After she left him in the lobby, she'd felt his gaze upon her, as if he was reluctant to let her climb the stairs without him.

It was best to leave him down there. She wouldn't have the willpower to keep him out of her bed, not when his kisses left her weak-kneed with want.

A ribbon of guilt swirled through her. He was on his way back to Gaylene, still waiting for him in the dining hall—and he had Juliette's kisses on his mouth.

She didn't know what relationship he had with the young woman. Perhaps he'd overstepped his bounds in kissing Juliette with such fervor, but somehow, she didn't think so. She'd discovered long ago that Tru loved deeply. If he was in love with Gaylene, he would never have kissed Juliette.

A tiny flare of hope formed. Could it mean that Father's betrayal—and her own—hadn't destroyed all the feelings Tru once had for her?

It should have. If the story Tru and Stan Parsons had told her was the truth—and she had the sick feeling it was—what Father had done was unforgivable. What right did Juliette have to want Tru to continue loving her? Why would he bother? She didn't deserve it.

Nor could she forget that Tru had established his life here in Nebraska. Juliette had done the same with hers in New York. If not for her need for the McCord land, she might never have seen Tru again.

Except somehow Camille had managed to nurture a love affair with Ryan. How could Juliette have been blind to it? Had she been so absorbed with her resort hotel that she'd ignored Camille's loneliness?

Obviously.

Her sister's reluctance to confide in her about Ryan troubled Juliette deeply. Her own selfishness had driven Camille to keep silent, and Juliette was terrified at the thought of losing her.

She wanted their old lives back. She didn't want Camille in love with Ryan. She didn't want them married. But most of all, she didn't want to return to New York without her sister.

Juliette groaned and jerked the drapes closed. Tru was long gone—swallowed up by the night. He'd be with Gaylene, anyway, having fun with their friends, and oblivious to the turmoil battling inside Juliette's head.

The room's silence closed in on her, and the night stretched interminably. Every small sound, every muffled voice outside the room raised hopes that Camille had returned.

But she didn't.

She should have.

The wait was maddening, and the lateness of the hour suggested Juliette had little choice but to ready herself for bed. She sat at the vanity, removed the pins from her hair and shook the tresses free. When she reached for her porcelain-handled brush, a cold chill slid down her spine.

Camille's toiletries were gone.

Everything. Her perfume, combs, soap. Juliette bolted toward the armoire and flung open the doors. All her dresses were gone, too. Her shoes and coat. Juliette yanked at drawers and found them empty of stockings, underwear and nightgowns.

She pressed her fingers to her mouth in horror. Camille had eloped. Oh, God. She was probably married at this very minute.

Juliette sucked in long, calming breaths. She had to ride out to Tru's place. He'd know what to do about their siblings. He'd make everything right again.

She only hoped it wasn't too late.

Shirtless, barefoot and ready to shuck his Levi's to climb into bed, Tru slid a final, frowning glance toward Ryan's side of the small cabin. His room was empty, the bed untouched, his things missing.

Well, hell. Considering how late it was, Tru was pretty sure his brother wasn't coming home. He was sure, too, Ryan was still with Camille. Had a wedding followed their dinner plans?

He cast another glance toward the old clock on the mantel. Juliette would be frantic. Tru admitted to a few worried moments himself. It wasn't like Ryan to go off without letting Tru know where he'd be and when he'd be back.

But then, Camille hadn't been part of the circumstances before. Funny how a woman could make a man do things he wasn't prone to do.

The sting of envy deepened his frown. Tru would give his eyeteeth to be in Ryan's boots right now—away late at night with the woman he loved. And married to her.

He'd never be in the same situation with Juliette. At some point in the last three years, he'd gotten over her, even prided himself on putting her out of his mind. But tonight, kissing her as he had—damn it, he'd discovered he never stopped loving her. And what a waste of time *that* was, when they didn't have a chance in hell in being together.

A sound outside the cabin stopped him from delving into self-pity, and he strode toward the door. He intended to give Ryan a few choice words for keeping Camille out this late. He might be crazy in love with her, but Juliette deserved the courtesy of knowing his intentions. For that matter, they both did.

Tru pulled the door open, and his heart dropped to his toes. Juliette had been riding hard, and she was out of the saddle before her mount came to a full stop.

"I think they've eloped, Tru," she said, breathless and clearly frantic. She rushed toward him, and he caught her in his arms. "Have you heard from them yet?"

Her hair was wild about her face, windblown and thick, and it was all Tru could do to keep his hands out of it.

"You rode all the way out here? Alone?" he demanded, hustling her into the cabin and out of the night's chill.

"I'd have come sooner," she said. "But I had a difficult time rousing the livery owner out of his bed. He charged me a fortune to rent a horse."

Tru muttered an oath. "It's nearly midnight, woman. Can you blame him?"

She whirled out of his arms, her cheeks flushed in the glow of the only lamp he had burning. "The time doesn't matter! Ryan and Camille aren't here, are they?"

"No."

"They may have eloped."

"I know."

Her breaths came in quick pants. "But I don't *want* them to be married!"

"They do, Juliette."

Her lower lip trembled. "I can't lose her, Tru. Can't you understand? She's all I have. I need her with me in New York."

"Why?"

At the point-blank question, she stared at him, her violet-blue eyes pools of sad dismay. "Because I've built us a life there. My work will support us if my hotel succeeds, and if I were to become a partner with Waite and Caulkings, it's even more imperative that she be there to share—oh, God."

She covered her face with her hands, and her shoulders

slumped. Tru feared she would burst into tears, and what would he do then?

"I'm not thinking of her at all, am I?" she said, her voice muffled and hoarse.

"No."

He knew what the realization cost her, that voicing it out loud had a way of making the truth painfully obvious. He clenched his hands into fists to keep from taking her into his arms just yet. Juliette had a few more "truths" coming. He couldn't let her womanly softness distract him.

"I want you to do something for me, Juliette," he said quietly.

Her hands lowered, and she straightened. He steeled himself against the shimmer of tears she fought hard to keep from falling.

"What is it?" she asked.

"Think back to the first day you arrived in New York. Remember what Camille was feeling. How she acted."

Juliette's brow puckered. "She was grieving for Mama and Father. We both were. She still hadn't regained her strength from her illness yet, and she was—" Juliette shrugged helplessly "—often sad."

Tru nodded. "Now think about the year after that. The next two years. Was Camille happy then?"

"Some of the time, I suppose. She didn't socialize much. Her studies consumed the majority of her days."

"What would make her happy? Name one thing."

She appeared frustrated at his persistence. "I can't think— wait." She held up a hand as if a thought just struck her. "Her friend, Sarah Evans, made her happy. She wrote constantly, and whenever Camille received her letters, she would smile for days."

He nodded in satisfaction. "There's something I need to show you."

He strode to Ryan's room, then returned with a plain

wooden box. He removed the lid and indicated the envelopes stacked neatly inside. "Letters, Juliette. Every letter Camille ever sent Ryan he saved." He paused. "You see, Ryan was Sarah."

Juliette paled. "I don't understand."

Tru removed one of the envelopes. His finger tapped the front. He didn't need to say anything more. Juliette could see for herself.

"Camille's handwriting," she whispered. "I never questioned the Omaha address as anything but Sarah's."

"That was the idea. We swore the postmaster to secrecy. He made sure that letters from a Blanchard in New York sent to Sarah Evans at the McCord address got to us. Ryan never missed anything Camille sent him."

Juliette pressed her fingers to her mouth. "Why didn't she tell me?"

"I think you already know."

"Oh, God." She turned away, raking the hair from her face. "After my relationship with you ended, I forbade her from mentioning the McCord name ever again. She knew how upsetting it was for me. There'd been so much ugliness between our fathers. Just hearing your name hurt."

"I know." Oh, he knew all right. Juliette Blanchard had torn him apart for years. He'd hated her and loved her, all at the same time.

"Even when we were in Europe, the three of us without Father, Mama refused to discuss any of you," Juliette continued. "Looking back, I can see it was how she coped with her guilt. By burying her feelings and pretending her affair with your father never happened."

"Would've been best to talk about it. Get what happened out in the open."

Juliette inclined her head. "How differently things might've turned out for us if we had. Mama would've stayed married to Father, of course, but Camille and Ryan—" She halted. "How had they met? School? Even then, they were smitten?"

"Yes. Even then." Tru took a step closer to Juliette. He didn't want to talk about Ryan and Camille anymore. All that mattered right now was Juliette, what they'd once had, what they'd lost. What did *their* future hold?

"Does hearing my name, saying it, still hurt?" he asked roughly.

Her gaze lifted to his, her eyes straightforward. Bold, even. Tru knew whatever she'd say next would be spoken in complete honesty.

"I never stopped loving you, Tru. With all that happened between our parents, I wanted to believe you and I were different. That what we had was genuine and precious and would last forever."

She still loved him. The knowledge sucked at his breath.

"So what made you change your mind?" he demanded, though he had a pretty good suspicion already.

"Father." The corners of her mouth dipped. "He couldn't say enough terrible things about the McCords. After a while, I suppose, I started to believe they were true."

Tru took another step closer. God, how he ached to take her into his arms. But he didn't. Not yet, not when so much remained between them, so much needed to be said. He assuaged the need some by reaching out and trailing a finger down her cheek.

"Do you remember the last night we saw each other?" she asked, her eyes shimmering again.

"How could I forget?" The memories reared up, but strangely, the old bitterness didn't. Had being with Juliette, talking with her tonight, somehow destroyed it?

"You stole into my room," she said, shaking her head a little, as if even now his recklessness astounded her. "Climbed the tree outside my window and crawled right in. It was nearly two in the morning!"

"Couldn't come to call on you in the normal way," he grunted. "Your father wouldn't allow it."

"I know." She sighed heavily. "You wanted me to defy him and run away with you." Her mouth softened. "I found it all most exciting, you know. Very romantic."

"Yeah?" It hadn't been his intent to be either, but his need for her overrode all else, including his good sense. "I had nothing to give you at the time, but I would've found a way to take care of you, though I know now I wasn't being fair to you. I wanted you for my wife more than anything, even at the expense of ostracizing ourselves from your father."

"He despised you for it. He heard us talking and came in—"

"—I had you in my arms—"

"—and I was wearing my thin summer nightgown—"

"—damn, but you felt good—"

"—I was allowing you far too many liberties—"

"—and I paid the price for taking them."

"Oh, God, you did." Suddenly, she flung her arms around his neck. "I'm so sorry for what he did to you after that. Setting your father up to be killed. It was *horrid* of him."

She buried her face in his neck, and Tru's arms tightened around her. His own world tilted from the old hurts, and he held on to her to keep from being buried beneath them.

"He threw me in jail on false charges of burglarizing the Blanchard home. I hated him for it, but it was worse when you didn't come," he said.

Her head lifted, her expression stricken. "I never knew! You've got to believe me, Tru. When I didn't hear from you, I thought Father had scared you away, that you felt I wasn't worth defying him for. And Mama wouldn't let me out of her sight. She was so frightened at what Father would do to us both if I met with you against his wishes."

In retrospect, maybe Elizabeth had been right to keep Juliette away from him, Tru mused. No telling what Avery would've done to retaliate. "Pa managed to scrape up enough money to bail me out of jail the next day. He was killed that night."

"Then we left for Europe," Juliette said miserably. "I never saw you again until yesterday."

She hadn't sent condolences on Pa's passing. Neither had Elizabeth. But Tru refrained from reminding Juliette as much. Young, impressionable, overwhelmed by her father's hatred and whatever part she felt she had in it—well, Tru had to cut her some slack. If he'd been in her shoes, he might've reacted the same way.

Juliette cupped his cheek, her fingers warm and tender against his skin. "I can't tell you enough how sorry I am for allowing Father to influence my thinking on you and James. Can you ever forgive me?"

Tru couldn't help hesitating. Forgive? Once, he didn't think it could've been possible.

And now?

"We have to put all the wrongs behind us," he said finally, and pressed a kiss into her palm. "Some days, I suppose it won't be easy, but we can't change what happened. Best not to dwell on it. Important thing is to learn from the mistakes so they don't happen again."

"Tru." As if humbled, unspeakably grateful, she drew in a quavery breath. Her eyes closed, and she rested her forehead against his chest. Words seemed to come hard for her.

"Do you see now why I refuse to interfere in Ryan and Camille's relationship?" Tru stroked her hair, relished the feel of the strands sliding through his fingers. "They're entitled to be in love. We can't take that away from them."

Her head lifted. "No."

The word came out hushed, maybe even reluctant, but he knew she wouldn't have said it if she didn't mean it. In his opinion, they'd talked about it long enough. He considered the discussion closed.

Bending, he slipped an arm behind her knees and lifted her into his arms. "As late as it is, Miss Blanchard, we can be sure the two lovebirds won't be coming. You're not going back to town. You'll spend the night here."

"With you? Just the two of us?" Curling her arms around his shoulders as he carried her toward his bedroom, her eyes widened.

"Alone. The whole night."

Her mouth pursed, as if she was considering the idea but didn't find the impropriety particularly worrisome. He laid her on his bed, then lit a lamp on the small table beside it.

Her hair splayed against his pillow, a tangled mass of silken strands that shimmered in the light's glow. God, but she was beautiful.

"I'd like to ask you something," she said.

He sat beside her, hip to hip. "I'm listening."

"Are you in love with Gaylene? Because if you are, I refuse to spend the night with you or let you kiss me ever again."

He wasn't sure if he should be offended or amused. "Gaylene is an old friend. And no, I'm not in love with her. You think I would've kissed you like I did back at the Paxton if I was?"

"Perhaps not," she murmured. "But is she in love with you?"

He lifted a shoulder. "Might be that she was once. Maybe she still is. But after you, Juliette—" he drew in a breath "—well, there'll never be a woman like you in my life again."

"Oh, Tru. I—" She bit her lip, holding the emotion in.

"You might as well know, too, I'll always love you," he added. "No matter what happened to us in the past."

There. He'd said it. A McCord damn near on his knees professing his undying love to a Blanchard. Most likely, Pa had done the same to Elizabeth. Certainly, Ryan to Camille. And now Tru himself…

Hell. What was it about the Blanchard women that affected McCord men like this?

Tru scowled. It unsettled him, baring his soul to her. He

felt naked. Vulnerable. Maybe he should've just kept his mouth shut. Let her stew on it for a while.

He stood. She looked small in his bed. Pure female. Fully clothed, but soft and luscious and ripe for his taking. He swallowed hard.

"There's nothing I want more than to make love to you right now, Juliette." There went his mouth again, saying words that insisted upon being uttered. "But whether or not you think so, a McCord has honor. When and if I bed you, it'll be when everything's right and proper between us."

She gasped softly, pressed her fingers to her lips.

"I'll sleep in Ryan's bed tonight, since he's not here to use it himself." Tru took a step back. Two, then three. "Good night, Juliette. I'll see you in the morning."

And though it was one of the hardest things he'd ever done, he turned and left her lying there, alone in his bed.

Chapter Seven

J uliette wasn't sure what awakened her—the shrill song of a distant rooster, the bright morning sunshine or the realization she wasn't in the Paxton Hotel.

She rolled to her back. She was in Tru's bed. In his room. Her curious glance took in all the things that were his—assorted books on a shelf, his Sunday-best Stetson hanging on a hook, shiny leather boots beneath. The room contained only a few pieces of furniture, none of them new, each simply made but sturdy and polished. Plain, cotton curtains hung at the room's only window, the fabric pristine and starched. Tru McCord, she learned, liked his things neat and tidy.

Her head turned, and there on the pillow next to her lay a bouquet of sweet clover and buttercups, their stems held together by a length of string. He must've brought them just a short time ago, for morning dew still lingered on the petals. Touched, Juliette reached for them and inhaled their sweet, subtle scent.

She'd seen exotic flowers artfully arranged at the Waldorf-Astoria in New York. She'd seen lavish bouquets at the Paxton, too, as well as other high-class hotels, and hadn't given them a second thought. But this unpretentious bundle of wildflowers, well, they were more beautiful than any of them.

Bemused, she slipped from the bed and stood in front of Tru's mirror. Her dress was wrinkled from her sleeping in it, and her hair needed a good combing. Dare she help herself to his toiletries?

His razor lay next to a wash basin, the towel beside it still damp from when he'd shaved. The clean smell of his soap lingered in the air and reminded her of him all over again.

There was something intimate in seeing the items a man groomed himself with every morning. Items a wife would soon take for granted. Since Father had employed a personal barber, Juliette hadn't witnessed them often. Even Mama had been denied the privilege.

But Father, it seemed, had a way of doing things most men didn't. Tru would think the idea of a personal barber ludicrous, and thoughts of all they'd discussed last night rushed forward. Two very different men, Father and Tru. Yet they both held a special place in her heart.

I'll always love you.

Her pulse fluttered at the words Tru had spoken last night. *There'll never be a woman like you in my life again.*

He'd wanted to marry her once. Did he still? After all that had happened between them, did she have the right to want him to?

She used his brush to remove the tangles in her hair, and battled waves of apprehension with every stroke. Daylight had a way of changing one's perspective. Would Tru regret declaring his love? Certainly, there was much between them yet. Her hotel, most notably. Solving that problem wouldn't be easy, and she grimaced at the prospect.

Leaving her hair loose about her shoulders, she left the room, taking the wildflower bouquet with her. She found Tru at the stock pen, an arm braced over the rail, his gaze intent on the cattle within.

She held back from joining him, compelled, instead, to study the land that meant so much to him. Three hundred acres of prime Nebraska rangeland, graced with a beautiful lake and as much green grass as the eye could behold.

Tru's home. Ryan's, too. And Camille's very soon.

Juliette drew in a breath. Oh, God. Daylight did have a way of changing one's perspective.

Tru must have heard her coming as she walked toward him. He turned, his dark eyes clinging to her.

"A pleasure it is, Miss Blanchard," he murmured.

Her blood warmed at the husky greeting. "Good morning to you, too."

"Sleep well?"

"Considering I was alone the whole night—" she batted her lashes with exaggerated coyness "—as well as could be expected."

He chuckled, clearly pleased with her response. "Are you always flirty first thing in the morning?"

"Only with you, it seems." She pressed a quick kiss to his cheek. "Thank you for the flowers. They were a lovely surprise."

His arm circled her waist before she could step away. "You could have them every morning, you know. A bouquet for each room in the cabin."

"If I married you."

"Yes."

What could she say, when their past collided with their future? He kept her against him for a moment, clearly waiting for a response. When she could give none, he released her. She turned from him and once again considered the lake in the distance. Had it been only a couple of days ago that Stephen Dunn and Charles Hatman were out here with her, as enthralled by her choice of location for the hotel as she was?

She squinted up into the endless expanse of blue sky. "There's one thing you haven't told me yet, Tru."

"Just ask."

"How is it that this land is still yours when you said your father lost everything to Ace Stillman at the Antler?"

He hooked a thumb in the hip pocket of his Levi's. "Pa put these three hundred acres in my name. One of the few smart things he ever did in his life."

"I see," she said pensively. "With your name on the deed, my father couldn't touch it."

"No one could. Pa intended this land to be my graduation gift. A place for me to open a veterinary practice." His mouth quirked. "Due to circumstances beyond my control, I never graduated. But the acres are mine, nevertheless. Fair and square. I'm using the land to breed cattle instead."

An image of the tall cowboy she'd met at Stan's Restaurant loomed in her mind. His name was Cal Workman, she recalled, and he was keenly interested in Tru's stock.

Yesterday, she'd been so intent on convincing Tru to sell his land that she'd paid his cows no mind. Now, however, her curiosity bloomed.

"Mr. Workman mentioned breeding his stock with a particular bull of yours." A pair of newborn calves lay on the ground, content to be cleaned vigorously by their mother. Given how captivated Tru was with them, Juliette guessed they were sired by this bull. "He's pretty important to you, isn't he?"

"More than you know. I had him brought over from Italy. Cost me everything I had, but he's worth it." Tru cleared his throat. "Want to see him?"

She saw the pride he tried to hide. Her mouth softened. "I'd love to."

He took her arm and led her to another corral. Inside, a heavily muscled, gray-colored beast ruminated his hay, oblivious to the attention they paid him. "His breed is larger than nearly any other in our country. He can survive on a range with limited grazing during drought years. He tolerates Nebraska's heat and bitter cold. Beef quality is excellent, and he gains weight fast."

She never claimed to have more than the most basic knowledge in the art of cattle breeding. After all, she was a city girl, through and through. But Tru's enthusiasm was catching, and she couldn't help being fascinated by this animal he'd had shipped from halfway across the world.

"I studied a hell of a lot of breeds before I decided on this one," Tru continued. "I'm the first to introduce the line to the United States. It'll be only a matter of time before word spreads about him. Cattlemen are constantly looking for ways to improve their stock. Cal's only the first to give him a try."

"Deciding to buy this animal was quite an undertaking for you," Juliette said quietly, thinking of the time and money.

The risk.

Tru reached out, gripped her chin gently and turned her toward him. "I intend to make a name for myself with him, Juliette. Ryan, too. If it's the last thing I ever do, the McCords will be respected. Most of all, trusted. And if I get rich in the process, well, that's even better."

His dark, grim gaze held her transfixed. Time fell away, and the pain of his past loomed up, sucked her in, swallowed her whole. All his life, he'd borne the shame of his father's reputation as a two-bit gambler. He'd been abandoned by his prostitute mother. Lived a hand-to-mouth existence with his younger brother.

Through it all, he'd survived. Kept on surviving, even after her father set out to destroy what little he had. He'd grown into a man who took responsibility seriously. He loved hard. Worked hard. He knew what mattered most in life.

And it wasn't money.

Tears stung Juliette's eyes. Perhaps James McCord hadn't been a failure, after all.

She couldn't say the same about Avery Blanchard. Or herself. Father and daughter, both driven by a need to achieve prominence in the business world, where their career and the desire to be important consumed their every thought and action.

At what expense to the people they loved most?

"So now you know why I'll never sell my land to you, Juliette," Tru said. "No matter what you say or do."

She held his gaze and thought of the challenge he'd made. "Not even if I married you?"

"Not even then. If you decide to marry me, I'm going to make damn sure *I'm* the reason, and not your fancy hotel."

All along, he'd never had any intention of allowing her resort to be built on his three hundred acres. Had he known her better than she knew herself? That she, a Blanchard, would never marry a McCord?

He'd outwitted her.

Or had he?

A strange calm came over her, an acceptance of the way things would be between them.

"Well, then, Tru McCord, it appears this discussion is closed," she said.

His mouth tightened. "Seems so." He placed a hand at the small of her back and gave her a firm nudge toward the cabin. "C'mon. We'd best head back into town. Might be Ryan and Camille left a message for us at the Paxton."

But at the sight of the young couple standing at the pen, peering at the cows inside, Tru and Juliette stopped short.

Ryan glanced up, and his face split into a wide grin. "Woohee, Tru! We got twins!"

It took Juliette a moment to realize he was speaking about the newborn calves. Even Tru appeared taken aback at first.

"Born just before dawn," he said with a slow nod. "Healthy as can be, too."

Pride shone on Ryan's tanned, lean face, which so resembled his older brother's. "Makes three babies now and more coming. Got a good start on our new herd, don't we? Real good."

"Where've you been, Ryan?" Tru asked, cutting to the chase. "Juliette's been worried sick about you two."

The grin faded. "Reckon so, and I'm sorry. Guess it couldn't be helped."

"She was entitled to an explanation of your intentions. We both were."

"Please don't be angry with him, Tru," Camille said, stepping forward as if to shield Ryan from the scolding. "It was I who refused to leave word of our whereabouts."

"Because you wanted to prove your independence to me," Juliette said.

Camille swung toward her. "Yes," she said, her chin held high, her demeanor signifying she was ready to do battle.

A battle Juliette had no intention of fighting. Not anymore. She inclined her head. "In that you succeeded. You look well, by the way."

Happy, too, judging by the glow in her cheeks. She didn't look so frail. Or shy. She carried herself with confidence, as if pleased with the turn her life had taken. She wore one of her newest dresses, with her hair upswept and perfectly curled. Wherever Ryan had taken her last night, she'd been well cared for.

Some of the fight seemed to leave Camille. She eyed Juliette warily. "Better than you, I think."

Immediately self-conscious, Juliette tucked a hank of loose hair behind her ear and made a futile attempt at smoothing the wrinkles in her skirt.

"I came out here in a bit of a rush last night," she admitted.

"It was late. I wouldn't let her ride back to the Paxton," Tru said. "She had nothing with her but the clothes on her back."

Camille's eyes widened a little. "So you spent the night here." Her glance bounced between them. "Just the two of you."

"I did." Juliette refrained from explaining any more than that, though she sensed Camille's curiosity about her relationship with Tru, given their battle of wills over his land and her hotel. Didn't she have an inkling of Juliette's curiosity about her own whereabouts last night?

Juliette cocked her head. "I'm not sure how I should address you this morning. Are you still a Blanchard? Or are you Mrs. Ryan McCord?"

Ryan slid a protective arm around Camille's waist. "I want her as my wife more than anything, Miss Blanchard. We talked about things a long time. The past, mostly. The future, too. We're not going to let what happened between our parents stand between us. Not like you and Tru did."

Tru shifted and scowled. Dismay curled through Juliette. Why hadn't she and Tru possessed the wisdom and determination their siblings did?

"But we're not married," Camille said. "Not yet. Oh, Juliette." Lip quivering, she threw her arms around Juliette and held on tight. "A wedding is a woman's most special time in her life, and I do so want to share it with you. I couldn't bear to get married without you there to witness it. I just couldn't."

A lump of emotion welled in Juliette's throat. It took a long moment before she could speak. When she was sure she could manage it, she set Camille gently away.

"Does this mean I can't be narrow-minded anymore?" she asked with a smile.

Camille scrubbed at a tear. "Absolutely not."

"Guess we could all use a cup of coffee right now," Tru said. "I've got a fresh pot already made. Give me some help, Ryan."

Ryan frowned and showed signs of protesting. After all, Juliette knew, he had an equal stake in the discussion. But Tru clamped a firm hand on his shoulder and urged him toward the cabin.

She was grateful for the privacy he gave her. Slipping her hand into Camille's, she led her away from the stock pen. They sat on the back lawn, their skirts fanned out between them.

"I know you're wondering where we stayed last night," Camille said, for the first time looking a bit apologetic.

"I am."

"You needn't have worried about us, you know. Ryan is the perfect gentleman."

"How am I to know that when you ran off without giving me a single hint of where you'd be?"

Camille wrinkled her nose. "I was feeling stubborn, I guess."

"Imagine that."

She shrugged off Juliette's sarcasm. "We stayed at a boardinghouse. I don't even recall the name of it, but some friends of the McCords own it. It was very clean and nice. Nothing like the Paxton, of course. But nice."

"And?" Juliette prodded, one brow arched.

"We had separate rooms, if you must know. I paid for my own from the allowance you gave me, even though Ryan didn't want me to." She leaned forward. "You needn't worry, dear sister. My virtue is still intact."

Juliette clucked her tongue. "Thank goodness for that, at least."

Given the McCord virility, any woman would be hard-pressed to keep from giving herself to either one, even without benefit of marriage.

Herself included.

Camille sat back. "What of you, Juliette? You seem to be getting along well enough with Tru. How was your night with him?"

"Well, I slept in his room." She paused a moment. "In his bed."

Camille gasped and pressed a hand to her breast. "You didn't! The two of you?"

"It wasn't what you think." She couldn't help a regretful sigh. "I was alone the entire night. Tru slept in Ryan's bed. I woke up with my virtue intact, too."

"He gave you wildflowers." Camille indicated the bouquet Juliette still held. "Very romantic."

"Very." Juliette inhaled their fragrance again.

Camille's eyes sparkled. "And I'll bet he kissed you, too, didn't he?"

An instant blush sprang to Juliette's cheeks. "That's none of your business."

"He did. I can tell. Don't even try to deny it."

She gave up. "Oh, Camille. He did." She fanned herself with the wildflowers. "Lord, the man can *kiss*."

They both burst into giggles, and the weight of Juliette's worries lifted off her shoulders and floated away.

"They're laughing, Ryan." Tru approached, a cup in each hand. He hunkered beside Juliette and gave her one. "A good sign there's no hard feelings."

"What's so funny?" Ryan asked, and handed Camille a cup of the steaming brew.

"It was nothing," Juliette said quickly. It'd be just like her sister to blurt out their conversation, and how embarrassing would that be?

"Woman's talk," Camille said, and winked. "Men aren't allowed to hear it."

The brothers exchanged an amused glance, then Tru gave Ryan an encouraging nod. "This might be as good a time as any to say what you've got on your mind."

Their humor faded in unison. Juliette's heart began a slow pounding. This was it. The moment she'd been expecting. She felt as if she stood on the precipice of a giant cliff, with nowhere to go but down. But for her sister's sake, she managed to smile in readiness.

Ryan threaded his fingers through Camille's. "Miss Blanchard, I want you to know I love your sister more than anything. I give you my word I'll take care of her to my last breath. Doesn't matter to either of us that she's a Blanchard and I'm a McCord. Main thing is, we want to be married." There seemed to be no apprehension in him. Ryan knew what he wanted, and he was willing to fight the odds to get it. "It'd mean the world to Camille and me if you'd give us your blessing."

Juliette thought of Father, the hatred that had consumed him. She thought of Mama and the mistakes she'd made for a man she never should have loved. And she thought of Tru, who'd risen above it all, instilled his ideals and honor into his younger brother and helped him grow into the person he was.

Camille was fortunate to have Ryan's love. How could Juliette deny either of them?

She reached out and covered their joined hands with her own. "On one condition."

Ryan and Camille held their breath in unison.

"You must promise to always call me Juliette. After all, we're going to be family now."

Chapter Eight

"Thank you," Tru said quietly.

She dragged her gaze from the cabin. Ryan and Camille had disappeared inside, presumably to celebrate their betrothal in private.

"It would be a travesty to trouble their marriage with anything less than my complete approval," she said. "I've no right to hamper their happiness, though God knows I've tried."

"Considering all Avery kept hidden from you, it's understandable your opinions of the McCords were what they were."

Tru's insight, his wisdom, humbled her. He, too, had been hurt by hard-hitting Blanchard ambition. And still he welcomed Camille into his life without reproach.

"Ryan will take care of her, Juliette. We're not rich, but we've got plenty to eat. Folks around here are friendly. She'll fit in as his wife with no problem."

"I know." Juliette sighed.

"Omaha's not as big or fancy as New York, but she's got the best of both worlds here. A trip into town will get her all she needs. Doctors included. And she'll have the advantages of clean living out here on the ranch."

"Yes. You're right, of course."

"So why are you still worried?"

"I'm not. Not really."

He appeared skeptical. "Hard to let her go. I know."

She drew in a shaky breath. "It scares me, actually."

He seemed about to say something, then thought better of it. Rising, he extended an arm toward her. She took his hand, and he pulled her to her feet.

"What's next, Juliette?" he asked. Keeping her fingers entwined with his, he lifted her hand to his lips and dropped a single kiss to her knuckle.

Her heart squeezed at the simple intimacy. Didn't he know? Didn't he realize the McCords had won? That she would never build her prized hotel on his land? That she'd lost Camille? That she had no choice but to go back to New York and start over?

"Everything has changed," she said. "I'll have to rethink my options, of course, but…"

Her voice trailed off. It'd been on her tongue to say "I'll find a way," but what if she didn't? With the failure of her resort project, the Waite and Caulkings architectural agency would refuse her dream of becoming a female partner. Since Charles Hatman and Stephen Dunn had pulled out of the deal, she'd lost her financial backing. Aunt Louise's reputation was compromised, too. And all the hard work from the past three years was for nothing.

Yet worst of all was the knowledge that no one needed her anymore. Not Camille or Ryan. And certainly not Tru, already on his way to becoming a respected stockman. He didn't need her hotel's money to find his success. He would do it all without her.

"I have something to show you, Juliette," Tru said.

Her troubled thoughts gave way to curiosity. He led her toward the front of the cabin, where their horses waited.

"Are we riding somewhere?" she asked.

"Yes, but not far."

"Where are we going?"

"You'll see soon enough."

Her curiosity increased tenfold. "We should tell Camille and Ryan our whereabouts."

"Ryan will know where I'm taking you.'

"A conspiracy among brothers, then?" she asked, climbing into the saddle.

A corner of Tru's mouth lifted. "Something like that."

They rode off McCord land, heading east as they circled the oxbow-shaped lake that Juliette had fallen in love with so long ago. They pulled up somewhere on the other side, and Tru dismounted.

"Ever seen the lake from this angle before?" he asked, helping her from the saddle.

"No." She scanned the thick growth of cottonwood and elm trees, the sprawling land with rolling bluffs beyond—not so different, really, than the McCord side. No roads led to this area, and it appeared virtually untouched by human hand.

"The Missouri's that way." Tru pointed east. "Steamboats bring folks and supplies in on a regular basis." He swiveled his stance, tugging Juliette to look with him. "Union Pacific's that way. West. Their trains haul passengers and supplies, too. Plenty of good, maintained roads leading from Omaha. Travel's not a problem, except in the worst weather."

"Yes," she said. The very things that had led to her decision to choose Tru's land for her hotel. From a businessman's perspective, each one was crucial for the success of the project.

"Council Bluffs, in Iowa, is just south. Not far at all. I've lived here my whole life, Juliette, and I know for a fact they don't have a resort hotel around these parts. *Anywhere.*"

Her pulse began to pound. She was afraid to think. To hope.

"What are you saying, Tru?" she whispered.

He stepped closer, slid his arms around her, holding her upright when she feared her knees might give way. "I'm saying build your hotel here. On this side of the lake. Might be you won't have to change your design much. Maybe not at all."

She clutched at his chest. "But the land's not for sale. I already checked with Charles Hatman. He would've told me if it was."

"Not for sale, no," Tru said, lowering his head and nuzzling her hair, her neck. "But if you offer the same top-dollar price you offered me, it will be. I guarantee it."

"How can you be sure?" She held on tight to hope, refused to let it fly free.

"I know the rancher who owns it. Gaylene's father. He's had rheumatism for years. Been wanting to slow down, spend his winters in Arizona. The money you pay him would get him there."

"Oh, Tru. What if you're wrong?"

"I wouldn't tell you all this if I wasn't pretty damn sure I was right." He drew her earlobe gently between his teeth and nibbled. Juliette closed her eyes to savor the sensation. "I've got plans to build a house. With Ryan getting married, there's no room for me in the cabin. Just say the word, and I'll include an office for you."

Her eyes popped open, and she drew back. "An office?"

"No reason why you can't design your buildings from here, Juliette. Might be that architectural agency that means so much to you would let you work for them in Nebraska. If not—" he shrugged "—you can always start your own."

"My own agency," she breathed.

"We'll all be right here. Camille and Ryan. Your career." For the first time, he appeared to hesitate. "And me."

Tru McCord was not a man who acted rashly. Everything he did followed a good deal of thought and preparation. Had she been on his mind so much? Had he pored over every possible solution he could think of to keep her in his life?

Yes, he had, and the knowledge filled her heart.

"I love you, Juliette. From the time I first met you outside that grocery store, I've loved you."

"Yes." She knew it. Felt it. Rejoiced in it. "I meant it when

I said I've never stopped loving you, Tru. I worked hard in New York to forget you. My building designs were my salvation. They kept me from dying inside." She speared her fingers into his hair. She ached for his kiss, to have his body pressed to hers. "I walked away from you once. I can't bear to leave you again."

"Then don't. Marry me so you never will again."

Elation soared through her. "Yes. Oh, Tru, yes. I will."

His love had righted her troubled world in more ways than she could've imagined, and she would spend the rest of her life in complete devotion to him. His mouth took hers, hard and hungry, proclaiming his own devotion in ways words never could.

Long, deliciously hot moments later, his head lifted.

"Can't think of a better time than spring in Nebraska to have a wedding," he said. "Can you?"

"There's nothing I'd like more." She kissed him again and thought of Camille and Ryan. She smiled. "Except maybe a double wedding."

* * * * *

Harlequin Historicals®
Historical Romantic Adventure!

SAVOR THESE STIRRING TALES OF LOVE IN REGENCY ENGLAND FROM HARLEQUIN HISTORICALS

ON SALE MAY 2005

THE DUCHESS'S NEXT HUSBAND
by Terri Brisbin

The Duke of Windmere receives word that he's going to die, and tries to get his affairs in order—which includes finding his wife a new husband! But as the duke's efforts go awry and he starts to fall in love with the duchess again, dare he hope they will find true happiness together—before it's too late?

THE MISSING HEIR
by Gail Ranstrom

Presumed dead, Adam Hawthorne returns to London after four years to discover his uncle passed away and the young widow is in possession of his inheritance. Adam is determined to uncover the truth, but the closer he gets to Grace Forbush, the more he desires his beautiful aunt-by-marriage—in his arms!

Harlequin Historicals®
Historical Romantic Adventure!

PICK UP A HARLEQUIN HISTORICALS BOOK AND DISCOVER EXCITING AND EMOTIONAL LOVE STORIES SET IN THE AMERICAN LANDSCAPE!

ON SALE JUNE 2005

SPRING BRIDES
by Stacy/Reavis/Crooks

Fall in love this spring with three brand-new stories of romance: In *Three Brides and a Wedding Dress*, a mail-order bride arrives in town expecting one groom, but ends up falling for his cousin instead! An Eastern miss discovers love can be wonderful— and complicated—in the harsh Wyoming wilderness, in *The Winter Heart*. And in *McCord's Destiny*, a female architect gets the offer of a lifetime from a man who once stole her heart—and wishes to steal it again.

HEART OF THE STORM
by Mary Burton

Lighthouse keeper Ben Mitchell rescues a beautiful woman when a ship sinks off the Carolina coast. While helping her recuperate, he is fascinated by the mysterious Rachel Emmons. She won't reveal her past, will only live for the present. Can Ben uncover her secrets before he loses his heart to her completely?

Harlequin Historicals®
Historical Romantic Adventure!

PICK UP A HARLEQUIN HISTORICALS BOOK AND DISCOVER EXCITING AND EMOTIONAL LOVE STORIES SET IN THE OLD WEST!

ON SALE MAY 2005

ROCKY MOUNTAIN MAN
by Jillian Hart

On the edge of a small Montana town, ex-convict Duncan Hennessey lives a solitary life. When widow Betsy Hunter delivers his laundry, he saves her from a bear attack. Will this lonely beast of a man fall for the sweet beauty—or keep her at arm's length forever?

HER DEAREST ENEMY
by Elizabeth Lane

Brandon Calhoun, the richest man in town, wants to break up the romance of his daughter and the brother of town spinster Harriet Smith. He needs Harriet's help. But the feisty schoolteacher won't agree. Can the handsome banker charm her into his scheme—and into his life?

If you enjoyed what you just read,
then we've got an offer you can't resist!

Take 2 bestselling
love stories FREE!
Plus get a FREE surprise gift!